TRUSTING
TAYLOR

PRAISE FOR SUSAN STOKER

"Susan Stoker knows what women want. A hot hero who needs to save a damsel in distress . . . even if she can save herself."
—CD Reiss, *New York Times* bestselling author

"Irresistible characters and seat-of-the-pants action will keep you glued to the pages."
—Elle James, *New York Times* bestselling author

"Susan does romantic suspense right! Edge of my seat + smokin' hot = read ALL of her books! Now."
—Carly Phillips, *New York Times* bestselling author

"Susan Stoker writes the perfect book boyfriends!"
—Laurann Dohner, *New York Times* bestselling author

"These books should come with a warning label. Once you start, you can't stop until you've read them all."
—Sharon Hamilton, *New York Times* bestselling author

"Susan Stoker never disappoints. She delivers alpha males with heart and heroines with moxie."
—Jana Aston, *New York Times* bestselling author

"Susan Stoker gives me everything I need in romance: heat, humor, intensity, and the perfect HEA."
—Carrie Ann Ryan, *New York Times* bestselling author

"Susan Stoker packs one heck of a punch!"
—Lainey Reese, *USA Today* bestselling author

Marrying Emily

Rescuing Kassie

Rescuing Bryn

Rescuing Casey

Rescuing Sadie (novella)

Rescuing Wendy

Rescuing Mary

Rescuing Macie

Delta Team Two Series

Shielding Gillian

Shielding Kinley

Shielding Aspen

Shielding Riley

Shielding Devyn (May 2021)

Shielding Ember (September 2021)

Shielding Sierra (TBA)

Badge of Honor: Texas Heroes Series

Justice for Mackenzie

Justice for Mickie

Justice for Corrie

Justice for Laine (novella)

Shelter for Elizabeth

Justice for Boone

Shelter for Adeline

Shelter for Sophie

Justice for Erin

Justice for Milena

Beyond Reality Series

Outback Hearts
Flaming Hearts
Frozen Hearts

SEAL Team Hawaii Series

Finding Elodie (April 2021)
Finding Lexie (August 2021)
Finding Kenna (October 2021)
Finding Monica (TBA)
Finding Carly (TBA)
Finding Ashlyn (TBA)
Finding Jodelle (TBA)

Stand-Alone Novels

The Guardian Mist
A Princess for Cale
A Moment in Time (a short story collection)
Lambert's Lady

Writing as Annie George

Stepbrother Virgin (erotic novella)

TRUSTING TAYLOR

Silverstone, Book 2

Susan Stoker

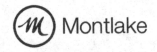

Text copyright © 2021 by Susan Stoker
All rights reserved.

Published by Montlake, Seattle

www.apub.com

Amazon, the Amazon logo, and Montlake are trademarks of Amazon.com, Inc., or its affiliates.

ISBN-13: 9781542021425
ISBN-10: 1542021421

Cover design by Eileen Carey

Printed in the United States of America

TRUSTING TAYLOR

Chapter One

Eagle sighed in frustration. He really hated grocery shopping. It was a task assigned to Shawn Archer, Silverstone Towing's newly hired cook, but he'd been given the week off with pay to spend with his daughter. Both of them needed it after what they'd been through. It would be a very long time before the man was comfortable letting Sandra out of his sight again.

Eagle couldn't blame him. If *his* child had been kidnapped, he'd have a hard time letting her do *anything* without him. It had been a very close call with Ricketts. The man had almost taken the most important thing in Shawn's life.

But the time off for their new employee meant that Eagle was back to doing the grocery shopping for the week. He could ask one of his friends to do it, and they would without issue, but since he'd always shopped for Silverstone Towing, he felt an obligation to continue.

He turned down the street where the grocery store was located and pulled into the lot.

The moment he parked, the lot suddenly filled with police cars.

Clearly something had happened, and Eagle sighed again. Of *course* he couldn't go to the store without there being some incident or another.

He got out of his Jeep Wrangler, glad that he'd parked in one of the farthest spaces from the store and wasn't in the thick of whatever was happening, and waited a few minutes before slowly walking toward the chaos, letting the officers do their thing. Eagle and the rest of his team-mates knew a lot of the officers who worked for the Indianapolis Police Department. They didn't work side by side with them, but Silverstone had offered its services a time or two.

As Eagle headed for the two closest officers, he noticed a woman standing by herself nearby with her arms around her stomach. She was biting her lip . . . and the expression on her face hit him like a punch to the gut. It wasn't that he hadn't seen nervous or scared women before. He had, both in his job at Silverstone Towing and when he had been in the military. But this woman seemed to be holding herself. She was uncomfortable, but he could also see resignation in her body language. As if she expected everyone in the vicinity to turn on her at any second.

It bothered Eagle deep down. He didn't like to see anyone look so . . . alone.

He'd never seen her before. Eagle would know if he had. He remem-bered every single person he'd ever met. His brain was wired differently from most people's, and he had a photographic memory when it came to names and faces. It was one of the reasons he was so invaluable to his team at Silverstone. He'd spent hours studying most-wanted lists, and if they ever came across someone on the lists, Eagle would know it.

The woman was average height, probably around five-seven or five-eight. She had on a pair of well-worn jeans, scuffed Converse sneakers, and a long-sleeve T-shirt. Her brown hair was curly and held back by a hairband, but even that couldn't seem to contain the curls.

Eagle had the insane urge to touch it, to see if his fingers got tangled in the wild strands.

She glanced up for a split second and caught his eye, and Eagle barely contained a gasp. The resignation was even stronger in her eyes. As if she expected him to judge her. Her eyes were dark brown—from this distance almost black. Even as he stared, he saw her bite her lip again, uncertainly.

And oddly, he hated that too. Hated that she was nervous, especially after seeing *him*. She didn't know it, of course, but he was as dangerous to her as a rock. He didn't hurt women . . . well, not those who weren't criminals. And Eagle's gut was telling him that this woman had lived a tough life and that she was no threat to him or anyone else.

"Hey, Eagle!" one of the officers called. Eagle recognized him as Emmanuel Brown, an officer he'd worked with in the past. The greeting snapped him out of his inspection of the woman. He had no idea who she was or why she was standing there . . . but he was going to find out.

He turned toward the policeman and gave him a small head jerk. "Hey. What's going on?"

"Altercation in the parking lot. Apparently two people wanted the same parking spot, and when one guy pulled into the space, the other guy took exception. He claimed he'd been waiting for it. They started fighting. One guy pulled a knife, and they both ended up bleeding. After they go to the hospital, they're both getting charged."

Eagle whistled. "Sounds messy." He really wanted to ask about the woman, but bit his tongue.

"It was. Crazy thing was that there was an empty space just two cars down. I'll never understand people," Officer Brown said with a shake of his head.

"Luckily there were lots of witnesses," another officer added. His badge said Nelson. Eagle hadn't worked with him before.

"Yeah?" Eagle murmured, encouraging the man to keep talking.

"Yup. Got statements from five bystanders, and it seems clear the man who was pissed he didn't get the spot started the whole thing."

He couldn't stand it anymore. Eagle motioned to the woman who'd caught his eye. "She a witness?"

Both officers looked over at the woman, then back to him.

Officer Nelson nodded. "Yeah."

"What's she waiting for?" Eagle asked. "I don't see any other witnesses around."

3

"Most have already left. We got their contact information if need be. But we're waiting for the approval of the captain to let *that* one go. She was right there from the second everything started, so she's the best witness, but there's an issue."

Officer Brown snorted. "That's an understatement. She's claiming she's got some disability—I don't remember what she called it—where she can't recognize faces. I guess it's some kind of *50 First Dates* kind of thing . . . remember that movie? With Adam Sandler and Drew Barrymore? It's hilarious. Anyway, sucks that she'll be no use as a witness. She won't be able to pick out the two perps in a lineup or if this shit goes to court. So we're trying to figure out if we should officially turn in her statement or just go with what we've already got."

Eagle couldn't help the surge of curiosity at hearing the officer's explanation. She couldn't recognize faces? God, there were times he *wished* he didn't immediately recognize people. "How long has she been standing there?"

Both officers shrugged.

Irritated on behalf of the woman, he made sure his facial expression showed nothing of what he was feeling. "Any problem if I go talk to her?"

"Nope. We expect to hear from the captain any minute now, and I'm guessing she'll be off the hook. No lawyer's gonna want to bring her in as a witness. She'd be torn apart by the defending attorney."

"What's her name?" Eagle asked.

"Taylor Cardin."

Eagle hadn't heard the woman's name before, but because of his unique ability, he knew he'd never forget it. "Thanks. Stay safe out there," he told the two men before turning and heading for the woman.

Taylor had been watching him talk to the officers and kept her eyes on him as he approached. She didn't wait for him to get to her before she spoke.

"I've already told the officers everything I saw."

"I know," Eagle told her. He held out his hand once he was in front of her. "I'm Eagle. Well, my real name is Kellan, but no one calls me that."

The woman looked down at his hand, but didn't reach for it. Her arms stayed wrapped around herself.

He continued to speak, dropping his hand. "I'm not a cop. I'm acquainted with a lot of them, as I work for Silverstone Towing, and I've gotten to know them over the years. Are you all right?"

She stared at him for a long moment before saying quietly, "You're the first person to ask me that."

Alarmed, Eagle's eyes raked over her slender frame, trying to determine if she was injured. "You're hurt?"

She shook her head. "No." She glanced over at the policemen, then back at him. "And I'm nothing like Drew Barrymore in *50 First Dates*," she said, quietly but firmly.

Eagle was surprised at the ferocity in her tone, especially considering how fragile she looked.

She went on before he could comment. "I have prosopagnosia, otherwise known as face blindness. There's nothing wrong with my memory. Tomorrow, I'll remember everything about what happened here, I just won't be able to identify the men who were involved."

Making a mental note to look up prosopagnosia the second he got to a computer, Eagle nodded. "I've got the opposite issue. I've never forgotten a face or a name in my entire thirty-six years. Sometimes I have trouble if I met someone when they were a kid and now they're grown, but I've never forgotten a name."

"Ever?" she asked with a tilt of her head.

"Ever," he confirmed.

Then Taylor smiled.

And it blew Eagle away. It transformed her face. He hadn't thought she was anything special, looking at her earlier. She'd seemed just average. But when she smiled? Holy shit, her whole face lit up, and it was almost as if he could see a bit of her soul shining through. A little cheesy, and people would tell him he was crazy, but Eagle didn't care.

"What are the odds?" she asked.

"The odds of what?" Eagle asked, still somewhat in a daze.

"Of us meeting. I don't recognize *anyone*, and you recognize *everyone*."

"Seems to me it's fate," Eagle told her.

Taylor rolled her eyes, and he could see her arms relax a fraction. The fact that he could relieve her stress meant a lot to Eagle. She was a stranger, but he could see a lifetime of pain in her eyes. Heard it in her voice when she had to defend her medical condition to him. He hated that.

He was concentrating so much on Taylor that Eagle didn't hear one of the officers he'd been talking to earlier come up to them. Jerking in surprise at the officer's voice, Eagle could only mentally laugh at himself. He couldn't remember the last time someone had snuck up on him.

"Talked to the captain. She said we have what we need from the other witnesses. If we need to talk to you later, we've got your info," Officer Brown said.

Taylor nodded at the officer, then turned and headed for the grocery store without another word.

Surprised at her abrupt departure, and somehow amused by the fact she'd completely turned her back on him, Eagle nodded at the officer and ran to catch up with Taylor.

"What's the hurry?" he asked as he fell into step beside her.

"I hate grocery shopping. I always seem to run into someone who knows me, and it sucks when I have no idea who they are. I thought coming early might prevent that from happening, but instead, all it did was put me smack in the middle of two idiots fighting for a damn parking spot. I'm tired, hungry, and sick of people looking down on me because of something I have no control over. I'm going to get my food, go home, and eat a dozen doughnuts to try to forget this disastrous morning."

"Mind if I tag along?" Eagle asked.

At his question, Taylor stopped in the middle of the entranceway to the store. She turned to look at him with a frown. "Why?"

"Why?"

"Yeah."

"Well, because I have to shop too. And like you, I hate it. Not because people might recognize me, though. But because I hate to cook. I suck at it. I'm also responsible for shopping for Silverstone Towing, and I always buy the wrong shit. It's like a game to everyone who works there, telling me everything I forgot to buy or how I bought whole wheat flour instead of the regular crap." He shrugged. "I thought maybe two people who hate grocery shopping could muddle through if we worked together."

Taylor stared at him for so long, Eagle was afraid she was going to turn around and leave him standing in the doorway like a fool. But she took a deep breath and held out her hand. "Hi. I'm Taylor Cardin."

Eagle grasped her hand in his and shook it. "Kellan Trowbridge, but my friends call me Eagle." Her palm was warm and smooth. His was covered in calluses from working on the tow trucks and from the missions he and his team went on.

She dropped his hand, and Eagle immediately wanted to grab it right back, haul her close, and see if her hair was as soft as it looked. But he did none of those things. He was attracted to the woman, but it was more than obvious she needed a friend. It was presumptuous of him to assume so, but there it was.

"I'm not sharing my cart with you," she quipped as she headed for the row of shopping carts. "You'll have to push your own."

"I'm okay with that," Eagle told her. "We just met—can't have our food touching."

She chuckled and shook her head at him, and just like that, Eagle wanted to get to know this woman. He wanted to know everything about her. What it was like growing up with prosopagnosia, who her friends were, where she lived, what her job was—everything.

He had a peculiar feeling that knowing her would change his life . . . for the better.

"I can hear you thinking," Taylor said as they walked through the produce section.

"It's just . . . I have about a million questions," Eagle admitted. "I've never met someone like you."

"Prosopagnosia is rare," she explained. "Only about two percent of the population is born with it. I can't recognize faces, even my own. If you showed me a lineup of pictures and included mine, I wouldn't be able to tell you which picture was me. I can make out individual features—like the fact you have blue eyes—but if you then showed me ten pictures of blue eyes, I wouldn't be able to pick out yours. But otherwise, I'm just like anyone else. I can make sound and rational decisions, and I wince when someone mixes polka dots and stripes in their outfits."

"And I'm the opposite," Eagle told her. "I wouldn't be able to tell you what's fashionable and what isn't, but if my second-grade teacher suddenly showed up in front of us, I'd not only be able to recognize her, but tell you her name."

He blindly reached for a bunch of bananas, and Taylor reached out and put a warm hand on his wrist.

Eagle glanced at her. He liked her hand on him. A little too much.

"You aren't seriously getting those, are you?" she asked with a little frown.

Looking down at the bundle of bananas he was about to put in his cart, Eagle shrugged. "Yes?"

"No," she said firmly, taking the fruit out of his hand and putting it back on the stand. She reached for another bunch and held it out to him. "Here. These are much better."

"Why?" Eagle asked.

"You said you were shopping for a group of people, right?"

"Yeah. There are over a dozen employees at Silverstone. They don't all work at the same time, but they're allowed to stop in whenever they want to hang out or to eat. Their families are welcome too."

"Right, so if you got that first bunch of bananas, they'd be bad within a day or two. If you get them a little greener, like those," she said, nodding to the ones she'd picked out, "they'll last longer. Besides . . . who wants to eat mushy bananas?"

"Hadn't really thought about it," Eagle told her honestly.

Taylor shook her head. "You really *do* suck at this shopping thing."

"I told you I did," Eagle said.

"I know, but I thought you were just hitting on me or something."

Eagle chuckled. "Unfortunately, no. I mean, I have a feeling you're pretty astute and would see right through any kind of flirting I might attempt. But I *do* suck at shopping. I just don't have the patience for it."

"Flirting doesn't really work with me," Taylor told him in a matter-of-fact tone, as if she was talking about the weather.

"What *does* work?" Eagle blurted, wanting to take the words back as soon as they were out of his mouth.

"Giving me time. Showing me with more than words that I can trust you."

Eagle stared at the woman next to him. At six-two, he was at least half a foot taller than her, and he had the urge to beat the shit out of anyone who'd broken her trust.

Inexplicably, he wanted to stand between her and the rest of the world. He couldn't decide if it was because he was sexually attracted, if her condition had him so intrigued, or if it was simply a matter of how vulnerable she seemed.

But regardless, one thing Eagle knew . . . he was going to do everything he could to prove to this woman that she *could* trust him. If that meant being a friend and nothing else, so be it. Earning her trust seemed more important than anything physical . . . at least at the moment.

"You *can* trust me," he told her.

She shrugged. "I've heard that before."

Eagle didn't like being lumped in with the other assholes who'd obviously let her down in the past. "You can," he insisted.

"What else is on your list of things to buy?" she asked, changing the subject.

Eagle let her, because at the moment, he had no idea how to convince her he was one of the good guys, let alone why he wanted to.

Well, not completely a *good* guy. He had a feeling if he told her that he and his friends traveled the world, ridding it of the worst of humanity, that wouldn't exactly earn her trust.

Instead of telling her what was on his list, he showed her. With Archer away, the employees took turns cooking, and they'd made a list of things for him to buy so they could put together meals. It was a hot mess, with ingredients scribbled in no particular order on the notepad kept on the refrigerator. Most of the time when he shopped, he just started at the top and worked his way down, having to backtrack several times throughout the store to get stuff from an aisle he'd already been down. It was a pain in the ass, and part of the reason he hated the chore.

"What is this?" Taylor asked, squinting at his list.

"Everything I need to buy," Eagle replied, telling her something she obviously already knew. "The employees at the station write down what they want, and I shop."

"Holy crap, this is awful," she told him. "No wonder you hate shopping."

Eagle couldn't help it—he laughed. "I was just thinking the same thing."

"Okay, first things first, we need to put some order to this," Taylor said, grabbing her cart and heading for an empty part of the produce section, out of the way of the other shoppers. She reached into her purse and rummaged around for a moment before pulling out a pen and a receipt.

"This isn't ideal, but it'll have to do," she mumbled. Then she propped his list on top of her purse, which was sitting in the child seat of the cart, and bent over the receipt. She'd turned it over and was writing on the blank back side.

"Okay, you've got muffin mix down twice, but they didn't say what kind, so I think you should get blueberry and cinnamon raisin. If they don't like it, tough, they should've specified. Eggs are on here three times, so maybe if you get two dozen, that should be good enough for a week. And if it's too much, they'll keep until next time. Fresh fruit? What kind? Jeez, they need to be more specific. No wonder you hate this; no one tells you exactly what they want, so they're setting you up to fail. Fine . . . how about apples, peaches, and grapes? If they want something else, they'll have to be more specific next time. Ground hamburger, chicken breasts, and shrimp . . . that's easy enough."

Eagle observed Taylor as she completely took over his list. She was scribbling furiously on the back of the receipt, and he couldn't help but smile as she continually mumbled under her breath while she wrote. It was as if the rest of the world ceased to exist. It was cute as fuck —but it also concerned him as well.

"Taylor?" a voice called out, making her jerk in surprise.

Eagle turned and saw a middle-aged woman coming toward them, smiling brightly.

"I thought that was you. How are you? It's been forever since I've seen you!" the woman enthused.

Glancing at Taylor, Eagle saw that she hadn't been lying about her condition . . . not that he'd thought she had. She had absolutely no idea who the woman standing near them was—the woman who was waiting to be acknowledged.

It truly dawned on him for the first time how frustrating and difficult not recognizing anyone might be.

Plastering a smile on his face, he stepped forward and held out a hand to the woman. "I'm Eagle, a friend of Taylor's. I don't think we've met?"

And just as he knew she would, the woman turned her attention to him. "Oh, hi. I'm Wanda Wright."

"Nice to meet you. How do you know Taylor?" Eagle asked as he shook her hand.

"We used to live in the same apartment complex," the chatty woman volunteered. "I moved out last year to another complex closer to my son's. His wife left him and their two kids, and I wanted to be closer to help out."

"How are Gail and Bobby doing?" Taylor asked softly from behind him.

Eagle dropped the woman's hand and took a step back.

"Oh, they're doing great!" Wanda gushed. "They're flourishing in school and are growing like weeds."

"And your son? He's okay?" Taylor asked.

"He had a hard time of it for a while, but I think he's finally realized the bitch he married did him a favor by leaving. The divorce went through, and he got full custody . . . not that she contested it at all. She was more concerned with her new twenty-year-old boyfriend to want to deal with kids. Her loss. And how're things going with you?"

Eagle tuned out the conversation and concentrated on observing Taylor. As soon as Wanda had approached, she'd tensed, her fingers curling into her palms. But she looked relaxed now. The two women talked about some of Taylor's neighbors and commiserated about the woes of apartment living.

"I've taken up enough of your time," Wanda said after a while. "It was great to see you again. I was happy to move closer to my grandbabies, but I was sorry to say goodbye to you."

"I'm glad things are working out for you," Taylor told her.

Wanda smiled huge and said her goodbyes.

After Wanda had pushed her cart away, Taylor turned to Eagle. "Thank you."

"For what?" Eagle asked, playing dumb.

Taylor frowned. "You know what. I had no idea who that was, and you seamlessly stepped in and made her introduce herself."

Eagle looked into her dark-brown eyes and said, "You don't know me, and like you said, you have no reason to trust me. But you absolutely can. I'm going to prove it."

She didn't say anything, but didn't drop her gaze either.

They stared at each other for a long moment before he nodded to the list still in her hand. "Is that salvageable?"

Sighing, Taylor shrugged and then said in a wry tone, "I'm not sure. I really did think you were throwing me a line about the not-good-at-shopping thing."

"I wasn't. I'm not."

"I see that now. I think I've got the original list reorganized according to the aisles in the store. We might still have to do a bit of backtracking, but hopefully not much. You really ought to get your employees to make an electronic list. I can barely read some of their handwriting."

"Archer will take care of it," Eagle told her.

"Archer?"

"He's the new guy. Shawn Archer. He's currently got the week off, but when he gets back, I have no doubt he'll take charge of all this, and those haphazard lists will be a thing of the past. Not to mention, he'll be the one shopping . . . thank God!"

"Good. Well, come on. I've already been at this damn store much longer than I'd planned, and if I'm going to help you, we need to get on with it."

She grabbed her cart and was about to turn it to continue shopping when Eagle put his hand on her arm, stopping her. "Thank you. For helping me. I'm man enough to admit when I'm in over my head. I'd have eventually figured that list out, but I'd have been in a piss-poor mood by the time I did. So thank you."

"No, thank *you* for making me not dread being here for once in my life."

And with that, she pulled away and headed back toward the apples. With no other choice, Eagle followed . . . not that it was a hardship to watch her from behind.

～

Taylor couldn't remember a time that she'd felt so relaxed in public. Normally she dreaded every single second she spent outside her apartment. Inside her safe space, she was Taylor Cardin, highly educated, much-sought-after proofreader, and confident in her abilities. She loved watching cooking shows and trying out new recipes. She had good relationships with her regular clients and was witty and funny in emails and on social media.

But the second she stepped outside, she turned into someone she didn't like very much. Meek, unsure, and standoffish.

She'd put off grocery shopping for as long as possible, finally setting out for the store that morning. Taylor knew she could shop online and do the curbside-pickup thing, but she didn't like the thought of someone else picking out her food. She was particular about her meat and fruits and vegetables. Besides, many times when she was wandering the aisles, she got inspired to try something new in the kitchen.

But she hated running into people she knew. Or rather, who knew *her*. It was always awkward. She either pretended she knew the person, or she had to admit that she didn't recognize them. People hated that. She'd lost too many friends to count over the years because she simply didn't know who they were when she saw them.

Forcing the depressing thoughts to the back of her mind, Taylor turned her attention to the man behind her and what had happened in the parking lot.

She could identify the men who'd been fighting based on their clothes, but as soon as they went home and changed, she wouldn't know them from Adam. Taylor was well aware that the officers were skeptical about her condition. Maybe even thought she was lying to get out of testifying, if it came to that. She'd felt awkward as hell as they'd discussed her disability, with regard to what they should put in their report about her, in front of the other witnesses, who, one by one, were allowed to go about their day while she'd been detained.

She felt as if *she'd* done something wrong, when all she'd been doing was trying to buy some damn food.

Then Eagle was there.

She'd known people like him existed; they were called *super recognizers* in her world. People with the opposite ability to what she had. She'd pretty much expected him to blow her off too, to make her feel as stupid as the officer had when he'd compared her to Drew Barrymore's character in *50 First Dates*. She hadn't meant to blurt out to Eagle that she wasn't like that character, but he hadn't even blinked.

She also hadn't expected him to introduce himself to Wanda. He could've stood there and watched her struggle to figure out who the woman was. But instead, he'd taken the initiative to help. She'd known that was what he was doing the second he'd introduced himself.

That conversation had been the most "normal" one she'd had with someone in a very long time. She'd actually enjoyed seeing Wanda again and hearing how she and her grandkids were doing. There wasn't any awkwardness on either of their parts.

Taylor didn't know anything about Eagle, except that he apparently was clueless about cooking and shopping for food. She also knew he worked at Silverstone Towing, which in itself said plenty, because the company was well known around the Indianapolis area. The police officers obviously knew him and were comfortable with him.

Hmmm, maybe she knew more about the man than she'd thought.

"Why the hell are there so many kinds of flour? It makes no sense," he grumbled.

Taylor couldn't help but chuckle.

He turned to her. "What? Look at this shit. There are rows and rows of fucking flour. It's stupid. All-purpose, cake, bread, self-rising, whole wheat, gluten-free . . . jeez."

Taking pity on him, Taylor reached for two bags of all-purpose flour and put them in his cart. "There're different kinds for different kinds of baking. But because your people didn't specify what they wanted, they get the normal everyday kind. If they want something else, they'll learn to be more specific."

Eagle simply grunted.

It was such a *guy* thing to do, she couldn't help but giggle.

"Are you laughing at me, woman?" he asked, his brows shooting upward.

"Yup," she admitted easily. And suddenly Taylor realized she was having fun. For the first time in what seemed like forever, she was *enjoying* herself while out in public.

"Before I lose my mind about all this food shit and how complicated it is, tell me more about yourself," Eagle ordered. "What do you do?"

Taylor knew she could blow him off and he'd let her change the subject, but she didn't want to. She liked Eagle. He was blunt, but he'd also made her laugh. That went a long way with her.

"I'm a proofreader."

He glanced over at her. "A what?"

"A proofreader. I take things people have written and read them to make sure there aren't any errors. Commas, spelling, grammar, that kind of thing."

"Books?"

"Yes. And speeches. And manuals for products, and even textbooks. You name it, I proof it."

"I didn't know that was a thing," he admitted.

"Most people don't. But you'd be surprised at the number of errors I find. Even if something's been edited over and over, there are still errors that slip through. I don't promise to find everything, as I'm human, but things like homophones, for instance, are some of the hardest things for people to catch."

When he stared at her blankly, Taylor explained, "Homophones are words that sound the same, but have different meanings. They're spelled differently depending on what they mean. Like, *right* and *write* . . . the first is a direction, and the second is a verb to put something down on paper. Or they can be spelled the same way, but mean something different. Like *pen*. It could be a writing utensil or a holding area for animals."

"I hadn't thought about it . . . except when I'm reading a book and the author's used *their*, t-h-e-i-r, when they meant *they're*, t-h-e-y-apostrophe-r-e."

"Or *there*, t-h-e-r-e," Taylor added.

It took Eagle a second, then he smiled. "Exactly."

"Right, so I'm a proofreader."

"I'm gonna be crass here, but it's just because I'm curious . . . does it pay well?"

Taylor didn't take offense. "Not at first. I took whatever jobs I could get, but after a while, I got a reputation for being superpicky, which is good for a proofreader. I got more and more work, and could raise my rates accordingly. I was working independently for a long time, but then got hired on by a textbook company. But I'll still proof just about anything. Websites, pamphlets, signs, books, speeches."

"Wow, that sounds interesting," Eagle told her.

Taylor chuckled. "It can be. But it's also really boring sometimes too. I remember when I had to proofread a biochem textbook. I thought I would never get through that thing."

"And it's something you can do from home," Eagle said with uncanny insight.

"Yeah. I've gotten really close to some of the people I work for, but I'll never go to any book conferences or anything. No one would understand how I could be so friendly online and completely standoff-ish in person. They'd think I was ignoring them, and it could hurt my business."

"I'm sure if they understood . . . ," Eagle started.

Taylor shook her head. "They don't. Think of your best friend," she requested. "Now, imagine coming face to face with them, and you have no idea who he is, even though you've spent hours and hours together, drinking, shooting the shit . . . doing whatever guys do when they hang out. How would that make you feel?"

"It would be hard," Eagle said without hesitation. "But if he was a true friend, someone who cared about me and loved me as I was, we'd have talked about my condition, and I'm guessing he'd just tell me who he was, and we'd continue on as normal."

"That's really easy to *say*, but it's not so easy for people to do time after time after time after time."

"Wrong," Eagle told her, stepping closer. But Taylor wasn't scared of him being in her personal space. She trusted him not to physically hurt her in a public place, like the middle of the cereal aisle in the grocery store. "It's not hard at all. When someone has a disability or a condition they were born with, like you were, *true* friends learn to do whatever's necessary to make each other comfortable. You adapt. For instance, from here on out, when we see each other after being apart, I'll call you Flower so you'll know who I am."

"And who *are* you?"

"I'm a man who sees you, Taylor. I see your distrust and your wariness, and I don't like it, even though I understand it. You know why I'm called Eagle?"

"No."

"Because I'm eagle eyed. I see everything. I know everyone. And I see *you*, Taylor. And I like who I see."

"You don't even know me," she protested.

"I know you're tough as hell. You'd have to be. You're funny and compassionate, but you keep the real you buttoned down in public. I'd like to get to know the Taylor you are when you're by yourself. When you don't have to worry about who you know and who you don't."

"I'm nothing special," she told him.

"I don't believe that."

"My mom gave me up when I was two," she blurted. "I guess I cried all the time. She couldn't deal with the fact that I couldn't recognize her. I'm sure it made it easier for her to separate herself from me emotionally."

"That's on *her*, not on you," Eagle told her. "And I hate that it's made you look at yourself differently. You say you're nothing special, but I firmly believe those people who've had the roughest times growing up end up being the most extraordinary adults. So . . . Flower," he repeated. "When you see me, that's what I'll call you so you'll know it's me." He grinned. "And not the flour you helped me buy," he clarified, adorably pointing out the homophone. "The way I see it, you're like a flower . . . an evening primrose. It's a flower that blossoms only at night, in the dark. You hide yourself away because of the way people treat you . . . but you still blossom. And I can't exactly go around calling you *all-purpose flour*." He winked. "So *flower*—meaning the beautiful plant—will have to be our code word instead."

Taylor swallowed hard and forced herself to take a step backward. He was overwhelming her. He was saying all the right things, but she'd heard them before. People telling her that her disability didn't matter. But eventually, it *did* matter. Girlfriends when she was in grade school, boys she'd dated, even a few clients who she'd opened up to . . . they'd all let her down.

"If we're going to get through this list of yours anytime soon, we'd better get on it," she said shakily, ignoring the whole flower thing.

For a second she didn't think Eagle was going to let it go. But he finally nodded. "Okay, Taylor. I can take a hint. You'll learn that I never say anything I don't mean." Then he grabbed ahold of his cart and continued down the aisle, throwing some oatmeal and Cheerios into his basket.

Taking a deep breath, she followed him.

Flower.

The man in front of her was lethal. Smart. Funny. Considerate. She had a feeling she was in big trouble.

∼

Brett Williams let himself into the home he shared with his mother and went straight to the basement. Anticipation flowed through his veins. It had been a while since he'd found a woman who'd interested him as much as the one today at the store.

Taylor Cardin.

He'd overheard her attempting to explain her disability to the officers.

Prosopagnosia.

He'd never heard of it, but the second he'd gotten into his car and looked it up on his phone, he'd known she was the one.

She didn't have the ability to recognize faces.

Which meant if she saw him tomorrow, she wouldn't know who he was.

Wouldn't know that he'd been a witness to the two idiots fighting in the parking lot.

He would always be a complete stranger to her.

But he knew who *she* was.

Eagerness rolled in his gut. He could have so much fun with her. He could mess with her mind for weeks . . . and she'd have no idea she was in his sights.

It had been almost seven months since he'd felt the high that came from having a woman completely at his mercy. He'd had the last one for five days, and at first she'd been fun to psychologically torture. She'd been scared out of her mind. It had made him feel incredibly powerful to watch her beg for her life, to see her cry as he'd choked her into unconsciousness time and time again.

After dumping her body, he'd had to lie low. Give the cops time to run in circles trying to figure out who'd killed her. But now that their investigation had grown cold, it was time.

He'd found his next plaything.

Taylor Cardin.

He could take his sweet time, play cat and mouse. All the while, she'd have no idea she was interacting with a serial killer again and again.

Smiling with anticipation, Brett looked at the pictures on the wall of his basement sanctuary. Old-school Polaroids of the women he'd killed. There were eleven.

He couldn't imagine not remembering them. He could recall every single second with each. How they'd begged. How they'd promised him anything he wanted if he'd just let them go. Every little sound and expression. Their faces were burned into his memory. He thought about them when he jerked off and when he simply needed a good memory to get him through his monotonous days.

And Taylor would be lucky number twelve.

Soon, he'd have her picture to add to his remembrance wall. Taylor might never remember his face . . . but he'd always remember hers.

"This'll be fun," he whispered to the sightless eyes staring back at him from the pictures on the wall. "Now to decide where and how to start my game with little Taylor."

Chapter Two

"And then Thomas took a huge bite—and spit it all out on the table. That made Christine and Shane gag. Leigh pulled out her phone and called for pizza," Eagle said.

Taylor giggled. "Are you lying?"

"Swear I'm not."

"How can you mess up spaghetti?" Taylor asked once she'd gotten herself under control.

No one had been more surprised than Taylor when Eagle had called her the night after they'd met at the grocery store. He'd asked for her number before they'd gone their separate ways in the parking lot, and she'd surprised herself by giving it to him without hesitation. There was just something about him that intrigued her . . . even if she wasn't one hundred percent sure of his motives. They'd only talked for about ten minutes during that first call, but then he'd called the next night. And the next. And the next.

It was now twelve days later, and they'd spoken every evening. She looked forward to their chats more than she wanted to admit.

"Hey, I'm a pro at screwing up food," Eagle said with a chuckle. "And . . . I'll deny this if you tell anyone, but I may or may not purposely mess up sometimes so I don't get asked to cook again for months."

"You're terrible," she told him.

"I know," Eagle said.

"Eagle?"

"Yeah?"

"It's been a long time since I've felt as if I've had a friend. Thank you." Taylor knew she could be making more out of this . . . whatever this was. This thing between her and Eagle. But she needed to let him know that she appreciated his friendship. "I've enjoyed our talks every night."

"Me too," he agreed. "You make me feel more . . . normal."

"You don't usually feel normal?" she inquired, pouring a glass of wine and sitting in the corner of her couch.

"No."

"Why?"

He was silent for a moment, and Taylor was worried about what he was thinking.

"When I started calling you, I admit that I was mostly curious about your condition. I've never met anyone who can do what I can, and the fact that you're the opposite is intriguing. But after that first call, I realized I didn't really give a shit about prosopagnosia or super recognizers or anything else. I simply enjoyed talking to you."

His admission upset her a little, but when he continued talking, she felt a warmth spread through her body. "Ditto," she said softly. "My condition shadows everything I do. I know I'm judged for it, even if people deny it. I admit it hurts a little to know that's why you wanted to talk to me in the first place, but I'm a pretty good judge of character, and I know if that was your only interest, you wouldn't still be calling me."

"I'm sorry. It was a dick thing to do," Eagle said.

"It's fine. You admitted it, which is more than most people would do."

"Even though it's been less than two weeks, I value your friendship," Eagle told her. "And in light of that . . . I'd like to tell you something about me."

"Okay," Taylor said slowly, not all that thrilled about the sudden serious tone in his voice.

"Not over the phone," he said firmly. "If I promise not to cook for you, do you think we could get together?"

Taylor's first instinct was to say no. She liked the relationship they had now. Talking on the phone every night. Discussing their day. It was easy. Relaxed. If they started hanging out in person, he would probably get irritated that she couldn't recognize him.

"Don't judge me by the assholes in your past," he said gruffly.

"How do you know what I was thinking?" she asked.

"Because I know you."

Those four words were scary as hell. Because he was right. He *did* know her. She'd opened up to him more in their phone conversations than she had with anyone else in her life. She had no idea what it was about Eagle that made her feel as if she could tell him anything, but it felt good. Really good.

"Okay," she said softly, deciding that if their friendship wouldn't survive face-to-face meetings, it was better to know now rather than down the line, when it would hurt more.

Hell, who was she kidding? She had a feeling that losing their nighttime talks would hurt plenty, even though it had only been two weeks.

"Good. I'm going to pick you up tomorrow around five. We'll come back to Silverstone Towing and eat a meal that Archer prepared. Then we'll sit and have a talk about what I do. I'll take you home whenever you want to go."

Taylor had to admit she was intrigued. She had no idea what it was Eagle wanted to tell her, but it sounded very secretive. "You don't have to pick me up," she told him. "I can drive over."

"Nope," Eagle said definitively. "I'm afraid if you come by yourself, you'll take one look at the compound and turn around and leave . . . and not take my calls anymore."

"Is it that bad? I thought you said Silverstone was doing well."

"It is, and we are," he told her. "But we've purposely made the buildings and the grounds look as if we *aren't* doing that well . . . to keep ourselves safe from anyone who might think we'd be an easy target for a robbery or other shenanigans."

Taylor was definitely intrigued now. "Really?"

"Really."

"Shenanigans? Who says that?" she teased, and was relieved to hear Eagle chuckle.

"I do, apparently. And . . . there's another reason."

When he didn't continue, Taylor asked, "What?"

"I want to prove to you that your condition doesn't bother me. That I don't care if you don't recognize me when you see me. I'll use our code word, and we'll continue on as we have over the last two weeks. Nothing changes, Taylor. I don't see you as less, and I don't pity you. Understand?"

Taylor wanted to agree. Wanted to believe him. But she'd been told that many times before, and ultimately, it always mattered. No one liked being looked at as if they were a stranger. Most guys' egos couldn't handle it.

"I understand," he continued when she didn't respond. "I'll just have to prove it to you. And I can't do that if we don't see each other. Five o'clock tomorrow, I'll be at your door."

"You don't know where I live," she protested.

Eagle chuckled. "You're cute."

"You *do* know where I live?" she asked.

"Yup."

"Do I want to know how you found that out?"

"I'll tell you tomorrow. Now . . . tell me what you did today. Did you get out of your apartment?"

Taylor wanted to know *now* how he could so easily have found her address, but even after just two weeks, she knew Eagle wouldn't tell her anything until he was damn good and ready. He was stubborn like that.

"I did," she told him. "I had to go to the post office. I have a PO box for my business stuff because it's more secure than the boxes here at my apartment complex, and I had to both send and pick up projects. I don't have too many clients who prefer me to mark up paper copies of their work, but when I do, I have to mail them back. So I got to take care of both with one trip, which I liked."

"How'd it go?" Eagle asked.

"Good, actually. I got into a chat with a guy while we were waiting in line. His mom needed stamps, and since she was handicapped and didn't want to order them online, he was there to help her out."

"Nice of him."

"It was. Of course, then the guy behind the counter asked me how I was doing and if I had any new cool clients. It was awkward because I had no idea what I'd already told him. I mean, I know that I've had discussions about what I do with several of the post office employees, but I didn't know what I'd told *him*. So I was vague, as usual, and luckily was done pretty fast."

"That's good."

"Yeah. Then I got some gas. Grabbed a fast-food burger on my way home, then spent five hours reading a book about an alien with a mail-order bride."

"I'm afraid to ask . . . was that a romance book or a sci-fi fantasy?" Eagle asked.

Taylor laughed. "Romance."

"Whew. I take it she wasn't eaten by the alien, then?"

"Welllll . . . ," Taylor drawled.

Eagle burst out laughing. When he could control himself, he said, "Wow, I walked right into that innuendo, didn't I?"

"Yup."

"It sounds as if you had a good day."

"Yeah. How about you? What'd you do?"

"I had a meeting with my friends in the morning, and then I went on a couple of runs."

"Anything interesting?" Taylor asked.

"A wreck, a tow because someone was driving on a suspended license, and two disabled vehicles," Eagle told her.

"I find it fascinating that someone who used to be in the Special Forces and obviously enjoys a good adrenaline rush can be satisfied with talking about the ins and outs of running a business and the arguably boring job of driving around," Taylor noted.

When Eagle didn't respond, she was afraid she'd offended him. "Eagle?"

"Yeah, I'm here. It's about balance," he told her mysteriously.

Taylor reminded herself that she didn't know the man as well as she sometimes felt she did, so she dropped the subject. "Well, since we've been talking, I've tried to become less of a recluse. I actually leave my apartment at least once a day now, just to get some fresh air. It's not bungee jumping or skydiving, but it's as much excitement as I want in my life."

Again, she got a weird vibe from Eagle's long pause, before he said, "I'm glad. Just because you have prosopagnosia doesn't mean you shouldn't get out and enjoy all life has to offer."

"I know."

"Good. I'm going to let you go. But I'll see you tomorrow afternoon around five."

"Okay. Thanks for calling."

"Thanks for answering," Eagle countered.

"See you tomorrow."

"Yes, you will," Eagle told her.

Taylor clicked off the phone and remained on the couch, staring off into space for a long minute. Some days she thought she knew who Eagle was, and other days, like today, she had a feeling she didn't know the first thing about him.

She supposed she should be worried that their friendship was moving so fast. But he hadn't asked her for anything. Hadn't done anything that made her nervous to talk to him. He hadn't pushed to see her before now, and he'd never done or said anything out of line. Other than the unintentional innuendo tonight, he hadn't hinted at anything sexual either.

And because things had been so good over the phone, she was reluctant to change the nature of their friendship. Over the years, she'd stopped trying to get close to others, simply because it hurt too much when her so-called friends decided it was too difficult to maintain the relationship.

And Taylor had *completely* written off romantic relationships after her last boyfriend had told her it was exhausting and depressing to have to tell her who he was every time he saw her.

Then, one morning, she'd woken up confused and disoriented because she'd legit forgotten he'd stayed over (which said something about how unmemorable sex with him had been) and momentarily freaked out when she'd seen a stranger in bed, which had been the last straw.

She'd tried to reassure him that she *did* remember him, remembered what they'd done in bed the night before (even if it hadn't been that good). But he couldn't get over the fact that she hadn't known who he was.

She really hoped Eagle was as thick skinned as he claimed.

Taylor also wished she had a girlfriend to talk to about Eagle, about how she already felt closer to him than just about anyone in her life. But she didn't. She could post on the prosopagnosia discussion board she belonged to, but she'd found over the years that it was more depressing than uplifting to read the posts on there.

Sighing, she reached for the remote control and clicked on the television. She didn't watch a lot of drama shows because she couldn't keep the characters straight, especially when they changed clothes throughout the episode. She turned on a cooking show instead and relaxed back into her cushions.

She was both excited and nervous about tomorrow, about seeing Eagle again. She tried to recall what he looked like and couldn't. He'd been wearing a pair of jeans, black boots, and a tan shirt when she'd met him, but other than that, she had no clue about his facial features.

She also had no real concept of what a good-looking man was. But she knew that the employee who'd helped her in the post office today had been wearing too much cologne. And the guy who'd been there to buy stamps for his mom had been wearing a pair of worn jeans with stains around the ankles. His shoes had looked brand new, and he'd eaten something with onions for lunch.

Her sense of smell was really good, and she had an uncanny ability to remember people's clothing, but when it came to their looks, she was clueless. Several people had told her that *she* was pretty, but that meant nothing to Taylor. When she looked in the mirror, she saw a stranger looking back at her. It was an odd feeling, one she didn't bother trying to explain to anyone anymore.

She couldn't help but wonder if Eagle might be one of the rare few who could understand. She had a feeling he would.

Sighing, Taylor turned her attention back to the television. Tomorrow was going to be a long day. She needed to finish up the proofread of the alien romance so she could start on the daunting task of proofing the six-hundred-page American history textbook she'd picked up at the post office while mailing out another manuscript she'd just finished. And the anticipation of seeing Eagle was daunting. She both dreaded seeing him again and was excited about it. She was a mess.

Her phone vibrated with a text, and Taylor realized she was still holding the cell in her left hand. She brought it up and chuckled when she read what Eagle had said.

Eagle: Stop worrying. If anything, I should be the one who's worried, not you.

Taylor had no idea what *Eagle* had to be worried about, but she took a deep breath. She'd learned over the years that worrying about something didn't actually lessen her anxiety. It only increased it. What happened would happen, and she'd deal. Just like she always did.

She typed out a quick reply.

Taylor: I'm not worried. Now hush, the heroine is about to find out that her alien has barbs on his penis and is wondering how in the world things between them will work out.

She had no idea why she'd written that. She'd finished the book earlier and was certainly not reading a romance at the moment, but she couldn't help teasing Eagle. She didn't like to think of him being concerned about whatever it was he wanted to tell her tomorrow.

Three dots came up on the screen, letting her know he was typing out a reply. When it came, Taylor could only shake her head and snort in laughter.

Eagle: Barbs? Jeez, as if I didn't already have an inferiority complex. How can I, a mere mortal, compete with barbs??!

Taylor: Thanks for making me laugh. I am nervous about tomorrow, but I trust you.

Eagle: Nothing's ever felt better than reading those last three words. Sleep well.

And just knowing she'd managed to make Eagle feel good made *her* feel good.

Taylor put her phone on the table next to her, chugged the rest of her wine, then snuggled down under a throw blanket and turned her attention to the screen. She *did* trust Eagle. He was one of the good guys. She'd bet her life on it.

～

Shit. Tomorrow, Eagle had to tell Taylor that he was definitely not a good guy. He wasn't exactly a bad guy, but he certainly wasn't good.

He hadn't lied to her. He'd been fascinated by her condition, and that was why he'd called her at first. But the more he got to know her, the more he genuinely liked her. She was smart as hell and way too good for the likes of him, but he couldn't make himself stop calling her every night.

Eagle had never had a female friend before. He'd slept with his fair share of women over the years, even thought he'd marry one once, but when he'd found out she was sleeping with half a dozen other men, he'd taken a long break from dating. He didn't want to be *that* guy, the one who distrusted all women because of one, but he was still smarting from her betrayal.

But damn if he didn't trust Taylor. There was something about her that called to him. And it had nothing to do with her condition, though he *was* concerned about her. Not being able to recognize anyone made her vulnerable in a way he wasn't comfortable with, and she seemed so cut off from the world. It was a self-imposed exile, but still.

He'd encouraged her to get out more. To ignore people who might look down on her because of her condition. And now that she *was* getting out, he couldn't help but worry about someone targeting her. He'd thought a lot about how her condition could make her even more vulnerable than she already was . . . and he didn't like it.

Shaking his head, Eagle knew he was fucked.

Taylor Cardin was the most interesting, most intriguing person he'd met in ages—and he was going to fuck it up tomorrow by telling her what he and his teammates did for Silverstone.

He wasn't going to make the same mistake Bull had. His friend had been head over heels in love with Skylar, and he'd told her about Silverstone just before going on a mission. After she'd learned what he did, they'd all thought the couple was done.

Eagle wanted to continue being Taylor's friend. Hell, if he was being honest with himself, he wanted more than that. But if she couldn't handle the fact that he was keeping the world safe by taking out terrorists, and others who had no respect for humanity, he was better off knowing sooner rather than later.

He hoped she could handle it, but he wouldn't blame her if she couldn't. She'd already wondered how he could deal with such a "boring" job after being in the military, and tomorrow, she'd find out that her assessment of him being an adrenaline junkie was spot on. He loved the intensity of the missions Silverstone went on. Got off on sneaking into and out of foreign countries. But his job at the garage was a necessary balance to the other side of his life.

Eagle hadn't talked to his friends about telling Taylor what they did, but he *did* want to make sure they knew to be on their best behavior tomorrow when he brought her to the garage.

The four of them were sitting in the safe room in the basement of Silverstone Towing. They'd discussed the schedule, gone over the reports from the drivers from the last few days, and written up Archer's preliminary employee report . . . which was nothing short of glowing. The man was a miracle worker, and all four men knew if he ever left them, Silverstone Towing would definitely be on the losing end.

"What's on your mind?" Gramps asked.

He was the oldest of their group, which was how he'd earned his nickname, but at forty-five, the man was in better shape than any of them. Nothing slowed him down. Ever.

"You've been acting weird lately," Smoke added. "Leaving work early, smiling more, acting all laid back. Something's definitely up."

Eagle chuckled. Smoke was only two years older than him but often acted like the father of the team.

"I'm guessin' it's a woman," Bull said, leaning back in his chair with a smirk. "I mean, I leave early every day so I can spend time with Skylar when she gets home from work."

They all knew Bull was still more than freaked out that his woman had willingly let herself be kidnapped by a child predator to protect one of the students in her class, who the man had developed an unhealthy obsession with—and had snatched off the playground at school. Now Bull had a compulsion to keep his eye on his woman as often as possible—not that anyone could blame him.

"It's a woman," Eagle admitted. "But she's just a friend."

Three pairs of eyebrows shot up as they all gave him nearly identical skeptical looks.

"Seriously," he protested. "I'm not saying I would mind if things progressed, but at the moment, I like what we have. I've only seen her once."

"At the grocery store," Gramps said with uncanny insight.

"The one with the facial-recognition thing?" Smoke asked.

"It's called prosopagnosia, and yes," Eagle said. "She's funny. And smart. And I can't remember when I've enjoyed talking to a woman as much as I do her. She's pretty amazing. I seriously can't imagine not being able to recognize anyone."

"That's because you recognize *everyone*," Bull said dryly.

"True. But think of the bigger implications. When she was bullied as a kid, she had no idea if someone walking toward her on the playground wanted to play with her or beat her up. In high school, she didn't know which boys were safe and which were to be avoided. And even today, if someone meant her harm, she wouldn't know if they were stalking her or not." Eagle shuddered. "I can't even think about it without wanting to throw up."

All three of his friends looked concerned now.

"I hadn't thought about it that way," Smoke admitted. "You think she's in danger?"

"No. Nothing like that. She hasn't told me about any skeletons in her closet or anything. In fact, she's pretty much been a recluse. People have treated her badly, to the point where she doesn't like to go out much."

"So if you've only seen her that once, how do you know so much about her?" Smoke asked.

"I've been talking to her every night. At first, I just wanted to pick her brain about her condition, but within minutes she had me laughing, and any thought of talking to her only about prosopagnosia flew out the window."

"*Every* night?" Gramps asked.

Eagle nodded.

"Well, all right, then."

"She's coming here tomorrow," Eagle informed his friends. "I want to introduce her to you all. But remember, when you see her next, she won't remember who you are. She'll remember meeting my friends, and being here and all that, but she won't know who you are from Adam. Just reintroduce yourself every time you see her and move on. Don't make a big deal out of it."

"She gonna know who *you* are?" Smoke asked.

"When I show up at her door and she looks through the peephole? No. I could be anyone."

"How's that gonna work?" Bull asked. "I mean, I'd think it would be weird."

"Right? If you ever get to the point where it's personal, what if she wakes up next to you and looks over and freaks because she has no clue who you are in her bed?" Gramps asked.

"Look, I don't have all the answers, but again, her *memory* isn't affected. She doesn't get amnesia from one day to the next. She'll remember my name, who I am, what we talked about. And if we ever sleep together, she'll definitely remember how she felt when she was with me. I'm guessing it has to be scary to look at someone and not recognize them. But she still *knows* me. I just need to tell her who I am, and it'll be fine."

"Maybe you should start wearing cologne so she can smell you," Smoke suggested.

"I know—you can eat onions all the time, so when she smells onions, she'll know it's you," Gramps teased.

"I could carve a giant *E* into your forehead so she can always recognize you immediately," Bull said with a smirk.

"Fuck off," Eagle retorted, knowing his friends were just messing with him.

"Seriously, though . . . ," Smoke said, "it has to be a very hard way to live."

"It is," he agreed. "She told me she doesn't have any pictures in her place because they mean nothing to her. That she can't recognize herself in photos, so what's the point of having them around? It would be like having pictures of strangers in your house."

Bull whistled. "That sucks."

Eagle nodded. "But don't feel sorry for her," he said. "You'll see when you meet her. She's fucking awesome. She's still really strong; she'd have to be just to have gotten this far in life. I want Silverstone to be a safe space for her."

"It will be," Gramps said resolutely.

"I can't wait to meet her," Smoke said.

"Are you gonna tell her about us?" Bull asked.

They all knew he was referring to their missions. They'd talked about this. That what they did should be shared only on a need-to-know basis. But everything within Eagle was telling him he could trust Taylor, that she'd be supportive. "I'm thinkin' about it," he told his friend honestly.

"You that sure about her?" Bull asked.

Eagle couldn't hear any censure in his friend's tone. "Yes."

Bull nodded. "If you want Skylar to talk to her, to help explain, I'm sure she'd be willing."

"My relationship with Taylor isn't like what you and Skylar had when you told her about Silverstone. I've got this," Eagle said, not letting any of his trepidation show.

Bull eyed him for a moment, then finally nodded. "Okay. You know we all trust you, and I won't interfere."

Eagle turned to stare pointedly at Gramps, one eyebrow quirked.

The other man held up his hands. "Hey, don't look at me. I learned my lesson. I won't butt in and tell her anything you don't want her to know."

Eagle nodded, then glanced back at Bull. "I'm picking Taylor up at five and bringing her back here. I already talked to Archer, and he's gonna make lasagna for us to eat. Do you think Skylar might be receptive to meeting her? I don't think either of them has a lot of girlfriends, and I suspect they'll hit it off."

"I'm sure she'd love to," Bull said. "I don't know if they'll hit it off or not, but it might make Taylor feel better if she's not the only woman here when she meets us."

"Leigh is working dispatch tomorrow night, and Christine's on duty, so she won't be the only female," Eagle said.

"You've clearly thought this through," Gramps noted.

"I like her," he said. "I admit I was fascinated by her condition, but I've learned she's funny, smart, and easy to talk to."

"Well, I'm happy you're hooking up, but don't think I'm gonna be next," Smoke replied. "I'm perfectly content being single."

"We aren't hooking up. We're just friends," Eagle protested.

"Don't knock it till you try it," Bull added with a smile, then he pushed back his chair and stood. "And speaking of which, time for me to get home so I can give my woman a few orgasms, then have wild monkey sex."

Gramps grimaced and covered his ears with his hands. "Jeez, don't talk about sex around me. It's been so long, I think my dick's forgotten how to work. Besides, I have to see Skylar tomorrow. I do *not* want to be thinking about you naked when I see her."

Bull merely chuckled. "See you guys tomorrow."

The others left not too much later, and Eagle closed the safe room and headed up the stairs. There were a few drivers hanging around the garage, and he spoke to each of them before heading out to his Wrangler.

He felt the same way right now as he did before leaving on a mission. Excited and a little jittery. He couldn't wait to see Taylor again. He wasn't sure how she would react to learning about Silverstone, but he had a good feeling. She was down to earth and practical. If anyone could see that Silverstone was doing the world a favor, it was her.

Chapter Three

Taylor was nervous.

Which was stupid, because she felt as if she knew Eagle pretty well. You couldn't talk to someone for two weeks straight and *not* know them.

But he was supposed to be at her apartment any moment now, and suddenly she wasn't sure if she should even be trying to move their friendship forward from a talk-on-the-phone kind of thing to an in-person thing.

She wasn't good at in-person friendships. She had twenty-eight years of history to prove it.

But here she was, pacing her apartment after having taken great pains to look nice. She'd showered that morning, blow-dried her hair, applied a bit of makeup, and put on a pair of jeans that hugged her ass and one of her favorite shirts . . . a scoop neck that showed off her assets. She'd never be a model, but she still didn't want to look like a slob when she saw Eagle again. Or when she met his friends.

It was obvious the men who owned Silverstone Towing were close. Eagle had mentioned his friends, of course. Bull, Smoke, Gramps, and Eagle had all been in the Army together and, when they'd gotten out, had decided to start up their company, but that was all she knew about the men.

"This is a bad idea," Taylor whispered nervously to her empty apartment.

Then she jumped when a knock sounded at her door.

Her heart rate accelerated. This was it. She figured it was Eagle who was waiting for her to open the door, but it could also be a neighbor, a maintenance man, or anyone else. She literally wouldn't know the difference between them.

Telling herself that it wouldn't be the end of the world if she and Eagle didn't click, if the connection they'd formed was only strong over the phone, Taylor walked over to her front door.

She looked through the peephole and saw a stranger standing there. Although, to be fair, everyone was a stranger to her. The man was tall, like Eagle, and had dirty-blond hair. He wore a dark-blue polo shirt, and she could just see some chest hair where it opened at his neck. He was cleanly shaven and had blue eyes.

"Who is it?" she asked through the closed door.

"Hey, Flower, it's me, Eagle."

The man didn't have an identifying accent, and there was literally nothing about him that she could recognize from looking at him through the small security hole in the door. But then she remembered his vow to call her Flower when he saw her. There hadn't been a need when they'd been talking on the phone.

Smiling at the memory of how confused Eagle had been when he'd tried to buy flour for his business, Taylor opened the door.

"Hi," she said a little shyly.

"Hi, Flower," Eagle replied, repeating their secret word. "I know this is outside your comfort zone, so thank you for agreeing to come to dinner with me at Silverstone."

"Do you want to come in?" she asked, holding her door open wider.

"No. I'll wait here. Unless you've changed your mind?" he asked, tilting his head in concern.

Taylor rushed to reassure him. "No, but . . . I admit that I'm really nervous about this."

"It's going to be fine. I hope it's okay, but I told my friends about your condition. So you don't have to get into any awkward explanations about it if you don't want to. I'll warn you, though, they're pretty curious." Eagle looked a little sheepish. "Much like I was when I first met you. But they're harmless. If you're uncomfortable, just say so. They'll back off and won't have any hard feelings. Promise."

Taylor wasn't sure about that. A lot of people got offended when she didn't want to talk about her condition. They asked downright rude questions, and when she tried to change the subject, they got irritated. She didn't admit that to Eagle.

But as she'd found over the last two weeks, he seemed to be on the same wavelength as she was anyway.

"You'll see," he told her. "Go on. I'll wait here while you get whatever you need."

Nodding, Taylor shut the door and went to get her purse. She trusted Eagle, but never leaving her door open was second nature to her now. It wasn't until she'd gotten her purse and had reopened her door to see Eagle leaning against the wall across from her apartment—she was aware it was him because of the navy-blue shirt he was wearing—that she realized she'd probably been rude.

"Sorry," she said with a small shrug. "Habit."

"I approve," he said, pushing off the wall and stepping toward her. "Ready?"

"Seriously, it was rude," she insisted. "I shouldn't have shut the door. It's not that I don't trust you, I just—"

"Taylor, it's fine," Eagle said firmly. "I wholeheartedly approve. I'm not offended, and I'm actually impressed. You should never leave your door open, even for someone like a delivery person or something. All it takes is a split second for someone to get inside and lock your door, then you're stuck in your apartment with someone who might want to harm you. Our society is too concerned about being polite and not offending someone instead of concentrating on their own safety."

That was exactly how Taylor felt. The connection she had with his man was almost scary. She gave him a small smile. She still felt a little off-kilter, which was normal for her. It always took her a bit of time to feel comfortable around someone she was already acquainted with, because while they looked like a stranger, inside, she was aware that they weren't.

Of course, Eagle seemed to sense it, and he didn't launch into awkward conversation or otherwise do anything to try to prove that she knew him. He simply gestured toward the hallway and walked next to her as they headed for the stairwell.

He kept quiet as they walked across the parking lot toward his Wrangler. He held open her door and waited until she was situated before closing it and walking back around to the driver's side.

It wasn't until they were pulling out onto the road by her apartment that she spoke. "So, what did you want to tell me?" All last night and most of today, Taylor had been wondering about what he might want to say to her. She was extremely curious.

"Nope."

"Nope what?" Taylor asked in confusion.

"I'm going to show you my business first. Introduce you to my friends. Then we'll eat. Then we'll shoot the shit with any drivers hanging around. I think Skylar—that's Bull's girlfriend—will be there at some point too. Then, once you're relaxed and comfortable, we'll talk."

Taylor supposed she should be irritated at Eagle for orchestrating their entire night without asking what she wanted to do, but nothing he'd planned was out of line, so she simply nodded. "Okay."

They talked the rest of the way to Silverstone Towing, and when he pulled onto a short driveway, Taylor could only stare in surprise at the complex in front of her. "Jeez, Eagle, you were right—it looks like a drug den or something. Razor wire on top of the fence, the tall weeds, the cameras . . . what are you hiding in there? Drugs? Gold?"

Eagle chuckled, not offended in the least. "Skylar said it looked like a motorcycle-gang clubhouse the first time she saw it."

"Yeah, that too," Taylor agreed.

She watched as Eagle lowered his window and leaned out to punch at least ten numbers onto a keypad. The gate in front of them opened surprisingly quickly, and when she looked behind them after they'd driven through, Taylor saw that it closed just as fast.

"It's not smart to have a slow gate," Eagle told her, obviously seeing where she was looking. "There's a sensor that knows when the vehicle has gone by, and it triggers the gate to shut. Two cars can't enter at the same time, and the fast motion of the gate is to try to prevent anyone from slipping in after a vehicle."

Taylor nodded, but that was honestly something she'd never thought of before. As they drove toward the largest of the buildings, she noted that while there *were* tall weeds around the property, they seemed to be more strategic than out of control. The grass up against the buildings was neatly trimmed, and there were no big bushes anywhere.

Eagle parked his Jeep toward the back of the building, at the end of a row of other vehicles, and glanced at her when he'd turned off the engine. "So?" he asked with a raised eyebrow.

"Impressive," Taylor told him honestly. "And you're right, I probably would've freaked if I'd driven myself here."

He smirked. "Yup. We purposely make this place look kind of shitty. Helps us fly under the radar in this neighborhood."

"You could move," she suggested.

"But the location is perfect," Eagle countered. "We're near the outer loop and I-65, and we can get downtown within ten minutes as well. Besides, a lot of our employees live not too far from here, and if we moved, that would inconvenience them."

He turned to get out, but Taylor put a hand on his arm, stopping him. Eagle glanced back at her.

"Why would that matter?" she asked, genuinely curious to hear his answer.

"Because our employees are the lifeblood of Silverstone Towing. Without them, we're nothing." And with that, Eagle climbed out of the car.

Taylor shook her head in disbelief. She hadn't met many business owners who cared that much about their employees. For most, it was all about the bottom line. Money. If it made fiscal sense to change location, that was what was done, and the employees had to deal. Altering the outward appearance of their business to try to match its location was a smart business move. But she had a gut feeling not moving was more about their employees than being close to the interstates.

Her door opened, and Taylor jerked in surprise. As she climbed out, Eagle put his hand under her elbow to help her stand, letting go once she was steady on her feet. Her skin tingled where he'd touched her.

He's your friend, she told herself. *Relationships don't work out for you, remember?*

It was hard to remember that when so far everything Eagle had done impressed the hell out of her.

He punched in another long stream of numbers on a keypad next to the door, and it opened with a click.

"I'd bring you in the front door, but then we'd have to walk all the way around the building, which would be stupid. So you won't get the full effect of the place, but I'll show you the front entrance later."

Taylor wondered what was up with the front entrance, but didn't have time to ask, because Eagle led her down a hall and into a large absolutely beautiful great room. The ceiling was high, and the room looked extremely homey and comfortable.

There were leather couches and chairs in the living area along with a huge television. A delicious smell permeated the room, coming from the fanciest kitchen she'd ever seen against the far wall. There were two huge refrigerators, a six-burner gas stove, and a granite bar that had at least a dozen stools pushed up under it.

"Welcome to Silverstone Towing," Eagle said softly.

Taylor turned to him with huge eyes. "I . . . this is hard to believe," she stammered.

Eagle chuckled. "I know. The outside looks like nothing special, but we wanted the inside to be a home away from home for everyone."

"You've succeeded. Wow," Taylor said.

"Hey, Eagle!" a man called out as he entered from a hallway on the other side of the room.

"Hey, Robert," Eagle returned. Then he put his hand on the small of Taylor's back and gently urged her forward.

Her belly rolled, but she pasted a smile on her face as they walked toward the man.

Eagle reached out and shook Robert's hand, then turned to her. "Taylor, this is Robert. He's one of our drivers."

Robert nodded at her. "It's nice to meet you."

"Busy tonight?" Eagle asked the man.

"Not so far. I'm just on a quick break for dinner. I was here when Archer was making the sauce earlier. I thought it smelled good then, but damn, now it's like an Italian restaurant in here."

Taylor couldn't argue with him.

"Who else is here?" Eagle asked.

"Bull, Smoke, and Gramps are downstairs in your room; Christine's in dispatch; Jose doesn't go on duty for another hour, but he's taking a nap in one of the rooms; and I think Thomas is on his way for lasagna too."

"Jose's baby is still colicky?" Eagle guessed.

"Yeah. His mother-in-law is here right now. His wife went out with friends for a break, and her mom kicked him out, told him to get some sleep before his shift," Robert said.

"Good," Eagle said with a satisfied smile.

Taylor could only listen in awe.

"Well, it was great meeting you," Robert told her. "But I need to get dinner before I'm called back on duty. Hope to see you around."

"Same," Taylor said, watching as the man made a beeline for the kitchen.

"You want a tour, or do you want to eat first?" Eagle asked her.

"Tour," Taylor said immediately. She couldn't wait to see more of the building.

Eagle smiled and held out his hand, indicating she should precede him. She walked through the large room and into the hallway Robert had come out of. She peered into a few of the rooms, seeing both small bedrooms as well as spaces set up so people could watch TV or play video games. There was a huge bathroom at the end of the hallway as well, complete with showers.

"I heard Robert say Christine was working dispatch, but I only see one bathroom . . ." She trailed off, not knowing how to ask her question without being disrespectful.

But Eagle understood what she wanted to know without her having to ask. "There's a private bathroom and shower downstairs for anyone who isn't comfortable using the communal one up here. We try very hard to be tolerant and accepting around here," Eagle told her. "As long as everyone's respectful of each other, we all get along fine. We're happy to make accommodations as needed too."

"Like the private shower," Taylor said.

"Exactly. When Leigh was first hired here, she said she absolutely couldn't pee or shower in the same room with a guy. She'd been assaulted and raped in the past. So we had the private shower and bathroom put in downstairs. It was the right thing to do."

Taylor liked that. No, she freaking *loved* how accommodating Eagle and his friends were.

"Come on, I'll take you downstairs," Eagle said.

They went down the stairway into another huge room. This looked more like a place people came to play rather than relax. There were more comfy chairs around the space, but also a Ping-Pong table, a few foosball tables, and video games. Taylor's fingers itched to play the pinball machine she saw in the corner, but she followed Eagle across the room instead.

He smiled when he saw where her eyes kept going. "I'll let you play a few games later," he told her.

"I don't have any quarters," she said.

His grin grew. "Don't need any. They're all set to free."

Of course they were. Taylor should've guessed. She saw a few doors and assumed one was probably the private shower Eagle had talked about, and the others were maybe some closets.

Eagle headed straight for a very formidable-looking door tucked away in the corner. Instead of a keypad next to this one, there was a biometric reader of some sort. Eagle put his thumb on a little black square, and she heard a lock disengage.

For a second, she thought about one of the romance books she'd proofread where the bad guys had gotten past the biometric lock by chopping off the guard's hand after they'd killed him and holding it up to the reader.

But her inane thoughts dissipated the second she walked into the large room, where three men stood as they entered. Taylor swallowed hard, feeling completely out of her element. She had no doubt these were Eagle's friends.

There was a round table to the left, as well as computers, a small kitchen, and a bathroom in the back, which Taylor could see because the door was open. She had no idea what Eagle and his friends talked about in this room, but it was more than obvious to her that it wasn't just a regular meeting space.

"Eagle," one of the men called out. He walked toward them and gave Eagle one of those man-hugs where they slapped each other on the back really hard instead of actually embracing.

"Hey, Smoke." Then he turned to the others and gave them a chin lift. "Bull. Gramps."

The other men returned the greeting.

"Everyone, this is Taylor. Taylor, these are the best friends a man could ever have. This is Smoke," he said, gesturing to the man who'd greeted them at the door. He was around the same height as Eagle, with dark-brown hair.

"The tall asshole is Gramps, and the guy with black hair is Bull."

Taylor appreciated Eagle pointing out the features of his friends. She didn't always remember what color hair people had, but it went a long way toward helping her keep the four men straight in her head.

"Hi," she said quietly, giving them a lame little wave.

"Come sit," Gramps said, gesturing to both her and Eagle.

Taylor did her best to memorize as much about the men as she could as she approached them. Gramps was indeed the tallest. He and Smoke both had shortish brown hair, so that wouldn't help her distinguish them, but their height would. Bull was also the only one of the three who didn't have brown hair; that would help her as well. Bull was wearing a red shirt, which would be easy for tonight, as the color reminded her of bullfights and waving red capes. Smoke was the only one wearing a pair of cargo pants, so that would distinguish him.

She nodded to herself, pretty confident that she'd be able to tell the four men apart. But when she saw them again—if she saw them again—it would be trickier since they'd be wearing different clothes.

"What'd you come up with?" Smoke asked when they'd all sat down at the table.

"What?" Taylor asked.

At the same time, Eagle said a little menacingly, "Careful."

"I was just wondering how she decided to tell us apart," Smoke said easily.

"Was it that obvious?" Taylor asked.

Smoke shrugged. "We're an observant bunch," he hedged.

Since she didn't hear any morbid curiosity in his tone, and the other men simply looked interested, she decided, *What the hell.* "I should be good for tonight, but after you change, I won't know you from Robert or Thomas or anyone else. But Bull's wearing red, like a bullfighter's cape, and has black hair; Gramps, you're the tallest; and Smoke, you've got different pants on than everyone else."

All three men nodded, as if in approval.

"She's not a fucking carnival sideshow," Eagle grumbled.

"What was the name of the woman who was in that car accident three weeks ago?" Bull asked. "You know, the one in the minivan with all the kids?"

"Meredith Oxgarden. Why?" Eagle asked.

"Didn't she have like five kids with her?" Gramps asked, smiling.

"Yeah. Billy, Carly, Riley, Aaron, and Christopher. Again, what does she have to do with anything?" Eagle asked impatiently.

Taylor tried to hide her grin. She knew what his friends were doing. She put her hand on Eagle's arm. "They're just curious," she said softly. "It's fine."

"Then why are they asking about Meredith and her kids?" he asked, completely confused.

Taylor chuckled. "They're making a point."

"Well, it's a shitty point if I don't understand it," Eagle griped.

"You remember everyone. I remember no one," Taylor said, still smiling. "We're different. It's probably fascinating to them. We make a weird pair."

"Fuck you guys," Eagle told his friends. "I can't believe you haven't gotten sick of doing that shit by now."

"It'll never get old," Bull admitted.

"And you guys aren't weird," Gramps told her. "Opposites attract."

"We're just friends," Eagle and Taylor said at the same time.

Bull, Smoke, and Gramps all grinned.

Taylor looked at Eagle and couldn't help but giggle. He looked so put out, but she thought it was hilarious. She turned her gaze back to his friends. "I know Eagle told you about my prosopagnosia. It's a pain in the ass, but there's nothing I can do about it. When I meet people, I do my best to memorize things about them that stand out. Scars, tattoos, things like that. Anything distinctive that helps me recognize them when I see them again. I was hoping at least one of you would have some huge wart or something on your face so I'd immediately know it was you, but alas, you're completely normal looking."

Smoke gasped and held a hand to his chest. "Normal? Aw, come on. We're the most handsome men on the planet. It's a shame you can't see that."

Everyone laughed.

"But seriously, we're just as interested in your condition as we are in Eagle's. That's where his name comes from, you know . . . because he's got an eagle eye. If we rib you about it, it's because we like you, not because we're being malicious."

Taylor nodded. She liked these men already. She didn't know them, but they'd done everything right. She felt comfortable giving them the benefit of the doubt.

"So you met Eagle at the grocery store, huh?" Bull asked. "He hates that place."

"I know, he told me," Taylor said.

"You weren't hurt in the altercation you witnessed, were you?" Gramps asked.

"No. Everything happened so fast. The guy in the convertible whipped into the spot so quickly, the man driving the van didn't even have a chance to get in there. He jumped out and started screaming, and then the fight was on. It was crazy."

"Did anyone try to stop them?" Smoke asked.

"No. They were beating the hell out of each other, and one pulled a knife," Taylor said. "No one was going to step into that. A few people videoed it, though, of course. Luckily there were lots of witnesses, so they didn't need me."

"Don't do that," Eagle suggested.

Taylor looked at him in surprise.

"We've talked about this. Just because you wouldn't be able to point them out in a lineup doesn't mean you wouldn't make a good witness. You were very clear in what you saw and what happened. You gave the cops a vivid picture of who took the first swing and who was in the wrong. The other witnesses were able to back up what you said. Don't discount what you can offer simply because you wouldn't recognize their faces."

They *had* talked about that one day on the phone, and Eagle had basically said the same thing then. Taylor had blown him off, thinking he was just being nice, but she could see now that he one hundred percent believed what he was saying. And it felt good.

"And that cop was out of line, saying what he did," Eagle added.

"What'd he say?" Gramps asked.

"He compared Taylor's condition to that movie *50 First Dates*," Eagle told his friends.

At their looks of confusion, Taylor quickly explained. "I take it you haven't seen it. Drew Barrymore has a condition where she doesn't remember anything that happens after going to sleep each night. So every day is a blank slate. Adam Sandler starts dating her, but he has to get to know her from scratch every day because she never remembers him. It's a comedy. But that's not anywhere near my issue. There's nothing wrong with my memory. I'll remember meeting you guys, seeing this amazing building, and eating lasagna. But tomorrow, if you all lined up in front of me, I wouldn't know who's who." She shrugged. "That movie's kinda been the bane of my existence."

"I can imagine," Bull said.

"That sucks," Gramps commiserated.

"I'm hungry," Smoke threw out after a moment.

Taylor giggled.

"And those are my friends," Eagle said with a sigh.

"What? We've been smelling the lasagna cooking all day," Smoke defended himself. "It's been torture."

"Skylar should be here any minute," Bull said. "She stayed late at school to change out her bulletin boards."

"Great. I want to show Taylor the dispatch room before we eat. Hopefully Sky'll be here by then," Eagle said as he stood.

Taylor followed, as did the others. She kind of wanted to look around the small room he'd shown her some more, but Eagle put his hand on her back and urged her toward the door. The heat from his touch felt good. Which made Taylor feel guilty.

Eagle was her friend. That was it. He couldn't be more. Wouldn't *want* to be more.

They all walked back up the stairs, and she and Eagle headed for one door while the other three continued on into the great room and toward the kitchen.

Eagle opened the door, and Taylor saw a woman sitting in front of three large monitors. She wore a headset and was obviously talking to someone.

"The accident is blocking the right lane, but you should be able to sneak around the traffic by using the shoulder . . . right, let me know when you're on scene."

Then she turned and smiled. "Hey."

"Busy?" Eagle asked.

The woman shrugged. "No more than usual."

"Christine, this is Taylor. You'll hopefully be seeing her around now and then."

"Hi," Christine said, her smile wide and friendly.

"Hey."

"Are you a new driver?"

Before Taylor could answer, Eagle explained. "No. She's my friend. She's the one who showed me which damn flour to get the last time I shopped."

"Oh!" Christine exclaimed. "Thank God you were there. Eagle's awesome, but he sucks at shopping."

"Hey, I'm not that bad," Eagle said.

"Um . . . yeah, you are. It's a good thing Archer's here now. Have you had some of his lasagna yet? Robert brought me a slice not too long ago. I inhaled it! Archer's a god in the kitchen. If he leaves, I'm quitting."

"No one's leaving or quitting," Eagle said in exasperation.

"I'm just sayin' . . . he's that good," Christine told her boss.

"Noted," Eagle said with a small shake of his head. "Any problems tonight?"

"Nope. All's good," Christine said breezily. "Go on, go get some of that lasagna. There might not be any left if you don't get there before Bull, Smoke, and Gramps. They've been salivating for dinner all afternoon."

"Shit!" Eagle swore, feigning panic and grabbing Taylor's hand and tugging her toward the door.

Taylor managed to turn and say, "It was nice meeting you!" as she was pulled toward the door.

"Same! Enjoy dinner!" Christine called out.

Taylor was too amused to protest as Eagle pulled her down the hallway. When he entered the great room, he bellowed, "Freeze!"

Gramps and Smoke were in the kitchen, and they immediately turned to stare at Eagle. Bull was standing on the other side of the room kissing a woman, who Taylor could only assume was his girlfriend, Skylar. Neither stopped their kissing at Eagle's loud command. There were two men sitting at the bar, and they comically froze with their forks halfway to their mouths.

"Step away from the lasagna," Eagle told Smoke and Gramps.

Both men grinned.

"Relax. No matter what Christine told you, there's plenty," Gramps said, turning to continue what he was doing. He plopped the biggest piece of lasagna Taylor had ever seen onto a plate in front of him.

"There'd better be," Eagle mock threatened as he headed for the kitchen. He hadn't let go of her hand, and Taylor didn't have the urge to remind him he was still towing her around. He started to reach for the handle of a cabinet when he finally realized he was still holding her hand. "Sorry," he said a little sheepishly, squeezing her fingers before finally letting go.

"It's okay," she told him softly.

Eagle grabbed two plates and headed for the pan of lasagna. There was only a quarter of the pan left, and Taylor frowned in concern when Eagle heaped a big portion of it onto one plate, and most of the remaining piece on the other.

"Um . . . I don't want to take the last piece," she said.

"There's another pan in the oven," Smoke told her. "Archer learned really quickly to make double and triple batches of everything."

Sighing in relief, Taylor watched in amusement as Eagle, after hearing there was more, put the last small piece of the delicious-looking lasagna on his plate. "Is that enough, or do you want more?" he asked, using the spatula to gesture toward the oven.

Taylor couldn't help it. She laughed. "I think the ten pounds you already put on my plate will be plenty."

A woman joined in, laughing as well, and Taylor turned. Bull had his arm around the woman's shoulders, and she was leaning into him. She was on the shorter side, but looked like she fit perfectly against Bull. She had curves Taylor envied and seemed completely at ease in the room filled with over-the-top alpha men.

"Hi, I'm Skylar," the woman said.

"I'm Taylor."

"It's really good to meet you," Skylar said.

"Same," Taylor returned. Eagle had told her a little bit about Skylar and how she'd been kidnapped. Looking at the woman now, Taylor couldn't find any hint of what she'd been through. She knew she was a kindergarten teacher at an inner-city school, and that she was loved and respected by both the students and faculty alike.

Taylor envied her. The other woman looked so put together and content, neither of which was something Taylor ever felt.

Skylar's auburn hair was pulled back into a bun on the back of her head, and she had on an honest-to-God jumper dress. It was so stereotypical and screamed *kindergarten teacher* so loudly, Taylor almost wanted to laugh.

She heard Smoke chuckle and looked over at him.

"I can guess what you're memorizing about Sky," he quipped. "She dresses like that Monday through Friday. Even I have a hard time recognizing her in jeans and a T-shirt."

Instead of being put out, Skylar grinned at Smoke's comment. "I know, I look exactly like what I am. But the school has a dress code, and after all the years of teaching, I find that I'm most comfortable in dresses and skirts when I teach now. But I do like my jeans on the weekends."

"Well, if I see you on a Saturday or Sunday, please remind me who you are so I don't get mad at Bull for making those googly eyes at another woman," Taylor said without thinking.

Skylar's eyes widened. "Oh crud, I forgot! Hang on!" Then she ducked out from under Bull's arm and rushed for the same door Taylor and Eagle had entered when they'd arrived.

"Where's the fire?" Eagle asked.

Bull shrugged. "I hope you don't mind, Taylor, but I told her about your condition. She asked me a million questions about it, and then said she had an idea."

Eagle brought both their plates over to an empty spot at the bar while they waited for Skylar to return. They didn't have to wait long. She rushed back into the room with a huge smile on her face.

She gave something to Bull. Then to Smoke, Gramps, and the two men at the bar, who'd finished eating their lasagna and were now sitting back, relaxing. Then she walked up to Taylor and Eagle and held something out to each of them as well.

"I thought about your condition and how hard it would be . . . especially to meet a bunch of people you don't know. I mean, who you *really* don't know. I had a hard time keeping everyone who works here straight when I first met Bull, and I don't have the condition you do. So I made name tags for everyone." She smiled uncertainly. "I thought maybe it would make it easier for you. If everyone wore them around here, you wouldn't have to wonder who anyone was. They're magnetic, so they won't poke holes in our clothes." She glanced at Eagle. "And they won't hurt the uniforms either. I know you guys decided not to put name patches on those overalls everyone wears, but I thought, at least around here, people could wear them?"

When no one said anything, Skylar continued on, talking faster, as if uncertain now. "I can make a board to put by the door that's magnetic. Everyone can leave them there when they go home, and pick them up when they come in. Maybe they can even wear them while they work. I mean, Bull made me see the error of my ways when I didn't call to confirm his identity when he showed up in his tow truck. The dispatchers could tell callers that their driver will be wearing a name tag, and what his or her name is."

Bull came up behind Skylar and pulled her back against his chest. Her brows were furrowed, as if she was worried about what everyone might think of the idea.

Taylor looked down at the name tag in her hand. It wasn't anything special. Oval shaped, plastic, black on the back side with the magnet and white on the front side, where her name was printed in black bold letters. Big enough to see from a good distance away. Looking over, she could see Eagle's name in the same large letters.

Swallowing hard, Taylor felt her eyes burn, and she looked back down at the name tag in her hand, trying to get control of her feelings.

Eagle lifted her chin and forced her to look at him. "Taylor?"

At the same time, she heard Skylar say, "I'm sorry! It was stupid. Just ignore me. I wasn't trying to be offensive. I just thought it might help."

Not wanting the other woman to think for one second that she was offended, Taylor turned to her. A tear escaped and rolled down her cheek. "This is one of the nicest things anyone's ever done for me. Thank you."

The sigh Skylar let out was not only audible, but visible as well. "Whew. I didn't want to overstep, but I couldn't imagine how it would feel to be surrounded by strangers every minute of every day."

And that was exactly what it was like. How Skylar understood that, Taylor didn't know, but it was obvious the woman was compassionate and empathetic. She had a feeling she was an amazing teacher.

"And it's a great idea for the drivers to wear the name tags on the road," Smoke added. "It might take some time for them to get used to wearing them."

"It's not *that* hard," one of the men from the counter said. "You think we're idiots or somethin'?" He smiled when he said it, so Taylor knew he was kidding.

"Hi, Shane," Taylor said, reading the name tag he'd attached to his overalls. "Jose," she said, nodding to the other man, who'd also put his tag on.

"Ma'am," both said, nodding at her.

It was stupid to be so emotional over being able to call someone by their name, but this was literally the first time in her life she'd been able to do so without introduction. Everyone always had to tell her who they were before she could greet them by name.

"This is a safe place for all of our employees," Gramps said quietly. "We try to go out of our way to make sure everyone has what they need here. You're no exception."

"Thank you," Taylor whispered.

"Did you save us any?" Bull asked, and Taylor was grateful for the change in topic. She was still too emotional to talk about how much Skylar's gesture meant to her.

Eagle held out her stool, and she climbed on, then he surprised her by stepping closer. Looking up, Taylor licked her lips, noting just *how* close he was. If she leaned forward even an inch, she could rest her cheek on his chest.

"You okay?" he asked softly.

It felt as if they were the only two people in the room, even though Taylor knew they were surrounded by half a dozen others. "Yeah."

"And are you really okay with the name tags?"

Taylor nodded. "It'll make things . . . better."

"Then I'll make sure everyone knows to put theirs on as soon as they step inside Silverstone Towing."

"It seems like overkill when I don't know that I'll be here all that much," Taylor said honestly.

"Why not?"

She frowned in confusion and shrugged. "Because I don't work here?"

"So? Many of the wives of our employees hang out here. And their kids too. You're my friend, so you're welcome to come by whenever you want. You need a change of scenery, you can hang out here. You get sick of your own company, you can come here. Sometimes I like hanging out at Silverstone more than my own apartment. I don't really like the quiet. I can't promise we'll have name tags for all the significant others, but if someone works for Silverstone, they'll wear one, and you'll know who they are."

Taylor wanted to cry again. "Why are you being so nice to me?"

Eagle shrugged. "Because I like you, Taylor Cardin. Your condition doesn't define who you are as a person. I don't care that you don't recognize my face. I know you know who I am here . . ." He picked up her hand and placed it over his heart. "And I don't say that lightly. I've told you more about myself in the last two weeks than I've told anyone other than my three best friends. And after tonight, you'll know all of it. If you still want to hang around me, you'll be more than welcome here, and anywhere else I am. Understand?"

She didn't, but Taylor nodded anyway.

Eagle's lips quirked, as if he knew she was lying when she agreed. He took a step back, and Taylor couldn't help but feel the loss.

"Eat, Flower. We'll talk after."

Knowing Eagle wouldn't tell her anything before he was good and ready, she clipped her new name tag onto her shirt and picked up her fork. She shoveled a piece of the pasta into her mouth and closed her eyes in ecstasy.

"Good, isn't it?" Skylar said from next to her.

Without even opening her eyes, Taylor nodded.

"Wait until you try his tamales. They're even better than this."

There was no way anything was better than this. She opened her eyes and glanced over at Eagle. He was watching her with a smile on his face. Deciding to concentrate on the joy of an amazing meal and the company of people who'd made her feel more welcome than anyone had in her entire life, Taylor forked another piece of lasagna into her mouth, her own small smile on her face.

Chapter Four

Eagle was having second and third thoughts about telling Taylor about Silverstone tonight. It was obvious how much Skylar's gesture meant to her, and now, after eating dinner, she was relaxed and happy. He hated to do anything to make her feel differently.

But before he got any more attached to her, and she to his Silverstone Towing family, he needed to explain what he and his friends did.

This was a huge deal. Bull, Smoke, Gramps, and Eagle had made a pact not to tell anyone about their missions. Not unless they trusted them one hundred percent . . . and they thought there was a chance they might spend the rest of their lives with the other person. Hell, they hadn't even told their families what they did. For all anyone knew, they were just the owners of Silverstone Towing. Period.

He felt in his gut that he and Taylor were on their way to being much more than friends. He was probably still jumping the gun in telling her everything, but Eagle felt a connection with her that he'd never felt with anyone before. Not even his friends. He had no idea if he and Taylor would ever have an intimate relationship, but he felt a deep compulsion to tell her.

And it scared the fuck out of him.

Because despite the fact that it had only been two weeks, she was important to him.

He wanted her in his life any way he could get her.

And telling her about Silverstone could ruin that.

But Eagle had never been one to shy away from tough things. Be they missions or discussions.

They were currently sitting on the couch upstairs. The television was on low, but no one was really watching it. Bull, Skylar, Smoke, and Gramps had all stayed to chat. And the drivers who were on duty had been coming and going depending on their callout schedule. They were all relaxed, and Eagle was thrilled to see how well Taylor got along with everyone. She and Skylar had talked about their jobs, and not once had the conversation lagged.

But it was time. Eagle needed to get the discussion with Taylor over with. He'd been stressing about it for too long.

Leaning over, he asked quietly, "You ready to talk?"

Taylor immediately nodded, and he wondered if she'd been as worried about what he wanted to tell her as he'd been.

"We'll be back," Eagle told his friends, not knowing if they'd be back to hang out or if it would only be to say goodbye as he took Taylor home.

Ignoring the looks his friends were giving him, Eagle steered Taylor toward the stairs. He liked touching her, but dropped his hand from her back as soon as they started down the steps.

They walked silently through the downstairs rec room toward the safe room once more. He unlocked it with his fingerprint and held the door open for Taylor. After entering, she stood uneasily in the middle of the room, as if not sure where to sit or what to do.

Eagle held out one of the chairs around the table for her, and she immediately sat. He took the one next to her and didn't beat around the bush.

"I've told you that my friends and I were in the Army."

Taylor nodded.

"We were Special Forces. Delta Force."

She nodded again.

"Do you know what that is?"

She frowned at him. "Of course I do. I'm not an idiot."

Eagle smiled a bit at that. "So, we were sent on highly classified missions all over the world. Some were hostage rescue, others were only to gather intel. Still others were to find and eliminate dangerous targets."

Taylor nodded, not looking the least bit alarmed at what he was telling her so far.

So Eagle kept going. "What I'm about to tell you can't go any further than this room," he warned her.

"I won't say anything to anyone," Taylor said seriously. "Who would I tell, anyway?"

"Right. So, our last mission was to Pakistan. We were to find and take out Fazlur Barzan Khatun, the leader of the Harkat-ul-Mujahideen terrorist group."

Her eyes widened. "Holy crap, that was you?" she whispered.

Eagle nodded. "Yeah. Khatun and his organization had claimed responsibility for killing almost fifty American and British soldiers in Afghanistan the year before. He was proud of what his organization had done and vowed to continue the killing."

Taylor put her hand on his arm. "It's good that he's dead, then," she said simply.

Her words made Eagle hope that this talk might turn out all right. "Yeah, it is. During the mission, we interrupted a meeting Khatun was having. We lined up everyone who was in the room and discovered that another well-known and most-wanted terrorist was there too. Nabeel Ozair Mullah."

"Holy crap!" Taylor gasped again.

"Yeah. He tried to pretend he wasn't Mullah, but I knew who he was the second I laid eyes on him."

"Because you'd seen his name and face before."

Eagle couldn't read her tone, but he nodded anyway. "Yes. I always study the FBI *Most Wanted* lists before every mission, just in case."

Taylor hadn't moved her hand from his arm, and she squeezed it gently. "That's amazing," she told him softly. "I mean, what an asset for your team and country."

She looked a little sad, and that wasn't what Eagle wanted. Not at all. "I'm not telling you this to make you feel bad," he told her.

"I know you aren't, and I'm okay," she reassured him. "There are times, however, it's really brought home to me how much of a disadvantage I have."

"There's more to life than being able to recognize terrorists," Eagle told her.

"I know. But you obviously have the ability you do for a reason. A very good one."

Eagle pressed his lips together for a moment. He'd always taken what he could do for granted. Had never really thought about it much . . . until he'd met Taylor and understood there were people who were exactly the opposite. He should've realized it way before now, but it just hadn't occurred to him. He cleared his throat and continued.

"Anyway, we killed Mullah too. There was no way we could've left him there. The Mujahideen would've promoted him, and I honestly believe he was worse than Khatun. There was just something in his eyes that made it clear he hated everything about the Western world and wouldn't be happy until he'd killed as many people as possible."

"I do vaguely remember reading about all that," Taylor said. "I mean, I'm not much of a news watcher, and I was in my early twenties, so it wasn't exactly on my radar, but there was some sort of big kerfuffle about them both being killed, wasn't there?"

Eagle snorted. "Yeah, there was a kerfuffle, all right," he told her. "The bottom line was that the Army wasn't happy with us for killing Mullah. Our only mission was to take out Khatun. We obviously weren't supposed to be in Pakistan in the first place."

"If you tell me you got in trouble for that, I'm gonna get mad," Taylor said fiercely.

Eagle felt a warmth move over him. He was used to people thanking him for his service in the military, but hearing Taylor defending him and his team without hesitation felt good. He put his hand over hers on his arm and squeezed. "We were reprimanded. Our Delta team was disbanded, and we were going to be separated, sent to bases all over the States. Then, when our reenlistment dates came around, we were going to be barred from being in the Army any longer."

"That's bullshit!" Taylor blurted. "Seriously, they should've given you guys medals, commendations. To kick you out of the Army is ridiculous! I mean, that's like telling the fastest runner in the world he's not allowed to compete anymore, that even though he could win the Olympics, he won't be allowed. Or . . . telling a world-renowned brain surgeon that he can no longer do the complicated surgeries that would save people's lives, that he could only open a family practice and treat people with the sniffles. Gah, I'm so pissed for you, Eagle!"

Eagle couldn't help but smile. He loved how passionate Taylor was.

"Tell me you protested and they changed their minds," she demanded.

Eagle shook his head. "We did, and they didn't," he said. But before she could break into another tirade, he went on. "The night we learned our fate, we were drowning our sorrows at a local bar, and a guy came in. Picture it—we were in a dive bar filled with dangerous-looking men, and in comes a Fed wearing a crisp white shirt and slacks, complete with spit-shined black shoes. But no one harassed the dude. He knew all about what had happened on our mission in Pakistan—*and* about the hearing we'd just had that day. And to know about both those things meant he had some serious connections.

"I'd never seen him before, which irritated me. I knew who a lot of the big players in the FBI were. I'd made a point to know. He said he worked for the FBI and Homeland Security and told us that he could get us out of our obligation to the Army the next day."

"What was the catch?" Taylor asked, interrupting him.

Eagle snort-laughed again. He hadn't thought he'd be laughing while telling this story. Not a chance. But Taylor had surprised him . . . in a good way. "That's exactly what I asked," he told her. "The guy somehow knew Smoke had inherited this garage from his uncle, along with a shit ton of money. He suggested we come here to Indianapolis and make a go of Silverstone . . . while still doing what we do best, with the help of the FBI and Homeland Security."

When Taylor's facial expression didn't change, he went on. "We talked about it and knew we'd never be able to make an actual garage work, as none of us knew anything about cars. Smoke suggested we make it a towing operation. So we did. Silverstone Towing opened, and we got to stay together as a team. We work with the FBI and Homeland Security—unofficially, of course. We get to decide who to go after and when."

There. He'd gotten it out. Taylor hadn't gotten up and stormed out of the room. He was counting that as a good thing.

"And?" she asked.

"And what?" Eagle asked.

"That's what you wanted to tell me?"

Eagle was confused. "Yeah."

"Okay."

"Okay?" he asked.

"Yes." Taylor shrugged.

"I don't think you understand," Eagle said. "My team and I use this room to research terrorists and drug dealers—the guys at the head of the organizations—serial killers and sex traffickers. We decide who we want to *take out*, and plan missions to do so. We're assassins," he said bluntly. None of them liked that term, but he needed to be absolutely clear with Taylor.

She leaned forward and met his gaze without flinching. "Good," she stated. "Someone has to, and it's obvious that you and your friends are very good at what you do. If you think I'm going to be upset that you're ridding the world of horrible, awful people, you're wrong. I know I'm not exactly worldly, but I remember reading after the fact about all the atrocities Khatun and Mullah had committed. They'd had no remorse for it, didn't care that the people they'd killed had families who loved them and were devastated. As far as I'm concerned, they *deserved* to be assassinated. I've always been thankful for our military men and women, but I'm even more so now."

Eagle closed his eyes and bowed his head. Every time he'd imagined telling Taylor what he did, he'd never thought this would be how she'd react. He'd thought she might be confused, worried, even disgusted, but immediately accepting? No.

"It's dangerous, isn't it?" she asked softly.

Eagle opened his eyes and looked at her. He nodded. He wouldn't lie about it.

"Yeah, of course it is," she muttered.

"I trust Bull, Smoke, and Gramps with my life," he tried to reassure her.

"Does Skylar know?" she asked.

"Yes. Although she didn't take it well at first," Eagle said. "She had a hard time wrapping her mind around it. Bull wanted to tell her before we went on a mission because he didn't want her thinking he was off cheating on him or something. She kinda freaked out, and Bull was a mess on that op. We thought it was over between them, because if Skylar couldn't accept what he did, there wasn't really any way for that relationship to work. But I guess she thought about it while he was gone and decided to discuss it with him some more. She loved him too much to just let him go without a longer conversation. Then she was kidnapped . . . and suddenly it didn't matter anymore."

Taylor nodded. "I can understand that. You said that I couldn't tell anyone, and I completely understand, but can I . . . is it okay to talk to Skylar about it?"

"Yes," Eagle said immediately.

She was quiet for a moment, then said, "I have a question, but I'm not sure how to ask."

"You can ask me anything," Eagle told her. *"Anything."*

"Why did you tell *me*? I mean . . . I'm glad you did, but we aren't . . . shoot."

"We aren't dating," Eagle finished for her.

She nodded.

"Honestly? I like you, Taylor. I could be wrong, but I think we clicked. From the first time I saw you in that parking lot, something drew me to you. We aren't dating . . . yet. I'm not saying we will for certain, but with the connection I feel with you? I wouldn't be surprised if that happened. But it doesn't have to. Even if we're nothing but friends, I'll feel lucky to have you in my life. I'm not explaining this very well . . ." He sighed, his voice trailing off.

"No, you are," Taylor said. "I feel the same way. I don't have a lot of friends—most can't handle my condition—but when I'm around you, and when I talk to you, I don't even think about it. And believe me, that's saying something, because it pretty much dictates everything I do in my life. I like you too, Eagle. A lot. But it scares me to think about being anything more with you, because I don't want to do something that will mess up our friendship. Talking to you in the evenings has been the highlight of the last two weeks."

"Nothing is going to mess up our friendship," Eagle vowed. "And everyone in your life who's cut you out because of your condition is an idiot. That's like not wanting to be friends with someone in a wheelchair, or someone who's blind or has some other medical condition. None of those things are the fault of the person who has them. I accept you as you are, just as you accept me."

A tear formed in Taylor's eye and slipped down her face. Eagle brought his hand up to wipe it away with his thumb. "Those aren't angry tears, right?" he asked with a small frown.

She shook her head. "No. I'm just . . . overwhelmed. My own mother rejected me when I couldn't bond with her, and ever since I was old enough to understand what was wrong with me, I figured I'd be alone."

"First of all, there's nothing 'wrong' with you. Second, your mom was stupid. A mother is supposed to love her children unconditionally. There were lots of different things she could've done to help you, even at a young age, but she didn't even try. Fuck her."

Taylor's lips quirked.

"The bottom line is that you're amazing," Eagle continued. "You're smart, and you already have my friends and employees wrapped around your finger. Hell, Skylar didn't even know you, and she wanted to help make your life easier with the name tags. You didn't take offense, which you would've had every right to, and instead made her feel really good about trying to help you. I wanted you to know about Silverstone. Not Silverstone Towing—that's a whole different thing. My team and I are proud of what we do, and before you become too important to me to let go, I needed to tell you."

"I'm honored," Taylor told him.

Eagle took a deep breath and dropped his hand from her face. He wanted to pull her into a hug, but wasn't sure if they were ready for that. He was encouraged by the fact that she hadn't insisted they were only friends; it gave him hope for the future. For now, it felt good that they were on the same page. They'd take it one day at a time, and whatever happened between them would happen.

"You want to go back upstairs and see if anyone's still here?" he asked.

"Actually, I want to play pinball," she said with a small smile. "I used to be really good at it when I was a teenager. I spent a lot of time at the mall so I wouldn't have to go back to my foster home, and I spent hours playing."

"You had a bad foster experience?" Eagle asked, harsher than he'd meant to.

"Not really. It wasn't bad . . . it just wasn't good either. I was just there. I found it was easier not to try to get close to any of my foster parents or siblings. I knew they wouldn't adopt me, I was just too weird."

"You *aren't* weird," Eagle said, angry now. "Didn't *anyone* try to understand your condition?"

Taylor shrugged.

He took that as a no. "Assholes," he muttered, then stood. "If you want to play pinball, that's what we'll do. Get ready to lose, though," he teased, trying to lighten the mood. "I'm the Silverstone champion."

"It's too bad your high score is going down, then," Taylor teased right back.

"Whatever," Eagle said.

"Wanna bet?"

Eagle stopped in his tracks and turned back to her. "Those are fightin' words," he told her with a grin.

"Bring it," she countered.

~

Taylor couldn't remember the last time she'd stayed out past midnight. It was now three in the morning, and she was lying in a recliner in the basement of Silverstone Towing, snuggled under one of the softest, fuzziest blankets she'd ever felt. Eagle was sleeping in another recliner across from her.

They'd played pinball until her fingers had felt sore from punching the flipper buttons. She and Eagle had been well matched. It had taken her a while to get into the swing of playing again, but once she had, she'd beaten Eagle five times, and he'd outscored her eight times. She hadn't beaten his best score, but she had no doubt that with more practice, she could.

After they'd gotten tired of playing, they'd raided the kitchen for leftovers and brought them downstairs, turning on the television and watching *Jurassic Park*. They'd agreed that the franchise should've stopped after the first three. Then they'd just talked. About nothing and everything.

Eagle had told her about some of the more memorable tow jobs he'd gone on, and had even opened up about some of the people he and Silverstone had rescued while they'd been carrying out their missions.

She'd gotten the impression that all they did was go in and kill bad guys, but in reality, they'd freed a good number of women, children, and even men who'd been held prisoner by whoever they'd set out to eliminate. It had been an eye-opening conversation, and even without details about who and where, Taylor had been impressed.

Hell, everything about Eagle impressed her. At one point, she'd told him he was a good man, and she could tell that he'd been uncomfortable with her assessment. He had changed the subject. She vowed that, one way or another, she would get him to see himself in a different light.

As she watched Eagle sleep, she studied him closely.

It was hard for her to pick out specific features on other people's faces. They all tended to blur together. She'd never understood when people described someone as having a strong jaw or a distinctive nose. When she looked at people, she simply saw a nose, a mouth, and two eyes.

Looking at Eagle, she could see he had a five-o'clock shadow. She bet if he didn't shave every day, he could grow a pretty impressive beard in a very short amount of time. His hair was short, and she thought his lips looked full, but she could just be imagining that.

Taylor didn't want to go to sleep. She wanted this day to go on forever. She'd never been invited to any sleepovers growing up. Had never been close to any of the girls in her classes. But eventually, her eyes drooped, and sleep overcame her.

~

Brett Williams sat in his car in the parking lot outside Taylor's apartment and scowled. He knew she wasn't home, as there were no lights on in her apartment.

"Where are you?" he asked out loud, tapping his thumb on the steering wheel.

He'd been watching his target for two weeks and had gotten a pretty good idea of her routine. She didn't go out much, but he'd been able to slip in behind her at the post office and talk with her a little bit. He'd wanted to test her condition—and he hadn't been disappointed.

He'd seen absolutely no recognition in her eyes, even though they'd exchanged a few words in the parking lot of the grocery store. He'd been positively gleeful.

Brett couldn't stop thinking about all the ways he could torture her when he got Taylor into his basement lair. He could pretend to be different people, maybe tell her that she'd been captured by a cult. And every one of the members was going to interrogate her. She'd think she was being hurt by a dozen different people. He couldn't wait to fuck with her head . . . and mark her body as well.

She had fair skin, which would welt up and bruise easily. Brett knew how to hurt someone without killing them. Yes, Taylor was going to be the most fun victim he'd played with yet.

But he wasn't ready for that yet. He wanted to know more about her. And the only way he could do that was to talk to her. Intercept her as she was going about her daily life.

Which he couldn't do if he didn't know where she was.

She hadn't come home tonight. *That* pissed him off. In the two weeks he'd been following her, she hadn't met with any men . . . or women, for that matter. She worked from home; she'd told him as much when they'd been in the post office. Where the hell could she be?

If she had a boyfriend, that would make his life more difficult. At one point, he'd toyed with the idea of trying to get her to fall in love with him, but decided he didn't have it in him to act like a loving boyfriend. No, he'd have to be a stranger until he made his move.

Looking at his watch and seeing it was three in the morning, Brett swore in frustration. He needed to get home. His mother had been locked in her room for eight hours. She'd probably already made a mess that he'd have to clean up. It would just get worse if he stayed away any longer.

"You can't hide from me," Brett whispered. "I'll always find you. Soon you'll be mine to do with as I please—and I can't wait to hear you scream."

And with that, Brett started up his car and drove out of the parking lot.

Chapter Five

Taylor jerked awake and blinked in confusion as she looked around. She quickly remembered. She was at Silverstone Towing. Her eyes went to the chair across from her, where she'd last seen Eagle sleeping, and saw it was empty. She was alone in the basement, which made her very nervous. She had no idea who was in the building, and even if she'd met someone the night before, she wouldn't know who they were this morning.

Glancing at her watch, she saw that it was seven thirty. She'd only been asleep for around four hours, and she was still exhausted. But she forced herself to get up anyway. It wasn't like she could sleep the day away. Eagle and his friends might need to use the safe room down here.

She went into the bathroom with the single shower and did her best to make herself look presentable. Her shirt was wrinkled and her hair a mess, but she finger combed it and decided it would have to do.

Taking a deep breath, she headed out of the bathroom and up the stairs. She figured Eagle wouldn't have left, since he'd driven her the night before, but she really had no idea. He might've been called out on a job.

When she stepped into the great room and looked around, Taylor froze.

There were five men sitting at the counter, and they all turned to look at her when they noticed her enter the room.

She remembered that Eagle had been wearing jeans and a dark-blue polo shirt the night before, but none of the men at the counter were wearing anything she recognized. If Eagle was there, he must've had a change of clothes here.

One man hopped off the stool he'd been sitting on and made a beeline for her.

Taylor stiffened and did her best not to panic. She racked her brain, trying to see anything about him that looked familiar, but came up blank.

When the man was still about ten feet away, he said softly, "Good morning, Flower."

And just like that, all the tension drained from her.

"Hi, Eagle," she said softly.

Eagle closed the distance, leaned in, and kissed her lightly on the temple, and Taylor inhaled deeply. He smelled clean, as if he'd showered recently. Looking into her eyes, he tilted her chin up with a finger and asked, "You sleep okay?"

"Yeah. You?"

"Like a baby," he said.

Something felt different between them this morning, but Taylor couldn't put her finger on it. Her eyes glanced around nervously, and she finally noticed he was wearing the name tag Skylar had brought over the night before. She'd been so panicked trying to figure out who he was as he'd been walking toward her, she'd forgotten about the name tags altogether.

"Come on, breakfast is ready. It's Saturday, and Archer doesn't work on the weekends, but he made an egg casserole for us to heat up. It's amazing," Eagle told her.

He grabbed her hand and led her over to where the other men were sitting.

Knowing she wasn't being subtle about it in the least, but unable to care even a little, Taylor checked out the name tags the men were wearing.

Smoke, Gramps, Shane, and Robert.

It felt really good to be able to put names to the men without having to ask them who they were. No one would comprehend the relief she felt.

"Good morning," she said a little shyly.

"Hear you beat Eagle in pinball last night," Smoke said with a grin. "Good job. Someone needs to put the asshole in his place. His head has gotten too big. No one else will play him, because when he wins, he throws his arms in the air like he's ten years old and does a ridiculous winner's dance."

Taylor giggled. "Oh, was that what that was?" she teased. "I thought he was having convulsions from the blinking lights or something."

"Hey," Eagle complained.

Everyone else laughed loud and long.

"She's got you there," Robert said.

"Yeah, well, you should've seen the evil little smirk on her face when she beat me for the first time," Eagle countered. "I swear she looked just like Wednesday from *The Addams Family*. It creeped me out and threw me off my game."

Taylor laughed. She knew he was teasing.

Breakfast was delicious. She didn't know if it was the subtle spices the amazing Archer had put into the eggs or if it was the company. All Taylor knew was that she'd never felt so comfortable around people she'd just met in all her life.

When they were finishing up, a man stuck his head out from the hallway and yelled, "Robert and Shane . . . got jobs for you. Smoke, Gramps, Eagle . . . are you guys working today?"

"You need us to?" Smoke asked.

The other man shrugged. "Wouldn't hurt. After Robert and Shane go out, we've got two more jobs stacked and waiting. They aren't urgent, but . . ."

"We can move our meeting to this afternoon," Gramps said. "I'm in."

"Me too," Smoke said.

"I need to take Taylor home, but I'll be back as soon as I can," Eagle chimed in.

"Thanks, guys," the other man said, then disappeared back down the hall, obviously to go back to the dispatch room.

"It was very nice meeting you," Robert told Taylor as he put his plate into the dishwasher.

"Same," Shane agreed, and he followed Robert across the room, heading for the door.

Taylor turned to Eagle. "I can call a cab if you need to stay."

"Nope," he told her, without seeming to be in a rush as he finished loading the dishwasher.

"But if you need to get to work—"

"Taylor," Smoke said, "we're good. It won't hurt anyone to have to wait an extra twenty minutes or so for a tow. Our dispatchers are very good at knowing what constitutes an emergency and what can wait. We don't *need* to work, but by doing so, it gives our employees a break. They can stop and get something to eat or just chill for a few minutes. We don't mind pitching in. Hell, when we started Silverstone Towing, we were doing *all* the driving. It's fine."

Taylor felt her respect for the men rise. She already liked them, and now she could see that they took their responsibilities very seriously. She liked that even more.

"All the same," she said, "I didn't mean to fall asleep here. I need a shower, and I've got a textbook that won't proofread itself."

Gramps walked over to her. "In case Eagle hasn't already said it, you're welcome here anytime. Doesn't matter if he's here or not. You need a change of scenery or want to play pinball, come on over."

"Thanks," Taylor said, feeling overwhelmed.

"What he said," Smoke quipped, coming over and pulling her into a hug.

Taylor felt dwarfed by the two men, but she wasn't scared of them or their size.

"All right, that's enough," Eagle bitched.

Both Smoke and Gramps smirked but backed away from her.

Eagle stomped over and took her hand and pulled her away from his friends.

Taylor laughed and turned to wave. "It was great meeting you!"

"Same!" both men called out.

Eagle stopped at the back door and took off his name tag, then placed it on the metal doorframe. Taylor had forgotten she was still wearing hers too. Feeling reluctant to take it off, she mentally shrugged and added hers to the doorframe. "Life would be much easier if everyone had to wear a name tag all the time," she said wistfully.

Eagle turned her to face him, and he waited until she looked up before he spoke.

"You're amazing," he said softly. "Don't let anyone else make you feel any different. The people who've shunned you because you can't recognize them at first glance . . . that says more about *them* than you. It has everything to do with other people's egos. Just because you can't pick me out of a group of men doesn't make me think you don't like me. A true friend doesn't care about shit like that. They care about having fun when you're around. About how you make them forget their troubles when you're around. They care if you've had a good day, and that you're home safe and sound."

Taylor wanted to cry. His words meant the world. "Thank you," she said softly.

"You don't have to thank me for being your friend," he told her. "I should be thanking *you*. Last night could've gone very differently. There was a sixty-forty chance that you would've been appalled at what I told you and demanded I take you home and never call you again. I wouldn't have blamed you either."

Taylor frowned up at him. "Why did you tell me, then, if you thought I might not be able to handle it?"

"Because I knew if you *could* handle it, our friendship would only get stronger."

She thought about something then. "Is your meeting this afternoon about going on a mission?"

Eagle shrugged. "We have meetings all the time—we try to stay on top of what's going on in the country and the world. We get updated info from our contact in the FBI, and we discuss where we think we should go next."

Taylor swallowed hard. She'd accepted what he and his friends did, but it was hitting home exactly how dangerous it was. "Are you going somewhere soon?"

Eagle leaned down until his forehead rested against hers. "I don't know. And I'm not just saying that. But I won't disappear without letting you know. I won't be able to tell you where I'm going or who our target is, but I won't just up and leave."

"Okay," Taylor said.

She liked being close to him like this. He always smelled good. Clean. And that got her thinking about how she probably didn't smell all that fresh. She pulled back. "I should probably get home and shower."

Eagle didn't let her go far. He leaned down and buried his nose in her hair.

She stiffened. "Eagle?"

"Don't mind me," he muttered into her curls. "I'll just be over here inhaling your vanilla shampoo."

She grinned. "That's the stuff I use to try to control my curls," she told him. "Not my shampoo."

"I love your hair," he told her, standing up and bringing a hand to her head. He pulled on one of her curls and watched it bounce back up. "I know this doesn't mean anything to you, and honestly, I love that about you even more . . . but you're beautiful."

People had told her she was pretty before. That her hair was amazing, that she had beautiful bone structure. She hadn't thought much about it. But Eagle telling her the same thing made goose bumps break out on her arms. "Thanks," she told him somewhat shyly. "You always smell really good." She winced. The words sounded okay when she'd thought them to herself, but when she actually said them, they were kind of lame.

He smiled. "Best compliment I've ever gotten," he told her.

Taylor rolled her eyes. "Right."

"Seriously. If you'd have said I was handsome in return, I would've known you were blowing smoke up my ass, because I don't think you have any clue what handsome really is. I mean, I could have a troll's face, and you wouldn't really notice. But using your other senses to tell me you like something about me? I know you're being sincere, and that means the world to me."

She couldn't even get upset at his words. He was right. For instance, she knew, intellectually and from reading social media posts, that Henry Cavill was supposed to be to-die-for handsome, but for Taylor, all she noticed was how, in his popular paranormal television series, his long hair looked like it needed to be washed all the time and how dirty he looked. She had little use for *handsome* with her condition. For her, it was all about how someone treated her.

And how he smelled, of course.

They stood staring at each other for a moment, then Eagle took her by the hand once more. He opened the door, and she followed him out into the parking lot. He held open the door of his Wrangler for her and shut it once she was settled. They drove back to her apartment in a comfortable silence. After he pulled into a parking space at her complex, he turned to her.

"Please take what Gramps said to heart. You're welcome at Silverstone Towing at any time. I know you're an introvert, but we aren't just saying that to be polite. Believe me, we don't invite just anyone to hang out there."

"Thanks. I'm not sure I'd feel comfortable going over there without you, but I appreciate the invite all the same," Taylor told him.

"I'm sure you could call Skylar, and she'd accompany you," Eagle told her.

Taylor nodded. "I liked her. She's nice."

"She's very nice," Eagle agreed. "And . . . if you ever have any questions about our missions, you can go to her if you don't think you can talk to me about it."

"Okay."

"I'll walk you up," Eagle said, unbuckling his seat belt.

"You don't have to," Taylor protested.

"Yes, I do," he insisted and opened his door.

Taylor got out on her side and met him in front of the Jeep. "I'm a big girl," she told him. "I've been walking up to my apartment by myself for a long time now."

"I know. But it would make me feel better to know I delivered you all the way inside safe and sound. Humor me."

She couldn't argue with that. They walked together into her complex and up the stairs. She unlocked her apartment door . . . and immediately felt nervous. "Do you want to come in?" she asked.

He smiled down at her. "No, Flower, I need to get back to Silverstone. But I'll take a rain check."

"Okay," she agreed. "Be safe out there."

"I always am," he said. Then he leaned down toward her.

Taylor held her breath as he got close. But instead of kissing her, he brushed his lips against her temple. "Have a good day," he said quietly, then straightened. "Lock this immediately behind me."

She could only nod. Then he was in the hall. He raised an eyebrow when she just stood there. Taylor forced herself to move and shut the door. She threw the dead bolt and heard his steps going down the hallway.

Taking a deep breath, she closed her eyes and leaned against her door.

What was wrong with her? She shouldn't have been expecting him to kiss her. And she definitely shouldn't have been disappointed when he hadn't.

"Get a grip," she said out loud. He was probably the best friend she'd ever had. She didn't want to do anything to mess that up, despite his suggestion that they might date in the future. And kissing would definitely change things between them. Wouldn't it?

Taylor was so confused. But she'd always been practical. Overthinking the situation wouldn't change anything about it. So she pushed herself off the door and headed for her bedroom. She'd shower and get to work on proofreading the history textbook she'd picked up at the post office the other day. When she had something as dry and technical as a text, she usually broke up the monotony by also proofing a shorter speech or a romance novel. It helped her brain stay focused. And today, she needed to forget about Eagle and Silverstone. At least for a little while.

So much had happened in a short period of time. She'd never expected to meet someone who would become so important to her this quickly. If she was smart, she'd put some distance between herself and Eagle, but Taylor knew that wasn't going to happen. She looked forward to chatting with him every night, even if they just talked about how their days had been. And now that he'd opened up and told her about Silverstone, something only a handful of people knew? There was no way she could hold him at arm's length.

She had no idea what Eagle saw in her, but she hoped and prayed he wasn't simply amusing himself. She hadn't realized how badly she needed a friend, and giving up Eagle might just break her.

~

It was a weird feeling to miss someone. Eagle had never felt as close a connection with anyone as he did with Taylor. After dropping her off at her apartment, he'd gone back to Silverstone Towing and gotten on the road. He'd worked for a few hours, then met his team back at the garage, and they'd gone over the day's intel they'd received from Willis.

But throughout the day, Taylor was always in the back of Eagle's mind. What was she doing? Had she eaten lunch? Had she made a dent in the new textbook she was going to start on that day?

Eagle had always been something of a loner. He'd dated women, but never felt as if he *needed* to talk to them all the time, to be with them constantly. He supposed that made him kind of an asshole, but none of the women he'd gone out with had seemed to mind. Everything had always been casual. Whatever the connection was that he had with Taylor felt anything but.

He'd wanted to kiss her when he'd dropped her off. *Really* kiss her. But at the last minute, he had forced himself to give her a casual brush of his lips against her temple. The last thing he wanted to do was mess up what they had. Taylor needed a friend badly, and he was going to prove that he could be one for her. People she'd known in the past were assholes for letting her condition scare them away.

So what if she couldn't recognize him by his looks? He'd seen the panic in her eyes that morning when he'd walked toward her at Silverstone. But the second he'd called her Flower, all the uncertainty had dissolved from her expression. If all it took to make her relax was a code word letting her know who he was, that was easy. Why no one else had bothered to try to help her in that way was a mystery.

But that was in the past. He'd seen how touched she'd been by Skylar's gesture. Name tags were a great idea. She could identify everyone at a glance and wouldn't have to rely on others to constantly introduce themselves.

Eagle would do whatever it took to increase her confidence and be the best friend he could be. He wouldn't screw that up by letting his feelings for her get in the way . . . at least not so soon.

With that in mind, he relaxed on his couch and picked up his cell. He punched in her number and waited for her to pick up.

"Hey, Eagle."

"Hi. I just wanted to see how your day went," he said. He heard the volume of the music in the background lower.

"It was good."

"What'd you do?"

For the next hour and a half, they talked about nothing and everything. She told him about getting started on the history textbook and how slowly it seemed to be going. When she asked about his meeting with his team, it felt so good to be able to be honest with her about what they'd discussed. He didn't share specifics, but when he explained that they'd read firsthand accounts of some of the women who'd been forced into prostitution in Amsterdam, she'd been extremely empathetic.

While prostitution was legal there, many of the women who worked in the brothels were doing so against their will, forced to have sex with dozens of men a day to keep their families safe from the evil men who'd blackmailed them. Silverstone wanted to find the man, or men, responsible at the highest level. Not the johns and pimps on the front line. They were small potatoes compared to the heads of the sexual-slavery rings.

He and Taylor had a long discussion about what could be done to help the women, which turned into a conversation about the pros and cons of legalizing prostitution. She brought up some good points that he and his team hadn't thought of. Eagle had known that Taylor was smart, but being able to have an intellectual conversation with her about a very controversial topic was more satisfying than he would've thought.

"What are your plans for tomorrow?" Eagle asked her.

"Same as today. Although I do need to go out for a bit."

"Where to?"

Eagle was surprised when Taylor didn't immediately answer him.

"I just . . . something I do every Sunday," she said.

He wasn't happy with the vague answer, but he told himself that even though they'd talked every day, there were a lot of things he still didn't know about her. "Cool. It's okay if you don't want to tell me, you're allowed to keep your life private."

"It's not that, it's just . . . it's something I started doing about a year ago, and at first I had mixed feelings about it, but now it feels like a calling for me."

"I hope you'll tell me about it sometime, but don't think I'm going to be sitting over here pouting because you won't."

She chuckled softly. "I can't see you pouting about anything. Except maybe not winning at pinball."

And just like that, she'd satisfactorily changed the subject. Eagle let it go, not wanting her to be uncomfortable in the least while talking to him. "I still think you cheated on that last round."

"How could I have cheated?" she asked. "Seriously, you're just a poor loser."

"Okay, that's probably true," Eagle admitted.

She laughed again. "Eagle?"

"Yeah, Tay?"

"I like this."

He knew exactly what she was talking about. "Me too. You're easy to talk to."

"Same."

"I'm going to let you go. It's late," Eagle said, glancing at his watch, surprised at exactly how much time had gone by. He'd never really liked talking on the phone, but with Taylor, he couldn't seem to get enough.

"Okay. Thanks for introducing me to your friends."

"Of course. And they're your friends now too."

She didn't comment on that, and Eagle knew she'd need to spend more time around them to really feel comfortable.

"I'll call tomorrow night?" he asked.

"I'd like that," she reassured him.

"Be safe tomorrow at whatever it is you're doing."

"I will. You too."

"Always," Eagle told her. "Sleep well."

"Talk to you later."

"Later." Eagle clicked off the phone and just sat on his couch, smiling and recounting their conversation for at least five minutes. Reluctantly, he admitted he'd rather spend the rest of his life in the friend zone if dating meant the risk of breaking up and losing her forever.

It had taken thirty-six years, but Eagle had finally found a woman whose happiness he'd put above his own. It felt scary, but so right.

Taylor Cardin didn't know it, but as of this moment, her life was going to get much better. He'd make it his mission to show her how fun life could be. She'd hidden herself away and protected her heart because of the assholes in her past. That was over.

Eagle nodded. He might never have the kind of relationship he wanted with her, but if Taylor lived her life unafraid of what others might think or say about her, Eagle, in turn, could find peace with that. She was an amazing human being, and the world needed more people like her. Hiding in her apartment, afraid to run into others she knew but didn't recognize, was wrong.

He'd make sure those who *did* know her changed the way they interacted with her. Make them learn to tell her who they were up front. He'd make everyone see her the way he did.

His decision made, Eagle got ready for bed with a lighter heart. He couldn't wait to see his Flower blossom.

Chapter Six

More than two weeks later, Taylor was cleaning up after her simple dinner when she realized she hadn't heard from Eagle all day, which was highly unusual. They'd continued talking or texting daily, and every couple days or so, he'd talked her into getting out of her apartment. He'd taken her to the zoo, they'd gone on a bike ride, she'd hung out with him at Silverstone Towing. He'd even brought her over to Bull's apartment one night, and she'd hung out with his friends and Skylar.

At first she'd been reluctant, but she'd come to look forward to his spontaneous invitations. He'd also finally agreed to come into her apartment, and she'd made them dinner one night. Nothing fancy—baked chicken and vegetables—but he'd told her that her cooking rivaled Archer's.

She'd recently gotten to meet the man who made such delicious food at Silverstone. Shawn Archer was a large guy whose laughter seemed to fill the room. It made Taylor happier just hearing it. She'd also met his daughter, a precocious little girl named Sandra.

All in all, not only had Eagle invited her into his world, but all his friends had also welcomed her with open arms. It felt amazing.

But for the first time in a month, she hadn't talked to Eagle even once today. Which surprised her. She'd texted him and gotten no response. She'd also called and left a message, but he hadn't returned her call.

Debating with herself, she finally picked up the phone and called Skylar.

"Hey, Taylor. Everything all right?"

"Yeah, I'm good. But I haven't heard from Eagle all day. I was wondering if you knew if he was okay?"

"Oh, I'm sure he is. They aren't on a mission, if you're worried about that."

Taylor hadn't even thought of the possibility. "Oh, no, he told me he'd let me know if they were headed out. I just . . . it's probably nothing. I've just gotten used to talking to him. I'm sure I'll get in touch with him tomorrow."

"I'll call Carson," Skylar said. "He's still over at the garage. He called earlier and said they were neck deep in research."

"Oh, okay. I'm sure he's just busy," Taylor told her. "Don't bother them."

"It's not a bother," Skylar said gently. "And it's not like him to not call. I'll see what I can find out and either call you back or tell Carson to have Eagle call. Okay?"

Taylor wanted to convince her to let it go, though she really *did* want to talk to Eagle. She suddenly had a gut feeling that something was wrong . . . but that was silly, wasn't it? They weren't dating, and Eagle could do whatever he wanted. He was an adult. He didn't need her nagging him and bothering him when he was working.

But she still couldn't shake the feeling that something wasn't right.

"Thanks, Sky. I appreciate it."

"No problem. I'll talk to you soon. You going to the garage this weekend?"

"I don't know," Taylor told her. It was Thursday, and she and Eagle hadn't talked about their weekend plans yet. It was silly, but she'd spent the last two Saturdays with him, so she'd simply expected to spend this one with him too. But that was presumptuous of her. He might have other plans . . . or a date.

She'd refused to let herself think of Eagle as anything other than a friend, but it was getting harder and harder. She liked the man. A lot. He'd gotten under her skin, and every time he touched her, she wanted more.

"Well, I'm sure I'll see you around soon," Skylar told her.

"I hope so," Taylor said. And she did. She really liked the other woman. She was fun and had such a positive outlook on life, especially considering what she'd been through. And the stories she shared about her kindergarten students were hilarious.

"Bye."

"Bye." Taylor hung up and bit her fingernail as she paced. Eagle didn't need to check in with her, of course. But her worry wouldn't go away.

Twenty minutes later, her phone rang, but it was Bull, not Eagle.

"Hello?"

"Hey, Taylor, it's Bull. I talked to Sky, and she said you called about Eagle."

"I did. Is everything all right? I mean, I'm probably being paranoid, but I haven't talked to him today, which is unusual."

Bull sighed. "We were reviewing a case today, and it upset him," he said after a moment. "Most of the time we can look at police reports and newscasts and compartmentalize, but something about the case we were looking at today really got to him."

Taylor's heart sank. "Where is he?"

"He said he was going home," Bull told her.

"I'll just head over there and see if he's all right," Taylor said.

"I'm not sure that's a good idea. Maybe you should give him some time," Bull said.

Taylor didn't believe that for a second. When you were alone with your thoughts, they seemed to get uglier. She would know. She'd spent most of her life alone, rehashing all the mean things people had said to and about her. After this last month with Eagle, she knew simply having someone to talk to released so many of those bad thoughts. Even if he didn't want to talk, she could at least sit with him. Try to make him laugh. Something.

"Okay," she told Bull, lying through her teeth. "I appreciate you calling to let me know."

"You're going to go over there, aren't you?" he asked.

Taylor pressed her lips together and didn't answer.

"Fine. But if he says anything out of line, don't take it personally. He's not himself."

"I'm not going to break if he yells," Taylor replied. "If he needs to let out his emotions, then I'll be there to take it."

"If you don't call me in an hour, I'm coming over there," Bull warned.

"That's not necessary," she protested.

"It is. Eagle's one of my best friends, but you're my friend too. I'm not going to let him abuse you or use you as a punching bag just because he's frustrated."

And now Taylor wanted to cry. "Thanks."

"Don't thank me. Text or call me, and let me know that you're both okay. I'm giving you an hour because I'm feeling generous . . . and I think you could be just what he needs. But do *not* take shit from him. Hear me?"

"I hear you."

"Good. And Taylor? Thank you."

"Later," she told him, already on the move.

"Later," he said.

Taylor shoved her shoes on and grabbed her purse before heading for the door. She'd been to Eagle's apartment twice, so she didn't have to think too hard about where she was going. Instead, she thought about what she was going to say to him. How she was going to help. She had no idea what the case was about, but it had to be bad for Eagle to lose his shit.

She pulled into his parking lot and hurried through the lobby. He lived in a fairly secure building, but the man who worked the desk simply nodded at her as she went by. Taylor had no idea if he was the man Eagle had introduced her to previously, but she didn't have time to be anything other than grateful he hadn't stopped her.

She hit the button for the second floor and waited impatiently for the elevator to rise. She practically jogged down the hallway and took a deep breath before knocking on Eagle's door.

For a second, she didn't think he was going to answer, but then the door opened, and a tall man was standing there.

He didn't say anything, just looked at her.

"Eagle?" Taylor said uncertainly. She knew it *should* be Eagle, but honestly, it could've been anyone standing behind his door.

He sighed. "Yeah, Flower, it's me."

Taking a deep breath in through her nose, Taylor suddenly decided how she was going to deal with this. She nodded and pushed past a surprised Eagle. She kicked off her shoes, letting him know that she was planning on staying awhile, and headed for the kitchen. She saw a bottle of Jack Daniel's on the counter and winced. Eagle wasn't a big drinker; for him to have broken out the booze meant he really was feeling like shit.

She opened a few cabinets until she found what she was looking for. She brought a pan over to the sink and began filling it with water.

"What are you doing?" he asked a little belligerently.

"Making you dinner," Taylor answered calmly.

"I'm not hungry."

"Too bad. I am," she said as unsympathetically as she could. The truth was, she wasn't sure she could eat anything with the way her stomach was rolling, but she'd do her best.

"Why are you here?"

At that, Taylor looked up and met his gaze. "Because you need me," she said simply.

She wasn't sure what she'd expected him to say or do, but it wasn't turning his back on her and striding into his living area to sit on his couch.

Mentally shrugging and deciding that his ignoring her was better than his kicking her out, she continued prepping a simple spaghetti dinner. He had ground beef and a can of sauce. He didn't have spaghetti noodles, but elbows would work just as well.

He didn't say a word for the thirty minutes it took to prepare the meal, but after she'd plated everything, set the table, and told him dinner was ready, he got up and came to the table to join her.

Sighing in relief that she hadn't had to force him to eat—not that she had any idea how she'd do that—Taylor sat next to Eagle. He picked up a fork and began eating unenthusiastically, but eating nonetheless.

She took a second to rest her hand on his thigh under the table and squeeze gently. She wanted him to know she was there for him. He didn't have to say a damn word, and she would still be there.

He stilled, but Taylor ignored that and removed her hand to reach for her fork. They ate in silence, but she swore that Eagle seemed a little less tense. He even helped bring the dishes into the kitchen when they were finished, but instead of letting her put the plates into the dishwasher, he took hold of her hand and not very gently towed her into the living room. He sat on the couch and pulled her down beside him.

Taylor immediately curled into him. Eagle grabbed a blanket off the back of the couch with one hand and covered her. Only then did he speak.

"I'm sorry I didn't call."

"It's okay," Taylor said. "I'm not your mom—you don't have to tell me where you are or when you're having a shit day."

"But as a friend, I should've at least texted."

Taylor nodded in agreement. He should've. But she wasn't going to hold a grudge. "I was worried about you."

She heard him inhale deeply through his nose before he said, "If the shoe had been on the other foot, I wouldn't have been happy if you didn't call me when you had a bad day."

Taylor didn't respond. She wasn't sure how to. She hadn't had *any* bad days since she'd met Eagle. But if she had, she was pretty sure the first person she'd want to talk to about it would be him.

"I've seen a lot of awful shit in my life," he said. "Babies lying dead in the dirt with their heads cut off. Women who have been so abused they're nothing but walking zombies. Men who've been tortured so badly they aren't recognizable as human beings anymore. I've seen more ways of killing someone than you could even imagine. Burning, stabbing, burying someone alive, shooting, beheading, hanging, starving someone to death, cutting out someone's heart while they're still alive . . . you name it, I've seen it."

Taylor shuddered but didn't interrupt him.

"But I'll *never* understand it. Never understand how someone can feel so much hate that they purposely want to torture someone else. We've been following the case of a serial killer in Albuquerque. He's been targeting sex workers. He kills them and takes them out to the desert and buries them in shallow graves. There's nothing particularly new about that. Men have been killing prostitutes for centuries. They feel as if they won't be missed, or that they're somehow 'less' of a person, which is bullshit. Anyway . . . the authorities believe it's been a while since he's killed. They thought he'd either moved or died. But we got the file today of a recent DB that was found just outside the city."

"DB?" Taylor asked quietly.

"Dead body. She was pregnant. Eight months. The killer cut the baby out of her body. The police suspect the mother was alive for that, as well . . . and that he possibly made her watch as he strangled her baby. Then he forced the victim to drink her own blood before sexually assaulting and killing her.

"I mean . . . think about that," Eagle said in a voice so tortured it made Taylor want to cry. "She was covered in blood from her *baby* being cut out, surely in utter agony, and he *raped* her." Eagle shook his head and closed his eyes. "I can't imagine what she was thinking—and that's what gets to me. What was she thinking? Was she wondering why no one was coming to help her? Why she'd been targeted? If he was going to do even more unspeakable things to her and her dead child when he was done getting his rocks off?"

Tears leaked from Taylor's eyes. His words were horrific, there was no doubt, but she cared more about the absolute agony Eagle was clearly feeling.

"I want to find him. To make him hurt as badly as he made his victims hurt," Eagle said. "But the police don't have enough information to track him down. It's almost unbelievable in this day and age that they can't find him. He needs to pay, Taylor. I want to *make* him pay, but I can't do that if I don't know who he is."

She buried her head in his chest and tried to hide her tears. She had no idea what to say to make him feel better, so all she could do was hold him.

"He could be anyone. He could be the guy in the grocery store bagging your shit up. He could be the nice middle-aged guy who lives next door. The man everyone thinks is quiet and introverted. All I need is a name and a face, and I'll hunt him down. He won't be able to hide from me," Eagle said, his voice breaking.

Then, as if he'd just realized he wasn't alone, his arms tightened around Taylor. She did her best to keep her sobs under control, but it was no use. Eagle lifted her chin with his hand and swore when he saw the tears on her face.

"Fuck. I'm sorry. I shouldn't have said anything. Now you're going to have nightmares about this shit."

Taylor shook her head. "I'm not crying because of what you said," she told him honestly. "I'm crying because you feel so bad. I don't know what to say to make you feel better."

He stared at her for a long moment before admitting, "You don't have to say anything. Just you being here is helping."

Taylor rolled her eyes. "Oh yeah, I can see how much it's helping."

His lips twitched. He didn't exactly smile, but at least he wasn't scowling anymore. "It does. If you hadn't come over, I'd probably have drunk that entire bottle of Jack. You fed me, and now you're holding me. Just feeling you in my arms makes me remember that the entire world isn't all bad. But it scares the hell out of me that there are people out there who could do that to another human being. I just don't get it."

He gently wiped her cheeks with his thumbs before guiding her head back to his chest once more. Then he surprised her by twisting and lying on his back, taking her with him. She was sandwiched between him and the back of the couch, but there was nowhere Taylor would rather be.

She moved her hand so it was resting under her cheek, and they both lay there in silence for a long few minutes.

"On Sundays, I go to the Dementia Senior Care Center," she said quietly. "I don't know why I didn't tell you before. It's not a big deal. I volunteer there a few hours every week. I feel a connection with the residents. I visit the same people week after week, and yet they never remember me. Every time I show up, I'm a stranger to them."

Eagle ran a gentle hand over her hair, his fingers getting trapped in her curls.

"I always explain why I'm there when I arrive, because I never recognize the person working at the desk, and I know they're probably exasperated or laughing behind my back because they know who *I* am, since I've been there so many times. I hate that, but not for myself . . . for the residents. Are the same staff members laughing at them too? One of the biggest fears I have is being put in a home like that. Being surrounded by strangers who don't bother to introduce themselves to me when they come into my room. Having them pull down my gown to listen to my heart or whatever, and having no idea if they're really a doctor or some pervert who just wants to get his jollies by looking at an old woman's tits.

"It's stupid, I know, but these are the things I think about. So I go every Sunday. I tell everyone I sit with who I am, and why I'm there. That seems to calm them, even if they don't remember me. Sometimes we have a conversation about something they remember from their pasts, but other times we just sit in silence."

Taylor felt stupid going on and on, but after Eagle had opened himself up to her, she felt compelled to do the same. And she'd told him one of her greatest fears, something she'd never told anyone else.

"Elder abuse is abhorrently real," he said quietly. "And I imagine it's even worse when the patients can't verbalize what's happening to them or can't really remember it. Those men and women are lucky to have you on their side."

"I don't really do anything," Taylor protested.

"Wrong. You show up week after week. You look after them, and the staff knows that. I'd like to think that they aren't purposely being mean to you, and you being there on a regular basis shows how much you care. I'm proud to be your friend."

Taylor was beginning to hate that word. *Friend.* But tonight was about him, not about how she felt about him . . . and how she knew she had to come to terms with the fact that they'd probably never be anything *but* friends.

"You want to know what I believe that woman was thinking?" Taylor asked.

Eagle stiffened, indicating that he understood what she meant. "Yeah."

"I think she was beyond pain," Taylor said firmly. "You can't be hurt like she was and not dissociate. Her nerves were probably severed, and she wasn't feeling anything he was doing to her. She probably felt as if she were floating. I bet when she closed her eyes, she could feel her baby's soul calling to her, and she was relieved she could join him or her in the afterlife." Taylor was crying again, but she didn't stop. "Whoever killed her was probably pissed he couldn't touch her thoughts. He wanted her to be afraid, to beg for her life, but I bet she refused. Didn't give him the satisfaction. People like that, they want their victims to be afraid. To feel power over them. But I'm guessing she didn't give him the satisfaction."

Taylor was talking out her ass. She had no idea what that poor woman had been thinking or feeling, but she wanted to believe that after having a child cut out of her womb, she couldn't feel much of anything afterward.

"Thank you," Eagle whispered.

"I know it doesn't make it better, but—"

"It does," Eagle interrupted. "I still want to find and kill him. But it helps."

Taylor nodded against him.

The last thing she remembered was thinking of how comfortable Eagle's chest was. She'd slept against men in the past, but none of them had made her feel as safe as she felt right at that moment.

~

Eagle felt Taylor's phone vibrating in her back pocket. She was fast asleep against him, and he didn't want to wake her. He pulled it out slowly and saw she'd gotten a text from Bull.

Bull: Everything ok? You've got five minutes to respond or I'm on my way over there.

He should've been pissed at his friend, but instead, all he felt was gratitude that Bull was looking out for Taylor. He put her phone on the table next to the couch and blindly felt for his own cell. After finding it, he unlocked it and typed out a quick text to his friend.

Eagle: Tay's good. Promise. Sleeping on me so I can't call. Will tell you all tomorrow. Thank you for sending her . . . and looking out for her.

Bull's response was immediate.

Bull: You okay?

Eagle: No. But I will be.

Bull: That was some fucked-up shit today.

Eagle: Yeah.

Bull: Yell if you need anything.

Eagle: Will do.

Eagle put the phone back on the table and looked down at the woman in his arms. He regretted what he'd told her tonight. He shouldn't have put all those images in her head. He knew better. Eagle had seen a lot of bad shit, but that didn't mean he had to share it with Taylor.

But she hadn't freaked.

Thinking back over the night, Eagle couldn't help but smile. She'd obviously been nervous, but she'd barged her way in, taken over his kitchen, and simply been there for him. Hadn't begged him to talk to her, to tell her what was wrong. She'd just taken him in her arms and held him.

And he loved her.

It'd only been a fucking month, but he loved her. They hadn't kissed, hadn't done more than hold hands every now and then, and he already couldn't imagine Taylor *not* being in his life.

She made a cute noise in the back of her throat and squirmed against him, trying to get comfortable. Eagle knew he should wake her up and get her home, but he didn't want to. He wanted to hold her. Wanted to feel her hair against his neck and feel her breaths against his chest. If this would be the only time he was able to hold her, he wanted it to last.

He leaned down and kissed the top of her head. "You're amazing, Flower," he whispered.

To his surprise, she mumbled, "You too," before going silent once more.

Grinning, Eagle put his head back and did his best to relax. He finally admitted to himself that when he'd read the report about the woman out in New Mexico, all he had thought of was . . . What if that had been Taylor? It was stupid. She wasn't a prostitute, wasn't pregnant. But just the thought of someone doing that to her, of hurting her, had made him lose it.

Tightening his hold, Eagle made a silent vow to continue with Silverstone for as long as he could. He wanted to keep people like his Taylor safe, and the only way to do that was to make sure those who wanted to hurt others never got the chance.

Chapter Seven

Things between Taylor and Eagle had been different ever since the night she'd gone over to his apartment. She'd woken up the next morning, and the first thing he'd said was, "Good morning, Flower." Then they'd continued on as they had before, and neither had mentioned her sleeping on top of him all night.

But something was still different, in a good way. Eagle had never not called her again. They talked less and less about superficial stuff. Although he still wanted to know what she did each day.

"How was your day?" he asked after she'd picked up the phone that afternoon, not too long after she'd spent the night at his apartment.

"It was fine, I guess. I went to the library to proofread for a change of pace and got into a long conversation with a guy there."

"About what?" Eagle asked.

"About American history. He saw the textbook I was proofing, and we got to talking about the Civil War. It was interesting, and he was nice."

"That's good. Want to come over tonight?"

"Yes," she said without hesitation.

"Good. I should be home around four thirty. I can pick up something for dinner on my way," he told her.

"Not necessary," she replied. "I can make something."

"Nope. You made us dinner the last two times."

"It's not a big deal," Taylor told him. "I *like* to cook."

"Let me spoil you," Eagle demanded.

How could she argue with that? "Okay. Fine."

"Want me to swing by and pick you up?" he asked.

"No. I can drive over there. I'm finishing up this last chapter, then calling it quits for the day. I do want to get through a few other smaller jobs before I come over, though."

"Okay. But text me when you leave so I know when to expect you."

"I will. Eagle?"

"Yeah?"

"Did everything go okay today . . . you know, talking about missions and stuff?" It had been a week since he'd had his mini breakdown, and she wanted to make sure he really was all right.

"Yeah. I'll tell you about it when you get here. It looks like we might be headed out relatively soon."

Taylor's heart skipped a beat. She tried to keep her voice as nonchalant as possible. "Yeah?"

"Don't panic," he said gently, and she realized he could read her better than anyone else in her life ever could, even over the phone.

"Impossible," she retorted. "I know you and your friends are supermen and all that, but I'm going to worry every second you're gone. You're just going to have to deal with that."

"I hate to cause you worry, but I have to admit, it feels kinda good," Eagle admitted.

There. That. Eagle saying things like *that* made her feel as if something vital had changed between them. But then he'd go back to being the buddy he'd always been. It was confusing as hell.

"And just for the record, you had two typos in the texts you sent me today. I thought as a proofreader you were immune to that kind of shit."

Yup. Right back to teasing her.

"Yeah, well, you know, I have to keep you on your toes," she retorted.

He chuckled. "That you do. I'll see you later, Flower. Drive safe."

"Always," she told him, echoing what he said to her when she told him the same thing. She clicked off the phone and closed her eyes.

She'd fallen hard for her best friend, and she didn't know what to do about it.

Did she tell him she was ready for more and risk making things awkward between them?

No. She couldn't do that. She'd just have to get over her crush, or infatuation, or whatever it was. The last thing she wanted to do was lose him in her life completely.

Forcing herself to concentrate on the textbook in front of her, Taylor did her best to put Eagle out of her mind for at least a little while.

~

At ten minutes past five o'clock, Taylor pulled out of her apartment complex and headed for Eagle's place. She was sitting at a stoplight when her car suddenly jerked forward, the seat belt tightening painfully against her chest for a split second.

She was confused for a heartbeat, then realized someone had hit her from behind.

"Shit," she mumbled. Looking behind her, she saw a man in an older-model Cadillac. It was dark brown and looked like it was on its last legs. She wasn't a car person, so she couldn't even guess what year it was.

He popped out of the driver's seat and jogged toward her. "I'm so sorry!" he said, leaning down to peer inside her car. "I've got insurance! If you want to pull over into that parking lot"—he pointed to a strip mall to the right of where they were—"we can exchange info. Again, I'm really sorry, I looked away to turn down my music and misjudged where you were."

Sighing, Taylor nodded, and when the light turned green, she pulled into the right lane and into the strip mall.

Looking around, she saw there were several people in the area. She wasn't in any danger where she was. She got out of her Kia Rio and looked at the damage.

Crap. Her back bumper was barely hanging on to the metal frame. She saw the Cadillac pull in behind her and noticed that it had a scrape on the front bumper, but she honestly couldn't say if that was from hitting her or if it had already been there.

The man once more jumped out and came over to her. "I really am sorry," he said with a headshake. "I feel horrible. Especially since my car doesn't even have a scratch."

"That's not from hitting me?" Taylor asked, pointing to the slight damage on his front bumper.

He winced. "No. This is my mother's car, and she did that not too long ago. I swear this car is bad luck. I only took it out today because mine's in the shop. I should've stayed home."

Taylor felt bad for the guy. He looked completely dejected. "It's okay. I'm sure the damage isn't as bad as it looks. Bumpers are meant to do that. I mean, their entire purpose is to take an impact, isn't it?"

The man brightened. "Yeah, I guess so. If you give me your insurance information, I'll call them this afternoon and make this right."

"Shouldn't we call the police?" Taylor asked.

"We could," the man agreed. "And you have every right to do that. But I'd really appreciate it if we just took care of this between the two of us. I've got a bit of a lead foot . . . I really need to learn to just slow down, and I have enough points on my license that if I get cited for this, I'm going to lose it for sure. My mom's sick, so I'm the only one she has to drive her to her doctor's appointments."

Taylor knew the man was laying on the guilt, but she had to admit it was working. "I'm sorry about your mom."

"Thanks. Oh, by the way, I'm Thanatos."

"Excuse me?" Taylor asked.

"That's my name. Thanatos. But I go by Than, because it's less of a mouthful."

Taylor gave him a small smile. "I'm Taylor."

"It's good to meet you, Taylor, but of course not under these circumstances. I'm serious, if you give me your info, I'll call your insurance company and get this taken care of for you. I'd just give you cash to keep it off my insurance, but I don't have it. The cost of my mom's medicine is kicking my butt. But I swear I'm all paid up on my insurance."

Sighing, Taylor nodded. "Okay. Give me a second." She walked to the passenger side of her car and opened the door. Than was beginning to irritate her. He was laying on the sob story really thick. Taylor leaned over to dig in the glove box to find her paperwork. At this point, she just wanted to get out of there.

After finding what she'd been looking for, she stood and turned—gasping when she almost ran into Than. He was standing about two feet from her car.

"Sorry. Didn't mean to scare you."

Taylor wished she was better at reading facial expressions. She couldn't tell if he was being sincere or not, and his tone was no help either. She sidestepped to get out from between him and her car. "Do you have a piece of paper I can write my info on?" she asked.

"Oh, I can just take a picture of it—that'll be easier," Than said, holding out a hand for her insurance info.

Taylor hesitated for a second, then handed it over. He quickly snapped a picture with his cell phone and handed the paper back.

"I'll call first thing tomorrow," he told her. "I'll make everything right."

"I appreciate it."

"Did I make you late for anything?" he asked.

Taylor felt a little awkward now. She wasn't sure she really wanted to make small talk with the guy who'd run into her, but she didn't want to be impolite either. "I'm on my way to my friend's place," she told him. Then lied and said, "My boyfriend." Maybe if Than knew she was dating someone, he'd back off a bit.

"Oh, well, I'm really sorry I ran into you. I hope he won't be mad."

It was a weird thing to say. "He won't. I mean, these things happen," Taylor said with a shrug.

"I appreciate you being so easygoing about it. You've got a good temperament," Than observed.

"Thanks," Taylor replied, feeling more and more uneasy.

"Dang, I didn't mean to make you feel uncomfortable," Than said astutely, taking a step back.

"It's fine," Taylor said.

"Your boyfriend isn't a big ol' bodybuilder who will track me down and beat the crap out of me, is he?"

Taylor smiled at that. "No. He actually works at Silverstone Towing, so I'm sure he'll know someone who I can bring my car to so it can be fixed sooner rather than later."

"Ah, that's good, then. You can't trust anyone these days."

Taylor nodded.

"With that, I'm going to let you get going. I'll be sure to be more careful from here on out. Someone else wouldn't have been as forgiving as you, Taylor."

Than gave her a polite nod, then turned and walked back to his Cadillac. She walked around the front of her Kia and nodded back as he pulled out from behind her and went on his way.

After he was gone, Taylor realized she should've written down his license plate number . . . or at least gotten his full name and number, so she could check back with him if she didn't hear anything from her insurance company. Sighing, and just relieved the entire encounter was done, she got back into her car.

She was going to call Eagle and let him know what happened, but figured she'd see him in ten minutes or so anyway. Besides, there wasn't anything he could do at this point. Her car was drivable, and she wasn't hurt.

Taylor arrived at Eagle's apartment complex and went into the lobby. A man was standing there, and as she walked toward him, he said, "Hey, Flower."

Surprised but pleased to see Eagle in the lobby, she smiled. "Hey."

"You okay?" he asked.

"Yeah, why?"

"You should've been here about fifteen minutes ago. I was worried. I texted but didn't get a response."

Taylor was surprised. He steered her toward the stairwell as they talked. "I'm really sorry. I didn't hear your text, otherwise I would've answered. And I'm late because someone hit me from behind when I was at a stoplight."

They'd just reached the second-floor landing when Eagle stopped in his tracks. "What?"

"Someone hit me—"

"I heard you," he interrupted. He put his hands on her shoulders. "Are you all right?"

"Yeah, I'm fine."

"Shit, Taylor. Why didn't you call me?"

Taylor frowned. "Because it was just a fender bender. It wasn't a huge deal."

"Come on, I'm not talking about this in the stairwell," Eagle said and grabbed her hand, practically dragging her down the hallway toward his apartment.

She wanted to point out that she wasn't the one who'd stopped and insisted on discussing why she was late before they'd even gotten inside his place. But she kept her mouth shut as he unlocked his door and gestured for her to precede him inside.

Feeling a little irritated at his reaction—and his assumption she couldn't deal with a fender bender—Taylor did her best to control her temper.

The second the door shut behind him, Eagle spoke. "Are you sure you're all right? Does your neck hurt? Do we need to go to the emergency room? What happened? Did you get a police report?"

Taylor held up a hand. "One question at a time, jeez," she said in what she hoped was a light tone. "I'm fine. My neck will probably be a bit sore tomorrow, but it's nothing a few aspirins won't fix. I wasn't moving, and the guy was only going probably ten miles an hour, if that. As I said, I was sitting at a red light, and he ran into me with his big boat of a Cadillac. We pulled off the road, and he got my insurance info, since there wasn't any damage to his car."

Eagle stared at her for a second, a muscle in his jaw ticking.

"What?" Taylor asked.

"You know that men do that shit to get their hands on women, right?"

Taylor felt her frustration rising. "What was I supposed to do, Eagle? Ignore the accident? That's against the law. Besides, we weren't in the middle of nowhere. There were plenty of people and businesses around."

"Give me his info, and I'll check him out," Eagle said, holding out his hand.

Taylor crossed her arms. She felt defensive that he was being so over-the-top obnoxious about a simple accident. "I don't have it."

"What? Why not? Isn't it on the police report?"

"There *is* no police report because we didn't call them. My car wasn't that damaged, just the bumper. It's gonna need to be replaced. He took my insurance info and said he would call them and get it taken care of. I didn't *need* to get his information."

"For God's sake!" Eagle exploded, turning his back on her and striding farther into his apartment.

Taylor followed slowly, watching as he paced back and forth. When he turned to face her, she braced herself.

"Did you even get his name?"

"Yes," she told him. "It was Thanatos. He goes by Than for short."

"What's his last name?"

She paused.

"Shit! You don't know it, do you? Thanatos could even be a made-up name. It's too stupid to be real," Eagle said in disgust. "Jesus, Taylor, he's not going to call your insurance company—and you handed over your info to a *complete stranger* without a second thought. Was your address on your paperwork?"

Now Taylor felt stupid . . . and she didn't like Eagle making her feel even worse than she already did. She pressed her lips together.

"And you can't recognize him if you saw him again," Eagle went on. "He's probably laughing his ass off right about now. Thrilled he hit someone so gullible she didn't even call the police. And he could walk right up to your apartment, since you gave him your address, and you wouldn't know it was him. He could hurt you or rob you blind, and you'd never be able to tell the police anything! God, how could you have been so stupid?"

The pain of his words took a second to register. And when they did, Taylor wanted to throw up.

For the first time since she'd met him, Eagle had made her feel like less of a person. He'd thrown her condition in her face and made her feel about two feet tall. And it hurt all the more because she'd been convinced he was her friend. That he would never judge her, no matter what.

Once more, she'd opened herself up in the hope that *this* time, things would be different, only to be reminded that her prosopagnosia would always make her an outcast. Someone to be ridiculed, made to feel like a pariah.

Knowing if she tried to say anything, she'd burst out crying, Taylor turned on her heel and headed for the door.

"Where are you going?" Eagle asked.

Taylor didn't answer, simply opened his door and started to step out into the hall.

Eagle stopped her by taking hold of her arm. "Taylor? We aren't done talking about this."

And that pissed her off enough for her to push back her sorrow, anger rising swiftly. "*We* weren't talking. *You* were. I get it, Eagle, I'm *stupid*. Not only that, I'm apparently going to get murdered in my bed because I won't know a bad guy until it's too late. Thanks for your vote of confidence and letting me know how you *really* feel." She yanked her arm out of his grip and took a few steps into the hallway, then abruptly turned back around.

"I thought you were different. That you saw *me*. But you're just like everyone else—you can't see past my condition. Well, I might not be able to recognize faces, but I know an asshole when I see one!"

And with that parting shot, Taylor turned again and walked as fast as she could without running down the hall.

But her heart broke when she got to the stairwell . . . and he hadn't come after her.

The door closed behind her, and the first tear fell.

Eagle had just broken her heart, and she wasn't sure she'd ever get over it. Over *him*.

$\sim$

Eagle stared at his closed door, adrenaline still pumping, and ran a hand through his hair.

What had just happened?

When he'd heard Taylor had been in an accident, he'd almost lost it. He hated that he hadn't been there, that she hadn't called him.

He barely remembered what he'd said, but he'd never forget her words to *him*.

He *had* been an asshole, but he'd been so worried about her. He'd seen too many crime scene photos of the aftermath of women not being smart about their safety. Pictures of mutilated and tortured women who'd trusted the wrong person. And the thought of Taylor ending up like that had made him lose his mind.

He needed to go after her, apologize, try to explain, but if he chased her down now, she wouldn't listen. Not that he could blame her.

"Fuck!" he swore, feeling sick inside. He'd fucked up. Big time. Now might not be the best time to talk to her, but he couldn't wait until tomorrow to say he was sorry.

He strode over to the kitchen counter, where he'd left his phone after he'd texted Taylor earlier, and picked it up.

He quickly typed out a text. He'd meant for it to be short, but once he started typing, he couldn't stop. There were errors throughout his apology, but he didn't bother to correct them.

Eagle: I'm sorry. I didnt mean anyting the way it sounded. I was worrid about you. I obviously did a shit job of letting you know that. I shouldve hugged you and said I was glad you were all rigt. You arent stupid. Shit, you're smarter than anyone I know. I'm the stupid one. Please, forgive me, let me mke this right. I see you, flower, and the person I see is the strongest person I know. I AM an asshole. Please let me know you got home safely.

He hit send and closed his eyes. He literally felt sick to his stomach. He knew Taylor's past. Knew how she felt about being belittled because of her condition, and he'd gone and done just that. In his defense, he'd been freaked out and worried, but that certainly wasn't the impression he'd given.

He went back to pacing. What if she refused to talk to him again? What if she decided she didn't want him in her life at all?

Eagle wasn't normally a man to panic. His experience as a Delta had pretty much beaten that emotion out of him—but he was panicking now.

He *needed* Taylor in his life. Couldn't imagine not talking to her every day.

Somehow he had to make this right, but at the moment, he didn't know how.

"*Shit!*" he yelled and slumped into one of his recliners. He held on to his phone with a tight grip and prayed she'd text him back soon and let him know she was home.

~

Brett sat in his basement and stared at the picture of Taylor Cardin's insurance information. He'd had so much fun this evening. He chuckled at the name he'd given her. Thanatos. She probably had no idea that it meant "he who brings death." Brett figured it was appropriate.

It was time to step up his game.

He had a lot more "random" encounters in mind for his Taylor.

He definitely wasn't happy that she had a boyfriend. That would make things a bit tougher for him. He'd assumed no one would notice when she disappeared. That he'd have plenty of time to play with her, then bury her body in one of the many state parks around Indiana. But if the guy she was seeing filed a missing person report, it could drastically cut into his time to do everything he wanted.

No. Fuck that.

Taylor was *his*.

No one would know he'd had anything to do with her. She wouldn't be able to describe him to her boyfriend. He'd seen her with a man once or twice, but for some idiotic reason, he'd never suspected they were dating. He'd just have to be more careful, make sure he was never seen by the man and that his interactions with Taylor were strictly when she was by herself.

Brett would be fine.

He knew there wouldn't be a problem this weekend when he showed up at the Dementia Senior Care Center that she visited every Sunday. She was always alone. She stayed for three hours, then left. He'd already visited the disgusting place himself earlier that week and gotten the lay of the land.

It was just another step in messing with little Taylor's head. He couldn't wait, once she was in his clutches, to let her know all the times their paths had crossed.

Looking behind him at the cot he'd set up for her, Brett smiled. He could picture Taylor there in his shackles. She'd cry and beg for him to let her go—they all did—and he'd let her think that was his plan, but there was no way she was going anywhere.

He could almost feel his hands wrapped around her neck, her breaths stopping. Her eyes would bug out as he choked her—she'd thrash under him, but she wouldn't be able to escape. He'd choke the life out of her—then breathe it right back in. Make sure she realized he had complete and full control. She'd be terrified . . . and it would be delicious.

Brett's dick hardened. He stood from his desk and went over to the cot to lie down. He unzipped his pants and took out his cock, turning his head to look at his pictures as he masturbated. The eleven faces of the other women he'd played with looked back at him from the wall. Soon, he'd have lucky number twelve. Taylor. She'd know what was in store for her when she saw those pictures, and he'd revel in her fright.

He got off on the terror his guests experienced. *He* decided how long they would live and when they would die. Nothing was better than having that control. He had none in his real life, so he'd take it here in his basement world.

His excitement over what was coming was too much to think about, and Brett exploded all over his hand.

"Donald?" he heard his mother call out from upstairs.

He scowled in disgust. Donald was his father, who'd been dead for over two decades. He hated that his mother was so pathetic. But he couldn't kill her. One, it would bring him no satisfaction; she wouldn't even understand what was happening. And two, he needed her social security and disability checks.

He'd keep the old bitch alive for as long as possible, and in the meantime, he'd take his enjoyment where he could get it.

After zipping up his pants, Brett wiped his hand on the cot and then stood, liking the thought of his Taylor lying on his come. With a satisfied grin on his face, Brett headed up the stairs to deal with his mother. He'd give her some drugs to knock her out, then he could come back downstairs and fantasize about seeing Taylor again.

Chapter Eight

Taylor could barely open her eyes the next morning. They were swollen from crying all night. She'd only slept in snippets; nightmares kept waking her up.

She leaned over and picked up her phone and reread Eagle's text . . . and knew that she'd overreacted. Yes, his words had upset her, but instead of admitting it, and talking with Eagle like an adult, she'd said things she hadn't meant, then run away like she was ten years old.

She'd also refused to text him back and let him know she'd made it home all right. But now in the light of day, instead of feeling as if she'd somehow "won," she just felt like shit. Guilty that maybe he'd worried about her all night, and ashamed that she'd reacted like she had rather than explaining how much he'd hurt her feelings.

Her head ached, and Taylor knew she wasn't going to get much work finished until she'd done what she could to make things right with Eagle. She pulled herself out of bed and headed for her shower. She could text him back, but she wanted to talk to him face to face. Wanted to tell him in person how much his words had cut her, but also let him know that she forgave him.

She needed Eagle in her life. She'd give him a second chance because she truly believed he was sorry for what he'd said.

After her shower, Taylor felt a little better. She put on a pair of jeans and an old comfortable sweatshirt. She brushed her hair and ignored the way her curls seemed to be more out of control than ever.

She headed for the kitchen, scooping up her phone along the way. Her plan was to eat breakfast, then haul her ass over to Eagle's apartment. If he wasn't there, she'd go to Silverstone to find him.

She'd just opened her refrigerator when there was a knock on her door.

Frozen in place and barely daring to breathe, she couldn't help but think about Eagle's words from the night before. Was this the guy who called himself Thanatos, come to hurt her like Eagle had said? It was an absurd thought, but now that the seed had been planted, and she could admit how stupidly she *had* acted yesterday, Taylor couldn't move.

It was too early for anyone to be at her door. Six thirty in the morning wasn't a time most normal people showed up at someone's apartment.

Staring at the door across the room as if it would somehow magically disappear and she'd come face to face with an ax-wielding murderer, Taylor jerked when the phone she still had in her hand vibrated.

She quickly looked down, ready to silence it, fearing that whoever was on the other side of the door would inexplicably be able to hear the vibrations.

Instead, she blinked in surprise at the text that had just arrived.

Eagle: It's me, Flower. I'm at your door. Are you awake? Let me in. Please?

What was Eagle doing there so early in the morning? Shit, was something wrong? Was he about to leave on a mission? Taylor would never forgive herself if that was the case and she childishly refused to see him. She'd already decided to find and talk to him anyway.

Closing the fridge, she hurried over to her front door and peered through the peephole. It was a stupid habit—of course she wouldn't recognize anyone standing there. But the man wasn't carrying a bloody ax, and he kept running his hand through his hair exactly the way Eagle did.

She kept the chain on the door and cracked it open. "Eagle?"

"Yeah, Flower, it's me. Can we talk?"

Without a word, she closed the door, took off the chain, and reopened it, gesturing for Eagle to come inside.

His shoulders were slumped, and he looked as tired as she felt.

The second the door was shut, Taylor said, "I'm sorry."

He said the same thing at the exact same time.

They looked at each other for a heartbeat, then, as if they'd planned it in advance, they stepped closer and wrapped their arms around each other.

Being in Eagle's arms felt so right, especially because she was so conscious of the fact that she'd almost lost him.

"I'm sorry," he repeated against her hair. "I was an ass, and you had every right to call me on it."

Taylor shook her head, but didn't move out of his embrace. He felt too good against her. "No, I should've stayed and talked to you. Not acted like a spoiled child by calling you names and stomping away."

It was Eagle who pulled back first. "No, you were right. Don't you ever take shit like that from me again. Call me an asshole, walk away, do what you have to, but don't stand there and let me hurt you with my words again."

After swallowing hard, Taylor admitted, "You *did* hurt me."

"I know," Eagle said without hesitation. "And that's why I haven't slept at all. I kept replaying my words and the look on your face. I might as well have punched you. I'll never forgive myself for it."

"Well, you're going to have to," Taylor said firmly. "Because you were right. I *was* stupid. I gave that guy my home address, didn't get his last name, his license plate number, or anything else about him. That's asinine for a normal woman, but for me, it's doubly so."

"You *are* a normal woman," Eagle insisted.

Taylor shook her head. "I'm not. And that's okay. I'm different, and it's taken me a long time to come to terms with that, but it is what it is. My brain isn't magically going to fix itself. I'm not going to wake up one day and recognize you or anyone else. I went through a lot of therapy when I was little, and none of it ever worked. I need to be more aware of my surroundings. Not everyone is as nice as you and your friends. I'm going to try to do better."

Eagle stared at her for so long, Taylor began to get nervous. "Eagle?"

He simply shook his head. "I'm just trying to understand how you can be so forgiving," he said. "I fully expected to have to grovel for hours just to get you to open the door."

"You hurt me," Taylor said, "but we're moving on. It's what friends do, right?"

He frowned slightly, there and gone. "Right," he said in a tone Taylor couldn't read.

"I don't want to lose you," she admitted. "I like having you in my life. I like talking to you and beating you at pinball. I like your friends, and I admire what you do. If I turned my back on everyone who ever hurt me, I'd be even more alone than I am now. I need to start forgiving and stop holding grudges."

"When you didn't respond to my text, I drove over here last night," Eagle admitted. "I had to make sure you'd gotten home safely. I saw your car in the lot and a light on in your apartment. Only then did I think I could get to sleep, but instead, I kept seeing your face, and knowing how much I hurt you kept me awake."

"You drove all the way over here?" Taylor asked incredulously.

"I did."

"Wow, okay, that's probably one of the nicest things anyone's ever done for me."

He huffed out a breath. "If that's the nicest, then I need to work harder."

They smiled at each other, and Taylor felt as if a ten-pound weight had been lifted from her shoulders.

"How do you feel this morning?" he asked. "Besides being tired and having a headache?"

"How do you know I have a headache?"

"Because you're wincing at the light from the kitchen. And your eyes are swollen, so it's obvious I made you cry last night."

It was amazing how he could read her. "I took some over-the-counter meds," she told him. "I'll be okay."

"Your neck sore?"

"Not as much as I thought it might be," Taylor said honestly. "I'm starving, though. I didn't eat dinner last night."

"Me either. Which is why I stopped by the Dancing Donut on my way over here."

Taylor smiled happily. "You did? I love that place!"

"I know," Eagle said. "Give me two minutes to run down to my car and grab the box. I'll be right back."

And before she could offer to go with him, Eagle was gone.

Sighing happily, and more relieved than she could put into words, Taylor went into the kitchen and grabbed two glasses. She poured them both some orange juice and got the coffee started. By the time she was done, Eagle was back.

He had not only one box, but two, and Taylor's eyes bugged out as he set them down. "Jeez, Eagle, how many doughnuts did you get?"

"Two dozen. I figured if you didn't like any of them, I could bring them to Silverstone later."

"Oh no. I get to keep them *all*," Taylor said. She loved doughnuts. She tried to stay away from them because she literally couldn't control herself. And the Dancing Donut was her absolute favorite pastry shop.

Eagle chuckled and took a step back from the boxes with his hands up in surrender. "Far be it from me to get between a woman and her doughnuts."

"And don't you forget it," Taylor teased, pointing a finger at him.

Eagle reached out and pulled her close once more. He wrapped one arm around her waist, and the other speared into the hair at the nape of her neck. She looked up at him.

"Thank you for forgiving me," Eagle said seriously. "I treasure your friendship, and I was sick that I'd said such horrible things to you."

Taylor licked her lips, and she saw his gaze flick to the movement before returning to her eyes. She wanted him to kiss her so badly, but she also didn't want to do anything that might hurt their truce. "You're not an asshole," she told him.

"I am, but I'm glad you think I'm not," he retorted.

"Do you . . . do you want to hang out here for a while?" she asked tentatively. "I think now that things between us are okay, I could get some work done. I was going to spend the morning tracking you down to apologize and to make things right. But now I can get something done, and maybe we can go and play some pinball later if you don't have to work?" She was aware that she was babbling, but she couldn't help it. Being in his arms made her nervous she was going to say or do something that would let him know how much she wanted to be more than a friend.

"You were going to track me down?" he asked.

Taylor nodded.

"I'd love to stay," he said. "I can take a nap on your couch while you work, if that's all right."

"It's more than all right," she told him.

"Are you going to the Dementia Senior Care Center this weekend?" Eagle asked out of the blue.

Taylor blinked. He hadn't let her go, so she couldn't hide her confusion. "I'd planned on it—why?"

"I thought maybe I could go with you."

Taylor frowned, and her stomach rolled with nerves. "Um . . . I'm not sure. It's . . . it's really personal, Eagle." She hated telling him no, but for some reason, she wasn't ready to let down her guard with him like that. The men and women she visited were so much like her, and that made her feel vulnerable.

"It's okay," he said, making her feel even worse because he was being so understanding.

"I just . . . I'm not saying never, but . . ." Her voice trailed off. She wasn't sure why she was so reluctant to have him accompany her this weekend.

"I understand. I made you doubt me last night. I'm going to make up for what I said, Flower. I swear. I'll make you trust me again if it's the last thing I do."

Then he leaned forward, kissed her forehead gently, and let her go. He lifted the lid of the top box of doughnuts, grabbed one, took a big bite, and headed for the couch.

Taylor took a deep breath. She wouldn't dwell on things. Eagle was here, they'd forgiven each other, they were moving on. And she had doughnuts. And a day that started with doughnuts was always a good day.

She brought the glass of orange juice and a mug of coffee over to Eagle, and he accepted both with a smile. "Thanks."

"You're welcome."

"If me being here bothers you, just let me know."

"No! It doesn't," Taylor said immediately. "I like having you here. When you knocked this morning, I scared myself by imagining a man with a huge ax was on the other side of the door."

Eagle winced. "I'm sorry."

"No, don't apologize. You were right," Taylor said firmly. "Giving that man my home address was ridiculously stupid. I'm going to have to be extra careful for a while as a result. It was right of you to point it out . . . and we're moving on. I'm glad you're here, Eagle. I swear."

"Okay. I'm just going to close my eyes. You do your thing, and when you want me out, just let me know."

"I don't want you out," she told him, sure he'd be able to read the longing in her tone, but he simply nodded and put the last bite of doughnut in his mouth and scooted down on the sofa, resting his head on the back cushion.

Feeling good that Eagle was there, Taylor went to her dining room table and opened the American history textbook. She was nearing the end. A good thing, since she'd received her next project, a three-hundred-page manuscript someone was trying to get published.

She was smiling like a fool but couldn't make herself stop. She'd woken up feeling so crappy, but now she felt on top of the world. She and Eagle were good—everything else felt insignificant.

∼

Later that afternoon, Eagle brought Taylor over to Silverstone Towing. Archer had made meatloaf for everyone to eat over the weekend, so they'd had an amazing late lunch and were playing pinball when Bull, Smoke, and Gramps appeared.

"We need to talk," Bull said in a tone of voice Eagle knew meant that shit had hit the fan.

He turned to Taylor, but she was already waving him toward the safe room. "Go. I'll be fine."

"You sure?"

"Eagle, *yes*. I'm good. I'll go upstairs and see who's still here and hang out. If everyone's out working, I'll watch TV or something. Hell, maybe I'll take a nap, since I didn't sleep well last night. The point is, you don't have to entertain me twenty-four seven. You guys have work to do, so go do it."

Eagle couldn't stop himself from putting his arm around her shoulders and hugging her to him for a beat. "Thanks for understanding, Tay."

"Hey, I'll never get in the way of you superheroes saving the world. Go do your thing."

And with that, Eagle nodded and stepped toward his friends. When the safe room door had shut, he asked, "What's up?"

Bull grabbed a chair and sat, pulling a sheaf of papers over to him. "You know the situation in Timor-Leste that we've been monitoring?"

"Yeah, what about it?" Eagle asked as he and the others all took seats around the table.

"It's time to move on that," Gramps answered.

"The leader of the rebels who started that coup last year has been a thorn in the Timor-Leste government's side for months," Bull said. "Everyone thought after most of the rebels had been caught, killed, or had given up, the resistance would die off. But there's a faction that *hasn't* given up. And they've changed their tactics in the capital city. Now, instead of harassing the government officials, they're targeting civilians."

"What do you mean, *targeting*?" Eagle asked. "They were always harassing them, right?"

"Yeah, but remember that American woman they were holding hostage and forcing to fight for them? The peace corps volunteer?" Gramps asked.

"Yeah. One day, she just reappeared in Southern California, and speculation about how she got away from the rebels was rampant. We all assumed some Special Forces group went in and got her out," Eagle said.

"Right. Because she never explained publicly. In the interview she gave the FBI—which Willis got us copies of—she explained exactly what they made her do, and what was done to her. But it was a relatively small group, and we all thought the rebels would eventually give up and fade back into the countryside. Apparently they're trying to rebuild their army. They're slaughtering families and forcing wives and children to fight. The stories coming out of the area are horrifying," Bull explained.

"And Willis wants us to go in and cut the head off the snake," Eagle concluded.

His three friends nodded. "The leader is in Dili, the capital city. We've got intel about where they're holing up. Willis believes if we take him out, his supporters will lose the will to fight. I agree," Smoke said.

"We all agree," Gramps said with a nod.

"When do we leave?" Eagle asked, anger coursing through his body at the thought of all the innocent men, women, and children caught up in a power struggle that the rebels were always bound to lose.

"We just wanted to make sure you agreed that we should go in," Smoke said. "We need to do a bit more studying of the layout of the city, and nail down the logistics of getting in and out of the country, but I'm guessing we can leave in two days."

Sunday. It was just as well Taylor hadn't wanted him to go with her to the Dementia Senior Care Center. Eagle had to admit . . . it stung to know she didn't want him with her, but he understood. Now, he was glad she hadn't agreed, since he wouldn't have to go back on his word and disappoint her by saying he couldn't go after all.

"I'll be ready," he said confidently.

"Good. Now, let's go over the layout of the city," Gramps said, spreading a large map out on the table.

～

Three hours later, Eagle and the rest of his team left the safe room and made their way upstairs. The sun was setting, and there had been a shift change at Silverstone Towing. Looking around, he didn't see Taylor in the great room.

"She's sleeping," Leigh said. "I swear that woman can sleep through a tornado. No one was quiet when they were here earlier, but even with the door open to the room she crashed in, she didn't move."

Eagle knew that was because she was exhausted after a sleepless night. He'd gotten a nice nap that morning while she'd worked, but she'd obviously finally crashed after a long evening and day.

"Thanks, Leigh," he told her, pleased to see that she was wearing the name tag Skylar had brought over. She'd made tags for all the employees, and no one had complained about wearing them. Even when Taylor wasn't around, everyone had gotten in the habit of putting on their tags when they came in the door.

He walked silently down the hall and found the room where Taylor was napping. She was on her side, with one arm stretched out, as if reaching for something. The other was tucked under the pillow.

Eagle hated to wake her, but he wanted to get her home. He ached to bring her to *his* apartment, to his bed, but since they'd just made up after their first fight, he figured he needed to move at her pace.

He loved her so much. Almost losing her with his careless words had affected him even more than he'd thought it would.

"Taylor," he said softly, sitting in the crook of her legs. She rolled toward him a bit, but didn't stir. "Flower, wake up," he said, putting his hand on her shoulder and lightly shaking her.

Her eyes fluttered, then opened in slits.

"Hey, Flower, I need to get you home."

"You done with your meeting?" she asked sleepily.

"Yeah."

"It go okay?"

"As good as it could," Eagle answered honestly.

"You leaving?"

He blinked at her insight, nodding. "Yeah."

"When?" she asked.

"Sunday. Probably early."

"That's only two days from now," she complained.

Wanting to smile because it was obvious she was still drowsy, Eagle merely nodded. "It is."

"Well, shoot. I know I said no earlier, but you caught me off guard. I wouldn't mind if you visited the dementia center with me," she told him. "I think I'd probably feel less vulnerable if you were there. It always takes me the rest of Sunday to feel normal again. Well, normal for me. But I think if you were there with me, I'd be able to get over the off-kilter feeling faster."

Her words meant the world to him. "Can I have a rain check?" he asked.

"Of course." Taylor pushed herself up on a hand. He was still sitting next to her, blocking her from moving her legs over the side of the mattress. "I'm ready to go if you are."

Eagle gently brushed her hair off her face.

"Eagle?" she asked tentatively.

Taking a deep breath, he forced himself to move. Standing, he held out his hand. "Come on, Flower, let's get you home."

She grabbed his hand and let him help her up. "I talked to some of your employees, and they said that I should take my car to Stanley Automotive. That he's the best around."

"They're right. I'll take care of it tomorrow for you."

"That's not necessary. I can do it," she said. "You've probably got a lot of stuff to do to get ready for wherever it is you're going."

She was right. They did have a lot to do, but he could take the time to bring her car to Stan. "It's not a problem, Tay."

"Okay. Thank you, I appreciate it."

"Stan'll have a loaner car you can use while he's working on yours. Although I don't think it'll take too long to replace that bumper . . . as long as nothing else was damaged. If I'm not back by the time he's done, he'll call you, and you can go and pick it up. Do you have enough to cover the cost?" he asked a little hesitantly.

"I do. I'm assuming you don't think Thanatos is going to take care of it?"

Eagle winced.

"No, don't answer that," she said before he could respond. "He won't. It's a lesson learned on my part."

"I'm sorry you had to learn it the hard way."

Taylor shrugged. "Do you know how long you're going to be gone?" she asked.

"Unfortunately, no. I don't want to even guess, because I don't want you to worry if we don't get back in my time frame."

"I understand. I don't like it, but I get it," Taylor said. "You'll be safe?"

"Yes," he reassured her. "We always are. We never take unnecessary risks. The last thing we want is for one of us to get hurt or killed. We're cautious, Taylor. Promise."

"Good." Then she stepped into him and rested her head on his chest and hugged him tightly. "I'm going to worry about you no matter what you say," she admitted.

Eagle hugged her back, loving how she felt in his arms. They'd gotten pretty touchy feely lately, and ever since they'd fought and made up this morning, they'd been touching each other even more. He wasn't complaining.

"I'll let you know the second we get back," he told her.

"Good." She pulled away. "All right, let's get going. There's a doughnut in my apartment calling my name."

"I can't believe how many you already ate this morning," Eagle teased.

"They're my weakness—I can't help it. And if you keep bringing them for me in two-dozen batches like you did this morning, I'm gonna weigh eight hundred pounds, so keep that in mind."

Eagle followed behind her as she walked down the hall and couldn't help but let his eyes land on her ass. It was round and gorgeous . . . and he'd already fantasized about how it would feel in his palms as she rode him.

If she thought she was anything but perfect, she was sadly mistaken. He'd bring her doughnuts for the rest of her life if it meant keeping her ass looking exactly how it did now.

"Did you hear me?" she asked as they crossed the great room.

"I heard you," Eagle assured her.

"That smile on your face makes me nervous," Taylor told him.

"It shouldn't. I have only your best interests at heart," Eagle said.

Taylor rolled her eyes, but chuckled.

After he'd taken her home and walked her up to her apartment and was driving to his place, Eagle began to strategize how he could move himself out of the friend zone. Nothing foolproof came to mind, but he had some time to think about it.

He was going to do whatever it took to maintain his friendship with Taylor, even while moving their relationship to the next level. He had a feeling it would be the best thing he'd ever done in his life. And he couldn't wait.

Chapter Nine

Taylor didn't want to think about where Eagle and his friends were going or what they would be doing. Well . . . she knew what they'd be doing, but that only made her more nervous. Intellectually, she realized they had to be very good at sneaking into foreign countries and taking out bad guys, but in her heart, the very idea scared her to death.

Earlier, she'd debated going to the Dementia Senior Care Center. What she really wanted to do was lie in bed with the covers up over her head, but if she didn't go visit the residents, who would? There was one man who didn't have any visitors except for her. And another woman only got to see her children once a month. Granted, both had no recollection of either of their families—or her, for that matter—but Taylor knew she'd feel guilty if she didn't go.

For the hundredth time, she wished Eagle was there. She didn't know what she'd been thinking, not wanting him with her. She had a feeling he would've made her visit so much easier. He had a way of cutting through the bullshit in her head and making her believe that her condition didn't matter in the larger scope of life. She was trying to believe that.

So here she was. Outside the center, sitting in the loaner car she'd been given to use while hers was being repaired.

Facing what her future might look like was always scary. A month ago, *this* had been her future. When she got old, she'd have to go into some home and be cared for by strangers. Because the nurses and doctors who worked in the home *would* be strangers. Every single person who came into her room would always be.

But now that she'd met Eagle, she'd begun to feel a glimmer of hope that maybe, just maybe, she'd have *him* by her side when she got old . . . and that future didn't seem so scary. Of course, that was ridiculous; just because someone was your friend didn't mean they always would be. Or that they'd stand by you when you needed them the most. She'd learned that more than once.

But she had no doubt that if Eagle said he'd do something for her, he'd do it. That was just how he was. *Who* he was.

Taking a deep breath, Taylor pushed open her door and got out. She needed to get inside. She had work to do at home; delving into a boring textbook would be just what she needed to keep her mind off missing Eagle and wondering if he was all right.

Taylor entered the care center, and the smell of the place hit her right in the face. It wasn't awful . . . she'd been in places that smelled worse than this, but it was still strong. Antiseptic, the bleach they used to clean the floors and surfaces, and a faint scent of urine. Some of the residents weren't ambulatory and inevitably soiled their linens.

She walked up to the desk. "Hi, I'm Taylor Cardin, and I'm here to volunteer."

The young woman sitting there glanced up from her phone. "Hi. I know it's you, Taylor. You come here every week." She sounded irritated. Taylor had told the employees about her prosopagnosia, but she didn't seem to remember, or care, that Taylor couldn't recognize her.

The employee grabbed a visitor's badge and handed it over. "Here you go. You know the rules."

And that was it.

Taylor was annoyed. For the safety of the residents, the person working the front desk should care a little more about who she was letting in and a little less about gossiping on social media. Knowing that saying anything would do no good, Taylor clipped the tag onto her shirt and headed down the hallway to her right. She would stop in and see how Mr. Clarkson was doing first. He was the man with no family who never had visitors.

She read the names on each door and was relieved to see Mr. Clarkson hadn't been moved since last week when she'd been there. Sometimes that happened, and she had to hunt for her favorite residents. She'd also once made the mistake of not checking the names on the door and had spent thirty minutes talking to a woman, thinking she was someone else. Which was like a comedy of errors—Taylor thinking the woman was another resident, and the resident thinking Taylor was someone from her past.

Pushing open the door, Taylor swallowed hard as the smell hit her. It was always stronger in the individual rooms. She'd mostly gotten used to it, though. Mr. Clarkson was sitting on the side of his bed, looking down at the floor. He was wearing a hospital gown instead of his usual flannel pants and T-shirt.

"Hi, Mr. Clarkson," she said softly. "It's good to see you."

"Ellen?" he said, his eyes lighting up as he looked to the door.

Taylor knew Ellen had been his wife. She'd died a few years ago, but Mr. Clarkson thought everyone who came through the door was his long-lost love.

"What are you doing just sitting there?" Taylor asked, knowing it was better not to deny she was his wife, that he wouldn't know who she was anyway if she said her name.

"Ellen, where have you been? I've missed you!" Mr. Clarkson said and held out his hand.

Taylor walked over and took it in her own. His skin was mottled with age, and his grip was weak, but she barely noticed any of that. She *did* notice the back of his hand was bruised all to hell, and it made her heart hurt looking at it. It was obvious he'd had to have an IV put in at some point since she'd last seen him. He looked even more fragile than usual. And the fact that he wasn't wearing his normal clothes was another cause for concern.

"Why don't you lie back?" Taylor suggested.

"Don't leave me!" Mr. Clarkson said, tightening his hold on her, his eyes going wide.

"I won't," Taylor reassured him. "Come on, lie down for me."

He did, managing to keep hold of her hand the entire time.

Taylor pulled a chair close to the bed and leaned her elbows on the mattress. "How have you been?" she asked.

"Not good, not good," Mr. Clarkson said. Then he went on and on about how terrible work had been lately and how their kids had been acting up. Taylor just sat and listened, making the appropriate sympathetic noises now and then so he knew she was there.

Over the months she'd been visiting him, Taylor had learned that he had a pretty tragic story. One of his children had been killed in a car accident, and the other, a daughter, was estranged. She'd gotten hooked on painkillers and was currently homeless, living out in Los Angeles somewhere. He had no siblings, and after his wife had died, there'd been no one to help take care of him at his home. He was literally all alone in the world, and it made Taylor's heart ache for him.

An hour later, she slipped her hand out of Mr. Clarkson's limp fingers and leaned over and kissed him on his wrinkled forehead as he slept. She wasn't sure she was making a difference in the lives of the people she visited, but she liked to think so.

The rest of her visits were shorter. Mrs. Allen wasn't in the mood to chat, Mr. Lloyd was too agitated for visitors, and a petite woman nicknamed Little Mama by her family was only concerned about the chocolates Taylor had brought and otherwise had no time to talk.

Her visits were always draining, so before driving home, Taylor went and sat in a small outdoor space. The care center was a huge square with long hallways of rooms, and in the middle, the developers had built a nice courtyard, a garden where the residents could sit without worrying the staff that they'd leave the grounds. There were a couple of residents there enjoying the sunshine, but Taylor made sure to sit away from them. She needed some downtime to get her head on straight before she went home to her lonely apartment.

Wishing Eagle was home so she could call him, Taylor sighed as she sat on a bench.

She'd only been there a few minutes when someone asked from nearby, "It's hard, isn't it?"

Looking up, she saw a man standing near her. Startled because she hadn't heard him approach, Taylor nodded.

"I'm Jim. Jim Warton," the man said, holding out his hand for her to shake.

Not wanting to be rude, Taylor reached out and shook his hand. It might've been her imagination, but she could've sworn the man held her hand a bit too long to be polite. When he did let go, she surreptitiously wiped her palm on her jeans and tried to think of a way to get out of conversing.

"May I sit?" Jim asked.

Mentally sighing and knowing she was going to be stuck talking to the man, she nodded.

He sat next to her, and it was only then that Taylor realized how small the bench was. She could feel the heat of his hip against hers . . . and it made her extremely uncomfortable.

"It's hard seeing loved ones like this, isn't it?" he asked.

Taylor nodded.

"You here visiting a parent?" he asked.

"No. I'm just volunteering," Taylor told him.

"Really? Wow, that's good of you. Most people don't want anything to do with a place like this. They're scared of the old people who act weird and can't remember anything."

For some reason, his words struck her as offensive. "They aren't weird," she defended them. "Most are just stuck in the past, and they're confused about where they are and why they can't be with their families."

"You're right," Jim said immediately. "I'm sorry, I didn't mean to imply otherwise."

He didn't sound all that sincere, but Taylor didn't call him on it. Instead she asked, "Why are you here?"

"I'm looking for a place for my mom," he told her. "I've been looking after her at home, but it's gotten more and more difficult, for both her and me. It's been the two of us for a long time, and I really don't want to do it, but she's not happy at home."

"I'm sorry," Taylor said, and she was. She was still getting weird vibes from the man, but she did feel for anyone who was trying to care for a loved one with dementia or Alzheimer's.

"Thanks. She's a wanderer. She's constantly trying to get out of the house, and that scares me to death. She thinks she's a prisoner. The last time she got out, she was telling everyone she saw that I was a horrible son and asking if she could live with them instead."

Goose bumps rose on Taylor's arms. The residents could say some pretty outlandish things, but most of the time their ramblings were rooted in memories of things that had actually happened in their lives.

The reason Eagle had been so upset with her the other night was really hammered home in this moment. He'd been scared for her safety. Because she'd given a complete stranger her home address. It had hurt when he'd called her stupid, but that was what she'd been. And she realized that she'd somehow gotten herself into another potentially dangerous situation.

Oh, she didn't think the man next to her was going to grab her and try to kidnap her; it would be impossible, since the courtyard had no external access. It was surrounded on all four sides by the walls of the building. But still.

She was sitting with a stranger who she'd never be able to identify. He had on a regular pair of jeans and a nondescript white T-shirt. He could literally be almost anyone. He had no distinguishing features whatsoever. When she inhaled through her nose, trying to calm herself, she realized that he smelled like the care center. Bleach and urine. She wondered if that was because he'd been visiting or because of the mother he took care of at home.

"I'm sorry, that sounds very stressful," she said carefully, doing her best to shift her body to the right so she wasn't touching him anymore.

"It is," Jim agreed. "So I came down here to check this place out. You volunteer here . . . what do you think? How's the staff? The security? Are the residents happy and cared for?"

She didn't want to talk anymore. She wanted to leave. But Taylor also couldn't be rude. It just wasn't in her. "Some of the staff could be more attentive," she said honestly. "But the residents seem to be happy."

"Hmmm, that's good. What about you? Are *you* happy, Taylor?"

Okay, that was it. She was done with this conversation. She should've politely greeted him, then immediately left the moment she'd felt weird vibes.

"I am," she said, then stood. "I'm sorry, but I need to get going. I hope you find what you need for your mother. It was nice to meet you." Then, without giving him time to respond, she turned and practically ran for the nearest door.

She glanced back when she reached the door and noted Jim was standing by the bench. He saw her looking at him and raised a hand, giving her a small wave.

But it was the odd little smile on his face that made her shiver.

Taylor considered visiting another resident just to hide out from Jim so he didn't catch her in the parking lot or something, but decided she just wanted to go home. She headed for the front desk and handed in her visitor's pass. With another look over her shoulder, and not seeing creepy Jim, Taylor rushed toward her loaner and locked herself in. She didn't see any sign of Jim as she exited the parking lot and sighed in relief when she pulled onto the road.

"Eagle being gone has made you paranoid," Taylor said out loud as she drove a little too fast back to her apartment. "You're fine. The man was just being friendly."

As usual, when she tried to bring up the man's features, she couldn't pull them all into focus at the same time to see a cohesive face.

When she was a little girl and in therapy, one of her therapists had told her to draw what she saw when she looked at other people. So she'd done as requested, had drawn a picture of her latest foster mother. She'd made her very tall, and put a bright-pink dress on the stick figure, since the woman liked to wear very bright clothes. She'd drawn long black hair on her picture and put long red fingernails on each hand. But inside the circle that she'd made to represent the woman's head, it was blank. No eyes. No nose. No mouth. It was easier that way, because putting together all the features she saw individually was too hard.

And that was what she saw in her head at that moment, trying to recall the man. A large menacing figure with no face. It had been scary when she was five, and it was equally terrifying now.

After she'd parked in a spot at her apartment complex, Taylor closed her eyes and brought Eagle to the forefront of her mind. His face was also a blank, but she concentrated on other features. His fresh clean smell. The way his arm muscles bulged when he played pinball. How he always ran a hand through his hair when he was frustrated or thinking intensely. The sound of his laughter when he was teasing her. How he made that sexy little noise in the back of his throat when he ate something he enjoyed.

She might not be able to pick him out of a picture lineup, but Taylor had no doubt that if she spent five minutes with men who were the same height and size as Eagle, she'd know who he was by his mannerisms and scent.

But five minutes was too long. She hated not being able to immediately know who he was. How could she not know someone who meant so much to her?

Realizing her thoughts were turning morose, she took a deep breath and got out of her car. She was halfway to her building when she stopped suddenly in her tracks, something occurring to her.

Jim had called her Taylor.

She'd purposely not introduced herself when she'd shaken his hand. Eagle's outburst had made her realize that it wasn't smart to give out so much information about herself when meeting someone, so she'd not given her name to the man.

So how had he known it?

The visitor's pass was generic, didn't have a name on it.

He might've heard one of the employees saying it when she'd been inside, but she hadn't really talked to any of the nursing staff that day.

A shiver ran through her, and Taylor looked around nervously. She didn't see anyone lurking in the parking lot, but she couldn't shake the feeling of being watched. She had no idea what kind of car Jim was driving. He could be anyone at this point. Watching her. Stalking her.

Shaking her head, Taylor realized she was stupidly standing in the middle of the parking lot, making herself an easy target for anyone who might want to hurt her. Hating how paranoid she felt, she made herself walk calmly toward the door.

She was done for the day. She was going to spend the rest of it locked inside her apartment, safe from anyone who might do her harm. Even though she couldn't think of a single reason why someone might *want* to hurt her. She was a nobody.

It wasn't until she was locked behind her apartment door that Taylor was able to take a deep breath. She felt safe in her home. And normally she loved living alone, always had. But for the first time, she didn't like it. She wanted to be able to pick up the phone and call Eagle. Just hearing his voice would reassure her that she was being paranoid.

But deep down, she had a feeling Eagle wouldn't dismiss her fears. He'd take them seriously. She hated that he was gone and prayed that whatever mission he and his friends were on would be over soon.

∽

Brett watched as Taylor stopped in the middle of her parking lot and looked around, as if she could spot whatever it was that had obviously made her nervous.

He'd pulled in behind her and had parked several rows away. His talk with her had gone exactly as he'd wanted it to. He'd even gotten to touch her.

Her skin was extremely soft, and Brett couldn't wait to mark it up. Run his knife over her palms and watch the blood well up there. He'd loved feeling the heat of her leg against his as well, though he had no desire to touch her sexually. He just enjoyed the feeling when his plaything's skin went from warm to cold.

He wanted her under him, his hands around her throat, choking the life from her, then bringing her back to him. Again and again and again.

His record was eight. Eight times he'd killed the same woman, choking the life out of her, then bringing her back.

He was going to break that record with Taylor. He grew hard just thinking about it.

He was going to keep her for as long as possible. He couldn't wait to see the life drain from her eyes, then resuscitate her and see the fear and panic return when she remembered where she was and what was happening. And he was looking forward to pretending to be a bunch of different men. One would be sadistic, using his knife to mark her pretty skin. Another would be the man who strangled her. Still another would be the nice guy.

Brett wanted to hear her beg for mercy, to swear to the "nice guy" that she wouldn't tell anyone what had happened if he helped her escape the "other men."

She'd literally have no idea he was her one and only captor.

The possibilities for torturing her were endless, and he was more grateful than he could say that he'd found her. Brett knew Taylor wouldn't be enough. He'd need to find others like her.

He'd finally found the perfect victim . . . and his playtime was coming.

Chapter Ten

Taylor's phone vibrated with a text, and hoping it might be Eagle telling her he was back, she quickly reached for it. She was having a hard time concentrating on the manuscript she was trying to proofread and welcomed any distraction.

Skylar: Hi, Taylor, this is Skylar. I was wondering if you wanted to go get some lunch with me?

Taylor was surprised to hear from her. One, because it wasn't the weekend, and Skylar should be at work. And second, because even though she really liked the woman and they'd exchanged cell phone numbers, they hadn't really hung out anywhere but at Silverstone Towing.

As nervous as she was about trying to get closer to Skylar, anything was better than what she was doing now . . . sitting in her apartment worrying about Eagle.

Taylor: Sure!

Skylar: Awesome. What about Rosie's Diner? It's close to Silverstone.

Taylor: I've driven by it, that sounds great. What time?

Skylar: Now? :) I'm starving. But if you're busy, we can go later.

Taylor: Now is fine. It'll take me fifteen minutes or so to get there.

Skylar: No problem. I'll grab us a seat.

Taylor hated to bring this up, but knew she had to.

Taylor: Sounds good, but remember that I won't recognize you waiting for me.

Skylar: I was planning on coming to get you when you entered the diner.

Taylor sighed in relief.

Taylor: Thank you.

Skylar: Of course. I'll see you soon!

Taylor punched in a thumbs-up emoji and pushed back from her dining room table, then hurried into her room to change into a pair of jeans and a nicer shirt. When she worked, she tended to wear stretchy pants and T-shirts. She pulled her unruly curls back into a messy bun at the nape of her neck and grabbed her purse before heading out.

The entire way to the diner, Taylor reassured herself that Skylar really would come to meet her when she entered the restaurant. It was always stressful to meet someone for an outing because she literally had no idea if they were already there or if she'd arrived first. It was awkward for everyone. At least it felt that way to Taylor.

After parking, she took a deep breath and headed for the door to the diner. She didn't have time to even look around before she saw a woman heading toward her. Taylor knew it wasn't Skylar, because this woman was older.

"Are you Taylor?" the woman asked.

Taylor nodded.

"Great! I'm Rosie. I own this place. Skylar asked me to keep an eye out for you. Said I'd know you on sight because of your amazing curly hair. And she's right—it's lovely. Come on, Skylar's over here."

Taylor relaxed. There was something about Rosie that made her feel comfortable immediately, which was quite a feat, as Taylor wasn't comfortable around many people in general.

Rosie led her toward a table in the back of the small diner, and a woman stood and smiled as they approached.

"Hi, Taylor, it's Skylar," the woman said brightly.

Taylor appreciated the easy way she let her know who she was without making a big deal out of it. Surprising herself, Taylor gave her a short hug. "Thanks for inviting me."

"Thanks for coming," Skylar replied.

"It smells amazing in here," Taylor said.

"That's because Rosie's a genius," Skylar replied, smiling at the older woman who was still standing next to them. "Although, I have to say, Shawn's giving her a run for her money."

"That's the guy they hired to cook for Silverstone, right?" Rosie asked.

"Yup. And seriously, he should have his own restaurant, he's that good."

"So why doesn't he?" Rosie retorted.

Skylar shrugged. "I don't know."

"Well, you tell him if he wants any advice or has any questions about starting up his own place, I'm happy to answer them for him."

"I will," Skylar said, beaming.

"Good. How're Bull and the rest of the guys?"

Skylar's easy smile slipped a bit, but Taylor had a feeling she was the only one who noticed. "They're all good. Busy as usual."

"Tell them I haven't seen them in way too long and they need to get their butts in here," Rosie demanded. It was easy to see the genuine affection she had for the men of Silverstone. Taylor couldn't blame her.

"I will," Skylar reassured.

"Good. I'll leave you guys to your lunch, then," Rosie said. "Enjoy."

"Thanks," Taylor said at the same time Skylar did. Then they both sat.

"Sorry I didn't meet you at the door. When I got here, Rosie wanted to know why I was by myself and where Bull was. She was asking so many questions that I used you as an excuse to distract her. She offered to bring you to the table, so I agreed."

"It's more than all right. She seems very nice."

"She is," Skylar said. "Bull brought me here for our first date."

"Really?" Taylor asked.

"Yup. I much preferred this place to anywhere fancy."

"I agree," Taylor told her.

They were interrupted by the waitress arriving at their table. They gave her their drink selections, and she said she'd be back to take their food order. Taylor examined the menu, and Skylar gave her some suggestions, but said that everything was delicious. She settled on a simple BLT sandwich with fries, and Skylar decided on a hamburger with a side salad.

When the waitress had left a second time, Skylar leaned forward on her elbows and asked with a smile, "So . . . what's up with you and Eagle?"

Taylor almost choked on the sweet tea she'd just taken a sip of. But Skylar looked so innocent and excited, she couldn't bear to be rude and tell her to mind her own business. Besides, wasn't this what friends did? Gossip and talk about their love lives? Taylor wasn't exactly sure, since she'd never really had a true friend, but she didn't want to chase Skylar off.

Slowly putting down her tea, she shrugged. "We're friends," she told the other woman.

Skylar looked skeptical. "Friends?"

"Yeah."

"But he told you about Silverstone," Skylar said in a quiet voice.

Taylor nodded.

Skylar sat up straighter. "I don't get it, then. I mean, I thought the guys agreed not to tell anyone about what they do unless they were ready to spend the rest of their lives with that person."

Goose bumps rose on Taylor's arms. She'd had no idea about that little detail. "Well, he told me that it wasn't something they went around announcing to the world, and that his family didn't know, but he said he trusted me."

Skylar stared at her for a long moment before nodding. "I understand."

"You do?" Taylor asked. "Because I don't."

"I obviously don't know everything about the other guys," Skylar said, "but Bull has told me a bit. I know that Eagle hasn't seriously dated anyone in a long time. He and the others have been very focused on making both Silverstone and Silverstone Towing successful. But I can see how he might take one look at you and decide you were it for him."

Taylor shook her head. "It's not like that," she protested, but deep down, it felt wonderful to know Skylar thought Eagle liked her as more than just a friend.

"Oh?" Skylar asked. "How often have you seen or talked to him since you met?"

Taylor blushed. "Just about every day."

"Right. Guys like Eagle—and Bull, Smoke, and Gramps, for that matter—are pretty straightforward. They don't lead women on, and they say what they mean. If you and Eagle are talking every day, it's because he *likes* you."

"You think so?" Taylor asked shyly.

"I know so," she said confidently. "The question is, do you like him back? I mean, would you consider dating him?"

"Consider it? Hell, I've dreamed about it," Taylor admitted.

Skylar beamed. "What are you waiting for?"

"I just . . . I don't want to lose him as a friend."

"You won't."

"You can't know that. Things are really good between us right now. Laid back, relaxed."

"Foreplay," Skylar said with a gleam in her eye.

"What?"

"It's foreplay. You're feeling each other out. Learning what the other likes and doesn't like. Tiptoeing around. I have a hunch that things will change in your relationship when you least expect it." Her voice lowered, and she grinned as she said, "And it's going to be *hot*."

Taylor couldn't help but chuckle. "I'm not sure I'm all that good at sex."

"Doesn't matter. You both could be complete virgins, but when you're with the right person, experience doesn't make one whit of difference. The first time I was with Bull was magical. It wasn't awkward in the least, and Lord, girl, the way he made me feel . . ." Her words trailed off, and she got a goofy look on her face.

Taylor knew she should probably be uncomfortable that they were talking about sex and relationships so early in their friendship, but instead, Skylar's honesty made Taylor like her all the more. "I love that for you," she said.

"Thanks. Me too. All I'm saying is that Eagle telling you about Silverstone *means* something. It's big. So I was just wondering if you were content to be his friend or if you wanted more."

"You wanted to see if I was in this for the long haul, didn't you?" Taylor asked with a small smile.

"Well . . . sorta. I like Eagle and the other guys. I don't want to see them hurt."

"I like them too," Taylor said. "If Eagle asked me tomorrow to be his girlfriend and wear his letterman jacket, I'd be thrilled."

"Awesome," Skylar said.

"And . . . I have to say . . . I like you too," Taylor continued, determined to get through this, even though it felt awkward. "It's hard for me to make friends, and I appreciate what you did with the name tags. It really makes things easier when I'm at the garage. But more than that, you didn't ask me a million annoying questions about my condition, and you didn't make things awkward today. Not many people are so understanding right off the bat."

"Which is stupid," Skylar said, a hint of irritation in her tone. "I mean, seriously. If you were blind, I'd help you get around. If you were deaf, I'd do what I could to help you understand what people were saying."

"But my condition is different. It's harder to understand because so many people have never heard of it. Most think I'm making it up."

"I've worked with a lot of children with a ton of different disabilities over the years," Skylar said. "And the biggest thing I've learned is to never underestimate them. All they want is to be given a chance to do the same things all the other kids are doing. Society has a long way to go with regard to discrimination and treating everyone equally."

Taylor nodded. "I agree."

The two women smiled at each other. Then Skylar lifted her glass. "To friends."

"Friends," Taylor echoed and clinked her glass with Skylar's.

"Except when it comes to our men," Skylar added.

Taylor laughed. "I'll drink to that."

The conversation during the rest of the meal was easy and light, and Taylor had never felt more comfortable with another woman in her life. When Skylar asked a few questions about her condition, it didn't feel as if she was fishing for juicy details, just honestly wanted to understand it. They talked about Silverstone Towing and what a great job the four men had done in making it one of the best businesses in the Indianapolis region, for customers and employees alike.

They finished eating, and when Skylar asked for the bill, the waitress informed them that it had already been taken care of. "A man who was here earlier paid for your lunch already."

Skylar looked confused. "Who was he?"

"I don't know," the waitress admitted. "I've never seen him before. But he got here not long after you guys. He had a couple cups of coffee, then asked to pay for your lunches."

"Wow, that's awesome. He didn't tell you to tell us anything?" Skylar asked.

"Nope. Just paid and left."

"Well, all right. Thank you."

"You're welcome. Stay as long as you want—we aren't that busy, so you're not keeping a table from someone else," the waitress told them.

"Thanks," Skylar said with a smile. When the waitress had left, she turned to Taylor. "I'm not sure that's ever happened to me before."

"I'd normally agree, but the other day when I went to get a hamburger, the guy in the car ahead of me paid for my lunch. I've read about things like that happening to other people, but I'd never experienced it before."

"Cool," Skylar said.

"Yeah . . ." But Taylor felt oddly anxious now.

Why would a stranger choose to pay for their meals? There were other people in the diner eating. Why *them*? And what were the chances she'd have someone pay for her meal twice in such a short period of time, especially when it had never happened before?

And of course, that made her think about the guy at the dementia care center . . .

So many weird things had been happening to her recently, and it was beginning to make her feel uneasy.

She and Skylar chitchatted for a while longer before Skylar said, "Thanks for coming out with me. I took a day off work—a mental health day, if you will—and I didn't want to spend it just sitting in my apartment being sad."

"How often does Silverstone go on missions?" Taylor asked.

"Not a lot," Skylar told her. "I mean, thankfully there aren't that many tens in the world."

"Tens?" Taylor asked.

"Yeah. Bull explained what Silverstone does this way: out of one to ten on the 'bad guy' scale, they only go after the nines and tens. They leave the rest to the police and other law enforcement."

"What constitutes a nine or a ten?" Taylor asked.

"Well, I thought the guy who kidnapped me and Sandra had to be an eleven. He was a pedophile who'd been in jail for assaulting someone else before. And he'd been watching Sandra for who knows how long before he snatched her."

Taylor leaned forward, fascinated. She'd heard about Skylar being kidnapped, but didn't know all the details and hadn't wanted to ask. "Were you scared?" Taylor asked.

"Terrified out of my mind," Skylar admitted. "But I knew without a doubt that Bull wouldn't rest until he either discovered where I was or, if I was killed before he could get to me, made sure the man paid."

Taylor shivered. "Holy crap."

"Yeah. Luckily for me, he got home from his mission and rallied the troops. But Sandra was the real hero in my rescue. If she hadn't been brave enough to run away from the house on her own, I know Jay Ricketts would've killed me. But back to the subject at hand. I considered my kidnapper to be a ten. But Bull told me that in actuality, he was more like a three or a four on the bad-guy scale."

"Wow," Taylor said, her eyes wide.

"Yeah, I was shocked too. Bull explained that Silverstone doesn't bother with threes and fours. If they did, they'd never be at home and would constantly be on missions."

"That's a pretty good explanation. And reasonable—otherwise they'd attract too much attention and open themselves up to lawsuits, and be accused of being vigilantes or something," Taylor mused.

"I guess. Does it make me a bad person to admit that I'm glad my kidnapper was killed when he was in prison awaiting trial?"

"He was?" Taylor asked in surprise.

"Yup. I had no problem testifying against him, even though it would've sucked. But we got word not too long ago that he was shanked one day while in the recreation yard. The guards had been doing their best to keep him away from the general population, but one day a fight broke out, and in the ensuing riot, he was stabbed. No one has admitted to doing it, and the video surveillance was no help because of the complete chaos that was happening in the yard. A large group of men were all clumped together, and when the dust cleared, Jay was dead in the dirt," Skylar said. "So Silverstone didn't kill him, but someone else took it upon himself to make sure a sicko like Jay would never be free to stalk and hurt another kid."

"I'm glad," Taylor said with feeling.

"Me too," Skylar whispered.

"Are you doing okay?" Taylor asked, reaching out and putting her hand on Skylar's forearm.

The other woman smiled. "I am. I admit that I sometimes have a nightmare or two, but Bull is almost always there to make me feel safe . . . and to distract me . . . if you know what I mean."

Taylor smiled. "I'm glad you have that."

"Me too. But anyway . . . I have a ton of sick leave because I'm amazingly healthy, knock on wood, and my principal doesn't mind the teachers taking mental health days if we have the leave time and honestly need a break. I just hope the guys get home soon. I miss Bull a lot."

"Do you think it'll get easier? That you'll miss him less as time goes on?" Taylor asked.

"No," Skylar answered without hesitation. "I'll always miss and worry about Bull when he's gone, but I would never ask him to quit. I've finally come to understand that what he does is important. It makes me uneasy, but that doesn't mean I'm not proud of him."

Taylor didn't feel the least bit weird about what Eagle was doing. She was glad he and his team were making the world a safer place. She'd seen the ugly side of people from a very early age. And while bullies and ignorant people weren't in the same category as the "tens" Silverstone was hunting, she couldn't muster any sympathy for anyone who did things that karma would make them answer for later in life.

Skylar smiled. "This was fun. Thanks again for coming out with me."

"Thanks for inviting me," Taylor told her.

"We need to hang out more."

"I'd like that."

"Great. Maybe we can go shopping sometime? You can keep me from filling a basket at Target when all I need is floor cleaner or something."

Taylor laughed. "You too? I don't know what it is about that place that makes me overspend and buy crap I don't need. I'm not sure I'll be much help."

Skylar grinned. "Fine, then we can roam the mall like we're fourteen again."

"Sounds good." And it did. Taylor couldn't remember when she'd felt so relaxed with another woman.

They stood up, and Skylar left a twenty-dollar bill on the table.

"I thought our meals were paid for?" Taylor asked.

"They are, but I always try to leave a big tip. The first time Bull brought me here, he left a very generous tip for the waitress, and I decided that was something I wanted to do too. Waiters and waitresses work really hard and have to put up with a lot of crap from customers."

Taylor nodded and reached for her purse.

"You don't need to leave any more, I've got us covered," Skylar protested.

Taylor dropped another twenty on the table. "It's fine. I like doing nice things for people. There's not enough kindness in the world—I know that firsthand."

Skylar nodded and linked her arm with Taylor's. "I knew I liked you when I first met you, and I'm thrilled for you and Eagle."

As they walked toward the exit, Taylor stayed silent. She wanted to hear more about why Skylar thought Eagle liked her, but that felt a little too middle schoolish. She had no idea if Skylar was right, but she hoped so. For now, she'd play things by ear and maybe, eventually, one of them would get up the nerve to make the first move.

Rosie called out a farewell, and when they were outside, Skylar promised to be in touch. Taylor was on her way home before she knew it, feeling happier than she had in a long time. She still missed Eagle and longed to talk to him, but she didn't feel quite as alone as she had before. Skylar was amazing, and much stronger than she looked.

Thinking about what Skylar had survived had Taylor shuddering again. She didn't think she could be anywhere near as strong as Skylar if faced with a life-or-death situation. But luckily, she lived a boring life as a proofreader and didn't come into contact with that many people. Certainly no one who would want to hurt her. Right?

Feeling that same sense of uneasiness from the diner, Taylor pushed it away. She'd had a good day, and no bad thoughts were going to ruin it. She was going to go home, finish proofing the manuscript she'd started earlier, and pray that Eagle would get back sooner rather than later.

Chapter Eleven

"Fuck," Eagle swore as he shifted in the airplane seat.

"You all right?" Gramps asked for what seemed like the hundredth time.

"Yeah, just moved wrong," Eagle said.

"You need me to look at that arm again?" Smoke asked.

No, he didn't need his friend to look at his fucking arm again.

Eagle was pissed. Mad that he'd managed to get himself shot. The bullet had grazed the fleshy part of his upper arm. He'd bled like a stuck pig, but he'd been lucky. Six inches to the left, and it would've gone through his heart.

One of the rebels in Timor-Leste had gotten off a lucky shot. *He* hadn't been as lucky, as Eagle's bullet had been the last thing he'd seen in this world. But now Eagle had to deal with an arm that throbbed and his friends hovering as if he were on his last legs.

"I'm fine," he told Bull, Smoke, and Gramps. "It's not my first graze and won't be my last. It's sore. It hurts. But I'll live."

"If you need more antibiotics or painkillers, just let me know," Gramps told him. "I can get more when we're home."

"Will do," Eagle told him. He knew he should go to the doctor, but a gunshot wound would mean a police report, and Silverstone did whatever they could to avoid that kind of attention. His arm would hurt for a while, but the butterfly bandages would do their job, as would the shit ton of antibiotics Gramps had shoved down his throat.

The only thing Eagle wanted right now was to see Taylor. It had been eight days since he'd seen or talked to her. He felt antsy inside. He needed to know what she'd been up to. How her week had been. Wanted to know if she'd been to Silverstone at all, or if she'd holed up inside her apartment like she'd been wont to do before he'd met her.

Their mission had gone well. They'd located the rebel leader, and while they hadn't been able to take him out as quietly as they'd hoped, he'd ended up with a bullet to his brain all the same. They all hoped the remaining rebels would lose interest in their obviously futile battle and fade into the night. It would take a bit of time for that to happen, but Silverstone, and Willis at the FBI, would keep an eye on the situation.

All in all, it had been another successful mission, but instead of feeling satisfied over a job well done, Eagle was impatient as hell to get to Taylor.

Was this how Bull felt about Skylar? He hadn't talked to his friend about what it was like for him, but he felt as if a conversation between them would be happening sooner rather than later.

Eagle loved Taylor. He had no doubt. But he didn't know how she felt about *him*.

A long three hours later, their small private plane finally landed in Indianapolis. Taking out his phone, Eagle turned it on—and sighed in relief at seeing all the texts Taylor had sent him while he'd been gone. He'd told her that he wouldn't have reception and wouldn't be able to read or respond to any texts, emails, or phone calls, but she'd communicated with him anyway.

Taylor: I miss you and you've only been gone a day. Ugh!

Taylor: My visit to the dementia care center was good, but why do I seem to attract creepy people? Nothing happened, but man, why can't I meet someone like Chris Hemsworth one day? lol

Taylor: I got my car back from Stan's, and I have to say, I missed my Kia!

Taylor: Why is it that I can think of all sorts of witty things to say when you aren't here to appreciate them?

Taylor: I went over to Silverstone Towing today, and I hate to be the one to tell you this . . . but I beat your high score. :)

Taylor: It's two in the morning, and I woke up because I had a nightmare that you were shot and lying on the ground, dying. You'd better be alive, Eagle, because I'll be pissed if you aren't.

Blinking, Eagle checked the date of that last text. He sighed in relief that she didn't seem to have some sort of psychic ability when he saw that she'd sent it two days before he'd actually been shot. He kept reading.

Taylor: I've been keeping to myself a lot since you left, because I realized that you make me feel safe. And now that you're not here, I see the boogeyman around every corner. I feel as if that makes me really weak, and I hate it.

Taylor: Shawn made the most amazing chicken Crock-Pot dish tonight. I decided I'm going to steal him from Silverstone and keep him in my apartment to cook for me every night.

Taylor: Why did the can crusher quit his job?

Taylor: Because it was soda pressing.

Taylor: HAHAHAHAHAHAHAHA!

Taylor: If you don't get home soon, I'm going to go out of my mind. I didn't realize quite how much I loved talking to you until you weren't here.

Taylor: I miss you, Eagle. I hope you're okay wherever you are.

Taylor: Thank you for making the world a safer place.

Eagle was amused by her random texts. But he also really loved that she obviously liked talking to him every day as much as he liked talking to her. They'd clicked so thoroughly that it felt wrong not to be able to talk to each other. He'd never felt that way with anyone else.

He needed to see Taylor . . . and he needed to see her *now*.

He shot off a quick text.

Eagle: I'm home, Flower. I'm on my way to you. I know it's late, but I need to see you.

He hoped she wasn't asleep, and he was thrilled when he saw three blinking dots in the text program, indicating she was typing.

Taylor: OMG!! YAY!!! It's never too late for you! I'll be up!

He chuckled at all the exclamation points she'd used. But couldn't deny the thrill of knowing she was as excited to see him as he was her. After promising to call the others tomorrow to check in and let them know how his arm was doing, Eagle rode the shuttle bus to the parking lot where his car was located.

He drove way too fast to Taylor's apartment and took the stairs two at a time and was in front of her door before he knew it. Two point two seconds after he'd knocked, he heard Taylor asking who was there.

"It's me, Flower. Eagle."

She wrenched open the door—and he'd never seen her looking more beautiful. Her hair was out of control on her head, curls sticking up everywhere. She had on a pair of loose pink-and-yellow pants and a tank top. He knew she slept in the tank and her undies, because she said anything wrapped around her legs made her feel trapped while she was sleeping. Her feet were bare, and Eagle noted that sometime in the last week she'd painted her nails light pink.

"Get in here!" she exclaimed, reaching out and grabbing the front of his shirt.

Eagle smiled and let her pull him into the apartment. She slammed her door, then threw the dead bolt and the chain before turning back to him.

"Are you all right? How was the mission? Did you find the guy you were after . . . or was it a woman? Either way, I'm assuming you guys were successful, which is awesome—one less asshole to worry about. How was your trip? Did you fly somewhere or drive? Are you jet lagged?

Do you want a cup of coffee? Or maybe you just want to sleep. Have you stopped by Silverstone Towing? Are you hungry?"

Eagle chuckled. "Breathe, Taylor. I can't answer your questions if you don't take a breath and give me a second between each one."

She blushed. "Sorry, I'm just so relieved you're home. I know you told me not to worry, that you and the others know what you're doing, but I couldn't help it. And I missed you. I swear I had no idea how much I'd gotten used to you being around for me to babble to."

"I missed you too," Eagle told her.

Surprising him, she threw herself against his chest and wrapped her arms around him.

Eagle couldn't help the pained grunt that left his mouth at her impulsive action.

Of course she heard him. Pulling back in alarm, she looked up at him. "What's wrong? I hurt you?"

"I'm okay," he said gently.

Taylor's eyes wandered over his face, down his chest—and stopped at his left arm. He was holding it gingerly to try to avoid its being bumped again.

She reached for his jacket. Slowly and carefully, she pushed it off his shoulders, ignoring the way it landed on the floor with a thump. He had on a short-sleeve shirt, and the bandage was clearly visible under the left sleeve.

Without a word, she grabbed his right hand and dragged him through her apartment, down the hall, and into her bedroom. Eagle hadn't been inside her personal space before, and he inhaled deeply, loving how everything smelled like vanilla.

She didn't give him time to examine her room before pulling him into the bathroom. It wasn't anything special, just a bath/shower combo and one sink, with a surprising amount of counter space to the left of it. The toilet sat to the right of the sink.

She turned him so his back was to the mirror and pressed a hand to his chest. "Stay," she ordered.

Eagle smirked at her bossiness.

She crouched to look in the cabinet under the sink, and Eagle did his best to ignore the way she was kneeling at his feet and how, if she came up on her knees, she'd be at the perfect height to remove his pants and . . .

Shaking his head, he repeated, "I'm okay, Taylor. I promise."

"Whatever," she mumbled. "You were probably in the wilds of some random country with more germs than people. And I'm sure you didn't stop to get proper medical care." She stood up with a commercial first aid kit in her hand. "I want to see it," she said, eyeing him sternly.

"It's not necessary," he said. "Gramps is worse than a mother hen. And Smoke is more capable than most doctors I've met. They cleaned me up and made me swallow a million antibiotics."

"Good. I still want to see it."

"It's ugly," Eagle warned, touched that she was so worried about him. Her concern felt different than that of his team.

"What happened?"

"Bullet grazed me," Eagle said bluntly.

All the color instantly leached out of Taylor's face.

Eagle swore and moved quickly before she passed out on him. He grabbed her by the waist, turned, and lifted her so she was sitting on the counter, ignoring the pain in his arm as he did so. He pushed between her legs and speared his hands into the hair on either side of her head. "Breathe, Flower. *Grazed.* It went right on by. Didn't hit any bones or anything important."

"You were *shot*," she whispered, her brown eyes huge in her face.

"Grazed," he repeated.

"Did you kill him?" she asked.

Eagle's lips twitched. "Yeah."

"Good!" she said fiercely.

He couldn't help but stare at her lips when she licked them.

"Eagle?" she asked.

Knowing he was probably making a mistake, but not able to help himself, Eagle lowered his head.

He gave her enough time to understand what he was going to do, and when she didn't pull back or ask him what the hell he thought he was doing—and instead reached up and put one hand behind his neck—Eagle closed his eyes and did what he'd been longing to do for weeks.

He kissed her.

Hard.

He'd wanted to go slow. To convince her that he could be more than a friend. Reassure her that they'd be good together. But Taylor ruined any chance he had of controlling himself when she all but devoured him. Her hand tightened on his nape, and she tilted her head to take him more easily. The moan in the back of her throat had his cock immediately ready for action.

As far as first kisses went, it wasn't perfect. Their teeth clicked together, and they had more enthusiasm than finesse, both of them desperate. But he'd never felt anything more perfect than Taylor's lips on his.

He pulled her to the edge of the counter, until his dick was pressing insistently between her thighs. Taylor moaned again and wrapped her legs around his ass, then hooked her ankles together, as if she was never going to let him go.

Their tongues dueled, tasting and learning each other's mouths. God, Eagle had never been turned on so fast before. Taylor lit up in his arms, acting as if she wanted to fuse her body with his.

Not even thinking about his arm, Eagle lifted her with his good arm under her ass and the other wrapped around her back.

She wrenched her mouth from his and gasped, "Eagle! Your arm!"

"It's fine," he breathed, then put his lips over hers once more. He couldn't stop kissing her. Didn't *want* to stop kissing her. Now that they'd crossed this line, he didn't ever want to go back to just being friends.

It didn't take too many steps to be at her bed. Knowing his arm wasn't going to allow him to prop himself above her, Eagle turned and sat. Taylor straddled him, and when he scooted backward and lay down, she was right there with him, kissing him the entire way.

She finally pulled back slightly and looked down at him. Her lips were swollen, and her cheeks were flushed. He wanted nothing more than to ravage her completely.

"Are we being stupid?" she asked uncertainly.

"No," he said immediately. "I can honestly say I've never wanted anything more than to be deep inside you."

"I don't want to lose you," she said.

"You aren't going to lose me," he said firmly.

Her nipples were tight under her tank top, and Eagle longed to strip off the top and look his fill. He'd fantasized about what she'd look like—but he wouldn't do anything if she wasn't one hundred percent on board.

He brought his hands back up to her face and ran his thumbs over her cheeks. "The first thing I thought of when that asshole's bullet grazed me was you. I worried about what would happen to you if I didn't come home. The pain was so intense—not from my wound, but from what I thought you'd be feeling. I knew right then I needed to stop fucking around and tell you how I feel about you."

He paused.

"And?" she whispered.

"I'm crazy about you. Have been for a very long time. I like everything about you, Taylor."

"I'm not going to get better, Eagle. I'm never going to recognize you."

"I don't need you to pick me out of a crowd, Flower. I'll always come to you. You'll know it's me by the way I look at you. You'll know it's me by the way I smell—don't think I haven't noticed you smelling me any chance you get," he teased. "You'll know it's me because I'll *tell* you it's me. I won't get tired of it, and I won't make you feel bad for something you have no control over."

Her eyes filled with tears. "Are you even real?"

"I'm real. And I'm yours . . . if you want me."

"I want you," Taylor said gently. "I have for a long time, but I figured you'd decided to just be friends."

"I didn't want to rush you," Eagle admitted.

"I missed you," Taylor said. "So many times I wanted to pick up the phone and talk to you."

"I missed you too. But now I'm back, and we can catch up . . . tomorrow."

She grinned. "Oh, because you're tired and want to sleep now, huh?"

Eagle snorted. "I'm not tired. And I don't want to sleep. But with my bum arm . . . this is gonna have to go differently than I'd like."

And just like that, the concern was back in her gaze. "Oh! I never got to look at your arm. Maybe we should—"

"You can look at it later. Right now, I need you to take what you want," Eagle told her bluntly. "I can't hold myself above you and fuck you, so you're going to have to be in control our first time."

He could tell Taylor was unsure . . . but he also saw the excited gleam in her eye. "You like that," he said. It wasn't a question.

"Yeah," she admitted.

"How about you start by taking off your tank so I can see what I've thought about more nights than I can count?" he suggested.

Taylor laughed. "I thought I was in charge," she replied, reaching for the hem of her tank.

Eagle wanted to respond, but it felt as if he'd swallowed his tongue.

Because she'd been in her pajamas when he'd knocked on her door, she wasn't wearing a bra, and the second the material cleared her head, his hands were there, cupping and squeezing her beautiful tits.

She had small areolas and nipples, but the fleshy globes were more than a handful. "Damn," he said softly.

In response, Taylor arched her back and pressed herself into his hands. Eagle's fingers went to her nipples and pinched them lightly. He was rewarded by a louder moan from between her lips. Taylor sat up straighter atop him and arched her back even farther. "Eagle," she whispered. He wasn't sure if it was a protest or an encouragement to continue.

"So fucking perfect," he said. Then he wrapped his right hand around her back and pulled her back down. He ducked his head, took one of her nipples into his mouth, and sucked hard.

"Oh shit!" Taylor said, throwing a hand out to catch herself. She leaned over him, her gorgeous breasts hanging down as he sucked on one nipple, then the other.

When Eagle felt her begin to squirm, he realized neither of them was going to last through much foreplay. He licked her once more before tilting his chin back to look up into her face. "Take off your pants," he ordered.

He'd meant to let her set the pace, to take control, but it literally wasn't in his DNA to lie there and let someone else dictate all their moves. He needed more of her. Needed to feel her naked body against his own. He simply needed *her*.

She scooted off him and stood on wobbly legs as she pushed her cotton pants and underwear down her legs. Eagle undid his jeans and shoved them off while she stood next to her bed, staring as he revealed himself to her. He wanted to rip his shirt off, but had to take the time to ease his left arm carefully out of the sleeve before removing the garment over his head.

They both stayed where they were, taking each other in for a long moment.

Taylor was perfect in every way. Perfect for *him*. Eagle knew, according to society's standards of *beautiful*, she wouldn't make the cut, but he didn't care. Her thighs were a little thick, and her stomach wasn't flat. She'd trimmed her pubic hair, which was sexy as hell. Her breasts moved with each excited breath, and he couldn't wait to feel her against him. To taste her. To feel her swallowing his cock in her hot, wet folds.

Eagle wasn't a vain man, but he was aware of his good looks. He worked hard to keep his body in top physical shape. He had to; his life, and the lives of his friends, depended on him being able to run, jump, fight, and simply be stronger than others.

And he loved the look of desire in Taylor's face as she slowly took him in. At the moment, her eyes were glued to his cock, and he couldn't stop himself from reaching down and caressing it, excited about what the night would bring for them both.

"Come here," he said after a moment, holding out his right hand to her.

Taylor licked her lips again and slowly crawled back onto the bed. She shuffled up to his left side, and he grinned. Using the strength of his good arm, he hauled her back over him until she was straddling his stomach once again. He felt the tip of his cock brush against her backside, and they both moaned.

"You're beautiful," she whispered.

Eagle knew he was smiling like a loon, but he didn't care. "I think that's my line."

She shrugged. "I like doughnuts too much."

"As far as I'm concerned, you can keep eating them. I like the way you look, and I love the way you feel against me."

She shifted, and the most delicious scent wafted up to his nose. Eagle inhaled deeply and smiled when she blushed again. "You smell fucking awesome," he told her. Then, without warning her, he scooted her body up, toward his face, his hand on her ass.

"Oh!" she exclaimed, shuffling forward on her knees so she wouldn't fall on top of him.

"That's right. Come up here," he said, his gaze focused between her legs. He could feel her wetness against his chest as she moved up his body.

Eagle settled his left arm carefully and gripped the back of her thigh. With his right, he grabbed hold of an ass cheek and pulled her right up to where he wanted her. Over his mouth.

Her smell was stronger now, and he couldn't wait to eat her out. To see if he could make her orgasm all over his face. He'd never done this before, not in this position, and he was so excited he could feel precome leaking from his hard-as-nails cock.

"I . . . I don't know about this," she said.

Eagle would back off if she really wanted him to, but he didn't think she did. She was just nervous. He played the sympathy card. "I'm afraid I'll hurt my arm if I do this any other way," he told her.

It was a fucking lie. He couldn't even feel his arm at the moment, but his words did the trick, because Taylor nodded.

But he truly wanted to make sure she was all in. He'd never forgive himself if she let him do this when she didn't actually want to. "I'll stop if you want me to," Eagle said quietly.

Her eyes got big. "You will?"

Eagle clenched his teeth and forced himself to look up into her eyes, rather than at the soft pink folds just waiting for him to dive into. "Yes."

"I'd have to hurt you if you stopped," Taylor finally said with a small smile. "But don't blame me if you suffocate down there."

He laughed. "What a way to go," he quipped, then pulled her down and licked her once.

Her taste exploded on his tongue. "Shit," he mumbled, feeling overwhelmed with how much he wanted her. Then he closed his eyes and got to work, making sure his woman enjoyed this as much as he did.

Chapter Twelve

Taylor's experience with a man going down on her wasn't vast. One man. One time. And they'd both been nervous about it. The guy she'd been dating clearly hadn't enjoyed her taste or anything about the experience, which had made her very self-conscious.

But from the second Eagle put his mouth between her legs, it was more than obvious he liked everything about what he was doing. He wasn't tentative, didn't start out easy. After the first lick, he acted as if he were a starving man, and she was the only thing giving him the sustenance to survive. He licked between her folds, pushed his tongue inside her, then slurped up the juices she knew were leaking all over his face.

Then he covered her clit with his lips and sucked.

Taylor jolted, and she felt his hand on her ass tighten, steadying her. She threw her hands up and propped herself against the wall, moaning. She stopped thinking that anything about this was weird and simply enjoyed herself. He alternated between licking her clit and fucking her with his tongue. Just as she thought she was going to orgasm, he'd change up what he was doing. It was maddening, and Taylor felt as if she was going to fly out of her skin.

Her hips began moving unconsciously, trying to follow his tongue, to get more pressure on her clit.

"You like this?" Eagle asked, and Taylor could feel the warmth of his breath against her. Practically panting, she nodded.

"Good. Because I fucking love it," Eagle muttered. "Could do this all night."

"Please," she said on a long sigh.

"You want to come?"

"God, yes! Please!"

"Love hearing you beg, Flower, but you don't ever have to beg for anything from me."

Then he lifted his head and latched on to her clit once more. Taylor realized that he'd been teasing her the entire time. His tongue felt like a vibrator against her sensitive flesh, and she wanted him to both stop and press tighter against her.

"Eagle . . . ," she moaned.

In response, he sucked harder.

That was all it took for Taylor to orgasm like she never had before. It felt as if every muscle in her body locked up. She quivered and shook, and she thought for sure that she blacked out for a second.

When she came back to herself, she was sitting on Eagle's chest. She didn't remember moving, but then again, maybe he'd pulled her down so she wouldn't actually suffocate him. For a moment, she was embarrassed, until Eagle spoke.

"So fucking beautiful," he said, licking his lips.

Taylor saw that his chin and cheeks were shiny with her juices—and she felt embarrassed all over again. But then Eagle grabbed her hip in his hand and began to shift her down his body.

"I need you," he said softly.

Yes. She needed him too. Reaching between her legs, Taylor took hold of his cock, loving how he inhaled sharply at her touch.

"Condom," he breathed.

"Where?" Taylor asked.

"In my wallet, in my pants."

It was ridiculous that she was disheartened to find he was so prepared. She should be thrilled he wanted to protect her. She wasn't on the pill, and they hadn't had a conversation about sexually transmitted diseases.

She leaned over and grabbed his pants, which hadn't quite landed on the floor when he'd taken them off earlier, leaving them within easy reach. She was glad for something to do so she could hide her feelings from him.

At least, she thought she had.

She opened his wallet and found the condom inside. She studied the wrapper, trying to reclaim the feeling of euphoria she'd had just a moment ago, after she'd climaxed.

But Eagle took the condom out of her hand and pulled her toward him. Taylor put her hands on the mattress on either side of his shoulders to balance herself.

"Look at me, Tay," he ordered.

Reluctantly, she did.

"That condom's been in my wallet for two weeks. That's it. I don't usually carry them around with me like a horny college kid. But I know myself. I've wanted you for a hell of a long time, and while I had no idea this was going to happen tonight, I know that I *wanted* it to happen. I haven't been with anyone in years. Didn't want to be. Until I met you."

Taylor closed her eyes in relief.

"Taylor," he said.

She opened her eyes once more.

"I can't promise not to be a dick. I'll probably piss you off a lot. I tend to spend too much time thinking about work, and I forget to do little shit like take the trash out and pick up my mail. But I *can* promise that I'll never purposely do anything to hurt you. Nothing that will put you in danger. And making love to you bareback before we talk about birth control or kids could be damaging. Not to mention, I want to get myself tested so you can see proof that I'm clean."

Taylor swallowed hard. "I am too. And I'm not on birth control."

He nodded. "This condom was always meant to be used with you. I swear."

"I believe you." And she did.

"Good. Now, lift up."

Obediently, Taylor sat up.

"All the way up on your knees," Eagle ordered. "And scoot back a bit."

She decided she kind of liked him being bossy like this. She went up on her knees and blushed when she could feel how wet her inner thighs were. She'd never been this wet before.

His eyes took her in slowly, from her head, over her breasts, down her stomach, to her pussy. Then she felt his hands brush against her folds, and she shivered. She was aware that he was putting on the condom, but she couldn't look away from his eyes.

He gripped her hip once more. "Take me inside," he told her.

Looking down, Taylor saw his hard condom-covered cock arching toward his belly button. She took it into her hand, loving how it jerked at her touch.

"Fuck," Eagle swore.

Taylor moved forward on her knees until she was hovering over him. She used the tip of his cock to caress herself for a second, and to spread her wetness all over him. She loved how long his cock was. It wasn't all that thick, but she had a feeling it might be hard to take all of him because of his length.

"Do it," Eagle urged.

Taylor notched his cock to her entrance and slowly began to sink down on him.

They both groaned at the sensation.

She stopped when he was only halfway in. It had been a while since she'd been with anyone, and the pinch of him deep inside her was slightly painful.

"Easy," Eagle crooned, and she was thankful he hadn't taken over and shoved himself all the way inside.

His hand moved between them, and he used his thumb to caress her still-sensitive clit.

Taylor jerked, taking a bit more of him inside her body.

"That's it," Eagle said. "Take your time. I can lie here all night and stare at your beautiful body. Your pussy's stretched so tight around my cock, and I've never seen anything more erotic in my life."

That did it. Taylor groaned at his dirty words and sank all the way down, taking all of him.

"Fuck, that feels so good!" Eagle cursed. "You're so hot and tight, you're practically strangling my cock."

Taylor felt extremely full, but in a good way. She swore she could feel him against her cervix. It was slightly uncomfortable, but not enough to make her want to pull away.

She wasn't stopping now—no way. It was almost unbelievable that Eagle was actually inside her. She hadn't planned on this when she'd opened her door earlier, but she couldn't be happier.

"Take as much time as you need," Eagle said.

Blinking, Taylor realized she'd been sitting stock still on top of Eagle while she'd been lost in thought. Slowly, she rose up off him, then eased back down.

Eagle didn't speak, but the intense look of ecstasy on his face said enough. Taylor wanted to please him. He'd gotten her off, and now it was his turn. She'd never climaxed during actual sex before, and she doubted she would now. But she wanted Eagle to enjoy this.

So she began to move. Up and down, clenching her inner muscles as she lifted up, doing whatever she could to try to make their first time good for him.

"You're trying too hard," Eagle scolded.

Taylor stopped moving, looking down at him. "What?"

"You're trying too hard," Eagle repeated. "Let yourself go. Do what feels good."

"Everything feels good," she protested.

"Do you trust me?" Eagle asked.

Taylor realized she must be doing something wrong if he could sound so normal in the middle of sex. She bit her lip and nodded.

"Lean forward a bit, and brace your hands on my chest," Eagle ordered.

Dubious, Taylor did as he asked.

"Now, lift your hips up, just a bit. There, stop. Right there. You comfortable?"

"Yes."

"Good. Don't move. No matter what. Understand?"

"But—"

"No buts—don't move," Eagle interrupted.

Taylor had no idea what he was thinking. How was she going to be able to fuck him if she didn't move?

But she didn't have time to wonder about what was going on, because she felt his fingers on her clit once more.

Gasping, she jerked again.

"Don't move, Flower. I mean it," Eagle scolded.

She froze.

His fingers didn't stop. They roughly flicked against her clit . . . and within seconds, she was once more on the verge of coming.

"Eagle!" she moaned.

"That's it. Fuck, I love feeling you clench against my cock. That's so fucking good. Come on me, Tay. I want to feel it."

She couldn't have stopped herself from coming if her life had depended on it. She flew over the edge violently as he expertly manipulated her body.

The second she started to orgasm, Eagle grabbed hold of her hips and slammed up into her. The shock of his body hitting hers made her cry out. But he didn't stop. Holding her still above him, Eagle fucked her hard and fast. His long cock driving into her over and over.

Taylor couldn't help but widen her stance, wanting more. The new angle allowed him to go even deeper, and her orgasm went on and on as he fucked her. Nothing had *ever* felt like this before.

It didn't take very long before Eagle groaned under her. He grabbed her hips even harder and, after one extremely hard lunge, pulled her down, holding her against him tightly.

Fascinated, Taylor watched as he swallowed hard, then his mouth opened, and he came with a long drawn-out groan. They were both sweating, and Taylor could actually feel him twitch and flex inside her body.

It took several moments, but Eagle finally let out a huge breath, as if he'd been holding it in. Taylor collapsed onto him as if she were boneless. She could feel his chest moving up and down with each labored breath, and his heart was beating fast under her cheek.

"Holy crap," she whispered.

Eagle chuckled. She felt a hand run over her hair. "You killed me," he joked.

Taylor lifted her head. "I thought you said I could be in charge?"

He smiled sheepishly. "I'd planned on it, but I couldn't stand the idea of you feeling uncertain. And once I felt you come on my dick, I couldn't hold back. Sorry."

"Don't be sorry," she told him immediately, putting her cheek back on his chest. "That was amazing. I've never . . ." Her voice trailed off.

"Never what?" he asked gently.

Deciding she wanted to be as honest with him as she could be, she said, "Never come during actual sex before."

"Really?" he asked.

Taylor nodded.

"Well, that sucks. But I promise that I'll do whatever I can to make you come both before *and* during, and maybe even *after* sex from here on out."

"After?" she asked drowsily.

"Yeah, who says fun times have to end once we make love?" he asked.

"Well, no one, I guess. I've just never had a guy who was interested in doing anything but sleeping after he comes."

"Please, don't talk about any other men in your bed while you're lying naked and satisfied in my arms," Eagle pleaded.

Taylor nodded. "Sorry. But you asked, I answered."

"True. Anyway, there might be times after I come that I'm enjoying myself too much to end things. I might eat you out again, or maybe I'll use a vibrator on you. Seeing you come is damn sexy, Taylor, and I think I might get addicted."

Taylor blushed. She felt his dick twitch inside her and realized he hadn't pulled out. She lifted her head and said, "Um . . . you're still inside me."

"I am," he agreed. "And it feels fucking fantastic."

"How is that possible?" she asked.

He grinned. "You may have noticed that I'm quite long."

Resisting the urge to roll her eyes and ask him if he'd measured his dick when he was a teenager and bragged about his length, she simply nodded.

"As long as neither of us moves, I can stay inside you all night, even soft," he informed her.

Taylor's eyes widened.

"Not lying," Eagle told her. "But unfortunately, I need to take care of the condom."

She frowned.

"I know. I don't want to move either. There's nothing I want more than to fall asleep inside you and wake up the same way."

She wanted that too.

"Shit, I felt your inner muscles clench. You like that thought, don't you?"

It would be silly to lie. Taylor nodded.

"Then that's what you'll get. After I get tested and prove that you can trust me. You'll need to go on birth control if you don't want to get pregnant. I have a feeling once I have you bare, I'm not going to want to go back to using condoms." Then he slowly moved her off his chest to his right, and they both groaned when he finally slipped out of her body.

"I'll be right back," Eagle said, leaning over and kissing her on the forehead. "Don't move."

As if she could. Taylor remained on her back and watched as Eagle strode confidently toward the adjoining bathroom. She heard the water running, and soon, he was coming back toward her. He was still naked, and still as beautiful as he'd been the first time she'd seen him on her bed.

But the white bandage on his upper arm was a stark reminder of how close she'd come to losing him.

He turned off the bedroom light on his way back to bed, and when he climbed under the sheet, Taylor immediately turned toward him.

"I forgot about your arm. Did we hurt it?"

"No," he said easily.

"Are you lying to me?" she asked skeptically.

Eagle chuckled. "No. I promise the only thing I was thinking about was how you felt on top of me, around me, over me."

Surprisingly, Taylor didn't feel all that tired. A second ago, she'd been ready to crash, but now that she was lying with her head on Eagle's shoulder, in her bed, something she'd never thought could ever happen, she wanted to stay awake and soak it all in.

"Your mission was successful?" she asked.

"Yeah."

"And the others are okay? They weren't hurt?"

"No, they're all good. Thank you for texting me while I was gone," Eagle told her. "I can't tell you what it meant to turn on my phone and see that you were thinking about me."

"I was. It was weird not to talk to you every day," Taylor admitted. "I've gotten really used to it over the last couple months."

"Me too," Eagle agreed. "There were so many times I wanted to reach for the phone, only to remember that I couldn't. Tell me about the creepy guy at the dementia care center?"

Taylor sighed. She shouldn't have told him about the guy in her texts. She didn't really want to talk about him. Not when she and Eagle were naked in her bed. But she did anyway. "He didn't really do anything. He was just talking, but I got a weird vibe from him. And after he said my name, when I hadn't told him what it was, I was done."

"You didn't tell me that part. He knew your name?" Eagle asked.

Taylor could hear the concern in his tone, and it actually reassured her that she hadn't overreacted with her uneasiness. Eagle could've immediately dismissed it, but he didn't. "Yeah. I mean, one of the employees might've told him what it was when he checked in, or one of the residents might've said something, but it just struck me as weird."

"It *is* weird," Eagle agreed. "And the employees have no right to be blabbing about you to other people."

"It happens," Taylor said, not sure why she was trying to convince Eagle that the guy knowing her name wasn't a big deal when, deep down, she thought it was. "Anyway, I left right after that, and didn't go back this week. I thought maybe . . . maybe you'd go with me this coming weekend?"

"Of course I will," Eagle said immediately.

"Thank you."

"You don't have to thank me for that. You know I've wanted to go with you for a while now. I was waiting for you to let me in, to trust me enough to let me go with you."

"Well, I certainly 'let you in' tonight," Taylor joked.

He snorted. "You know what I mean."

"I do," she said seriously. "I don't know why I was reluctant before. I guess it's just because dementia cuts a little too close to home for me.

I know what they're feeling. They can't express their thoughts in words, not really, but I *know*. And it scares the hell out of me. And a lot of the residents don't have families who visit them very often. They're alone, like I am."

Eagle tightened his arm around her. "You aren't alone anymore," he told her sternly.

"You don't have a crystal ball, Eagle. You have no idea what the future holds."

"You want kids?"

The question startled Taylor. She hadn't expected it . . . and the pain she felt anytime she thought about her own childhood bloomed inside her belly. "I'd make a horrible mother," she said.

"You're wrong. And you didn't answer my question," Eagle said calmly.

Taylor felt anything *but* calm. All the good feelings from the earlier orgasms were gone now. She should've just gone to sleep, after all. "It doesn't matter if I want them or not," she told him. "The fact of the matter is, I wouldn't be able to even recognize my own *children*. If I take them to the park, I wouldn't know which child was mine. When I went to pick them up from school, I'd have to wait for them to come to me. I'd be a horrible mom."

"Wrong," Eagle said vehemently. "You'd be an amazing mom. As for the park, you'd know what he or she was wearing, and you'd keep your eye on them. Same thing for school."

Taylor merely shook her head. "My childhood was horrible," she told him quietly. "You know I couldn't emotionally connect with my own mother, and she gave me up. It was the same with the foster homes I was in. And friends? Forget about it. I was bullied every day, straight through my senior year. The last thing I want to do is pass my condition on to someone else."

"Is prosopagnosia genetic?" Eagle asked gently.

"It appears to run in families," Taylor told him. She felt his fingers under her chin, lifting her head until she had no choice but to look at him.

"I think you'd be an exceptional mother . . . whether your kid had prosopagnosia or not. You'd learn to recognize your child by his or her mannerisms. A head tilt, the way he or she walked, the sound of their voice. You said it yourself, your sense of smell is heightened too. I have no doubt you'd find a way to recognize your child, even if that means giving him a Mohawk or letting your daughter put a streak of pink in her hair.

"And I can't think of anything better for a child with prosopagnosia than having a parent with the same condition. He or she could always talk to you about it . . . think about what a great resource you would be. You'd truly understand what your child is experiencing. And . . . you'd have your husband at your side as well. You wouldn't be alone, not for a second."

Taylor's eyes filled with tears. "Why couldn't I have met you years ago? Before I became so cynical?"

"Everything happens for a reason. If you'd met me five years ago, you wouldn't have liked me. I was bitter about everything that happened in the Army, and I was a dick. We were meant to meet when we did. I have no doubt about that."

"Thank you," Taylor said softly.

"You don't have to thank me for thinking you're pretty amazing," Eagle told her. "You just need to believe it yourself."

Taylor nodded, and Eagle lifted his head and kissed her hard on the lips, then let go of her chin.

"What else happened while I was gone?" he asked.

Glad he'd changed the subject, but feeling better after his encouragement and faith in her, she said, "I didn't feel like cooking one night, so I went out to grab fast food. And for the first time in my life, I had one of those experiences where, when I got to the front of the line to pay, the cashier told me the car in front of me had already paid for my meal. It felt awesome, so of course I had to pay for the person behind *me*."

"That's great, Tay. What else?"

"I went to lunch shortly after with Skylar, and someone paid for our lunches . . . which was a crazy coincidence right after the fast-food thing. Another day, I went to Silverstone Towing because I was missing you and figured I might feel closer to you if I was there. I already told you about beating your high score at pinball—sorry, not sorry—and Skylar showed up. We talked for a bit, and we made plans to go to the mall. We went a couple days ago, and I swear I felt like a teenager trolling the mall again. Skylar is hilarious. I really like her."

"I have it on good authority that she likes you too," Eagle said with a smile.

"I've never really had good experiences with friends," Taylor admitted. "But Skylar is so down to earth. I really hope things work out with us."

"They will."

"I got lots of work done too. It was a good distraction from worrying about you," she said.

"I'm sorry you were worried, but you know what? I've never had someone worry about me like that before."

Taylor traced a finger over a few long-healed scars on his chest. She had no idea what they could be from, but she knew life as a Special Forces soldier, and now working for Silverstone, wasn't exactly like working in an office. It was much more dangerous.

Eagle went on. "I'm not close with my family. I mean, we get along okay, we're just completely different people. My brother is ten years older, and I never see him. My mom and dad mean well, but they never approved of me going into the Army. They have no idea what I do now. And I've never had someone waiting for me when I get home from missions. I think I like it."

Taylor snuggled into him and was rewarded by his arm tightening around her. "You know what I like?" she asked.

"What?"

"This. Being able to talk to you in person right before I go to sleep, instead of on the phone." It was a risk, letting herself be vulnerable by admitting that, but it was too late to take it back.

"Me too," he agreed.

"I'm going to want to see your arm in the morning. You never did let me look at it."

A chuckle rumbled through Eagle's chest. "Okay, Flower. I'll let you examine me and kiss it all better."

"Wow, that sounded dirty," she told him with a small shake of her head.

"Well, your man's got a dirty mind," he retorted.

Her man. Taylor liked that.

"But he's also exhausted," Eagle told her. "My plan was to talk for a while, then take you again, but I'm not sure I can keep my eyes open that long."

"It's okay. I'm kinda sore," Taylor admitted.

"Shoulda run you a bath," Eagle said sleepily.

Just the fact that he'd even thought about it made Taylor melt. "It's okay."

"Missed you, Flower," he slurred. It was obvious he was almost out.

"Missed you too," Taylor replied.

Then all she heard was his deep breaths as he fell into a restful sleep.

Inhaling his scent into her lungs, Taylor closed her eyes as well. The night hadn't turned out like she'd thought it would . . . it was so much better.

Chapter Thirteen

The last few days had been idyllic. Eagle was the boyfriend Taylor had always dreamed about. He was incredibly attentive, and she'd had *no* idea what she'd been missing in the bedroom. He always made sure she got off several times.

But even outside the bedroom, he was amazing. He didn't hover. He left her to do her proofreading work while he went off to do his own thing and never made her feel bad if she needed to get some work done instead of hanging out with him.

He'd spent the entire day after returning from his mission at Silverstone Towing, debriefing with his friends. And after examining his arm, Taylor saw that it really had only been a graze. But that didn't mean she stopped worrying about him and whether he was in pain.

Taylor had also gone to dinner with Skylar one evening, and the other woman had taken one look at her and somehow known that Taylor and Eagle had taken their relationship to the next level. It still felt weird to talk about her love life with another woman, but it was reassuring that Skylar had most of the same fears when it came to the safety of the guys when they were gone on a mission.

There hadn't been any more creepy men trying to make conversation with her, and even the trip to the Dementia Senior Care Center with Eagle had been a success. He was amazing with the residents, staying back when it was obvious someone was uncomfortable with his presence, and engaging in a thirty-minute conversation with one of the veterans.

All in all, Taylor couldn't remember being happier—which scared her to death. Because it seemed as if every time she let down her guard, life threw her a curveball.

Today, she was sitting at her kitchen table proofreading a new book she'd been sent. It was a thriller by a *New York Times* bestselling author, and she was actually having a hard time concentrating on her job and not getting lost in the story, when there was a knock on her front door.

Surprised, Taylor looked down at her phone. Eagle usually sent her a text when he was on his way over, but she hadn't heard from him in a few hours. Feeling the butterflies in her stomach take flight at the thought of having to deal with someone she might or might not know, she walked to her door. Looking through the peephole, she saw a man standing there. He had on a gray T-shirt and a pair of blue overalls. He was also wearing a baseball cap.

"Who is it?" she called out, not willing to open the door to a stranger.

"Maintenance, ma'am," the man told her, looking up at the door.

She could see he had brown eyes, and he was smiling. He held up the large flat item he was carrying in his right hand and a flyer in his left. "I'm here to change your air filter."

Sighing in relief, Taylor remembered seeing the same notices posted around the complex. The managers always let the residents know when there would be someone coming around to do routine maintenance on the units or to spray for bugs. She'd forgotten about it until right this second. She undid the chain and dead bolt and opened the door.

"Hi, sorry about that," she told him.

The man shrugged. "You can't be too careful these days. A pretty woman like you could find herself in a bad situation if she wasn't paying attention." With that, the man pushed past her and entered her apartment.

The relief she'd felt instantly disappeared, and Taylor regretted opening the door. But it was too late now.

Then something else struck her. As the maintenance man had passed, his strong scent had wafted up to her nostrils.

Bleach, antiseptic, and urine.

He smelled exactly like the dementia care home . . . and the man she'd met there.

Taylor racked her brain, trying to remember anything about the man who'd creeped her out the other week while she'd been volunteering, but of course nothing stuck out. She remembered what he'd been wearing, but that didn't help her right now.

Realizing she was still frozen in place, Taylor moved a little farther into her apartment but didn't close the door. She might need a quick escape, and if she had to take the time to open her door, he might be able to prevent her from leaving. Because it was the middle of the day, most of her neighbors were gone, out working their day jobs. There likely wasn't anyone around who might hear her yelling for help.

She hated being so suspicious of someone, but she had no idea why the maintenance man would smell like the residents from the care center. It didn't make sense, and maybe dating Eagle had made her more paranoid . . . but something wasn't right here.

For the first time, Taylor realized that she was still holding her phone. Thank God.

Glancing up to see where the man was, she saw he was kneeling in the hallway, tinkering with the grate that covered the filter for her air conditioner. As if he could feel her eyes on him, he looked up.

"So . . . most of the residents aren't home this time of day. You work from home?"

Not wanting to make small talk, and with her intuition screaming at her to get the hell away from the man, she clicked on Eagle's name and brought her phone up to her ear.

"Hey, Tay, what's up?"

"Hi, Kellan. I got your text. You're on your way over now?" She hoped that by using his given name, she could make Eagle understand immediately that something was wrong. That, and the fact that he hadn't texted her and certainly wasn't on his way to her apartment.

"What's wrong?" Eagle growled.

"Great. The maintenance guy is here changing out my filter, but we can head out as soon as he's done."

"Someone's there? In your apartment? Are you all right?"

"Yeah, he just got here. But I'm sure it won't take long, right?" Taylor asked the man still kneeling in her hallway. She couldn't decide if it was her imagination that he looked irritated now or if she was simply panicking.

"Right," he mumbled, and turned his attention back to the filter.

"I'm on my way," Eagle told her, and Taylor could hear the engine of his car start up. "Stay by the door."

"I am," she told him.

"And if he does anything that makes you nervous, just leave. I don't care that you're leaving him inside your apartment—*nothing* is more important than your safety."

"Okay," she said. "I'm thinking I'm in the mood for pasta for lunch."

"You're doing great," Eagle told her. "Keep talking. I'm not going to hang up until he's gone or I'm there."

"Good," Taylor said in relief. She kept up a one-sided conversation about nothing in particular while keeping an eye on the maintenance man. Eagle kept encouraging her and giving her updates on where he was and when he would get there.

"That's it," the man said as he stood. "Good as new."

"Thanks," Taylor told him, not taking the phone away from her mouth. She was aware that it was rude, and if this really was a maintenance man, she'd feel guilty as hell later for doubting him . . . but she couldn't get that smell out of her nose.

He walked toward her, and it was all Taylor could do not to back away as he approached.

"He's leaving?" Eagle asked in her ear.

"Uh-huh."

"It was nice seeing you," the man said. "Have a nice day." Then he nodded at her and headed for her open door.

After he disappeared through it, Taylor gave him an extra ten seconds to make sure he was far enough down the hall. Of course, he could be lying in wait just outside the door, but she hoped the fact she was on the phone with someone would prevent him from doing anything crazy . . . if that was even his intent.

It wasn't until the door was shut and she'd thrown the dead bolt that she dared to breathe.

"He gone?" Eagle asked.

"Yeah," Taylor said in a shaky voice.

"It was nice *seeing* you? What the fuck was that?" Eagle growled.

Taylor hadn't even caught that part. Wouldn't most people say it was nice to *meet* someone? Shit, now she was *really* freaked.

"What was he wearing?" Eagle barked. "I'm almost there. I'll see if I can find him in the parking lot and have a chat with him."

"Gray shirt, overalls, baseball cap," Taylor told him. She was relieved he hadn't asked her what the man looked like. Most people wouldn't have thought twice about their question, but it was obvious Eagle knew better.

"I think he had brown hair," she offered. "I couldn't see much of it because of the hat. And he had on white tennis shoes."

"Okay, baby. I'm about to turn into the parking lot."

"He smelled," she whispered.

"What?"

"Smelled. I recognized it. Like the care center. I immediately thought about the creepy guy who sat next to me in the courtyard . . . but it can't be him, can it?"

But instead of reassuring her, Eagle said, "I'm going to hang up now. I'm here, and I'm going to look around before coming up. I'll text you right before I knock so you'll know it's me. Okay?"

"Okay. Be careful."

"Always," he said, as she'd known he would, then hung up.

Taylor backed away from the door and held her phone to her chest. Her heart was beating a million miles an hour.

Why would the man from the care center come here? How did he know where she lived? Was there even a connection? Maybe the man really *did* work for the apartment complex . . .

Nothing made sense—and that scared the shit out of Taylor.

She stared at the door from inside her apartment and prayed Eagle would hurry up.

~

Eagle wasn't happy that Taylor was freaked. When he'd left her that morning, she'd been sleepy and sated. She had no problem with her memory, but he was more than willing to remind her each day that *he* was the man in her bed. Every morning, as soon as they were both awake, he immediately said, "Good morning, Flower," and the relief and love in her eyes almost did him in.

He knew it was love. Because he felt the exact same way. Neither had spoken the words, but he couldn't deny the feeling was there.

Hearing her call him by his given name had jolted him out of the mellow mood he'd been in all morning. She *never* called him Kellan, and he'd known immediately something was wrong. He hated the way her voice had quivered; he'd been moving before he'd even thought about it.

The rest of the guys were out working, so he didn't have them for backup. His only thought was to get to Taylor. But now that she was once again locked behind her door, relatively safe for the moment, he took the time to call Gramps as he slowly drove around the parking lot, looking for anyone matching the description Taylor had given him.

"Hey, Eagle. What's up?" Gramps said as he answered the phone.

"I need your help. And the other guys too."

"Why? What's wrong?"

"I don't know. Maybe nothing, but I'm not willing to risk Taylor's life." He explained about Taylor calling him, and how she had a feeling the man who'd claimed to be maintenance was the same man who had creeped her out when she'd visited the dementia center.

"I'm in the parking lot," Eagle told his teammate. "I'm going to look around, but I could use some help."

"You got it. I'll call Bull and Smoke," Gramps promised without hesitation. "I'm finishing up a call, but I'll be there as soon as I can. You going to be all right until then?"

"Yeah. Taylor is in her apartment, so she's safe enough for the moment. Thanks, Gramps."

"You don't have to thank me," Gramps told him. "See you soon." Then he hung up.

Eagle hadn't seen anyone who remotely resembled the maintenance man, which was a clue in itself. If he really had been an employee of the apartment complex, he'd be around somewhere. Knocking on someone else's door, getting more supplies from a vehicle or a storage room, something. But the only people he'd seen walking around were obviously residents.

Though, Eagle also knew the man could've changed clothes to blend right in. Because Taylor couldn't identify him by his features, Eagle was at a definite disadvantage. It wasn't a situation he found himself in very often, and he didn't like it. Not at all.

He sent a quick text to Taylor.

Eagle: Everything's okay. I'm waiting for my team to help me scope things out. You all right?

She responded immediately.

Taylor: Yes. I'm okay. I feel kind of stupid, actually. I'm sure he was probably just the maintenance man. I'm sorry for bringing you out here on a wild goose chase.

Eagle's plan had been to wait for the guys and search every nook and cranny of the apartment complex and the surrounding area, but he needed to take a second and talk to Taylor face to face.

Eagle: I'm coming up. I'll be there in a minute or so.

Then he headed up the stairs, taking them two at a time, and he was in front of Taylor's apartment within forty-five seconds. He took a deep breath before he knocked, trying to get himself under control. Her panicked call had shaken him more than he cared to admit.

He'd faced down terrorists, murderers, and people whose only goal in life was to kill others . . . but Eagle didn't think he'd ever been as scared as when he'd realized Taylor was alone in her apartment with someone who may or may not want to hurt her. He had no idea who might want to harm his Taylor—if that was the case—but he was going to do everything in his power to keep her safe.

He was Delta. Special Forces. He and his team had the training and the ability to do what it took to make sure no one touched her, but . . . how did you fight a ghost? Taylor couldn't describe the man, and being able to identify him by the way he smelled wasn't exactly going to work in a manhunt.

Eagle rapped three times on Taylor's apartment door. "Tay? It's me, Eagle. Open the door, Flower."

The second he said their code word, he heard the locks disengage. Then she was in his arms. Eagle walked her backward, not letting go, and kicked her door shut. He looked around and didn't see anything that seemed out of the ordinary. He breathed out a sigh of relief and buried his face in her hair for a moment.

As usual, her curls were in disarray, and for a second, Eagle pictured her lying hurt and unmoving on her floor, those beautiful curls surrounding her head like some sort of macabre death halo.

Shaking his head, Eagle refused to think about Taylor's life being snuffed out. No, he'd just found her. He wasn't losing her now.

He pulled back and put his hands on either side of her head. She looked up at him, holding his wrists in a tight grip. "You're okay?" he asked, needing it to be true.

She nodded.

"Tell me what happened. From the beginning."

"There was a knock on the door. I knew it wouldn't be you because you always tell me when you're coming over, and I couldn't imagine who else it might be. I looked through the peephole and asked who it was. He said he was with maintenance and was here to change my air filter. So I let him in. He looked the part, Eagle. And he had one of the flyers that have been posted everywhere around here for the last few days, letting us know someone would be by. I wouldn't have opened the door if I didn't believe he was who he said he was."

"I know, keep going," Eagle said.

"Right, so he had an air filter in his hand, and when he passed me after I opened the door, I smelled him. I'm not crazy," Taylor said firmly. "There's no way a maintenance man should smell like he did. Bleach, disinfectant, and urine. I've been to the care center enough to know that smell."

"I believe you," Eagle reassured.

Those three words seemed to calm her.

"The smell freaked me out. I remember the guy from the care center who sat too close to me—he smelled like that too. So I kept the door open in case I needed to run out of here and then called you. I didn't really want to let him know that I was uneasy, although I think he knew anyway. As I was talking to you, he finished changing out the filter and left. He didn't say much, really."

"You did good," Eagle reassured her.

"What's going on, Eagle?" Taylor asked.

He leaned down and kissed her forehead reverently. "I don't know. But I'm going to do my best to figure it out."

"Okay."

One word had never meant so much. Taylor trusted him to keep her safe. To figure out if this guy was the same one from the care center. To find out what the fuck his issue was. He wasn't going to let her down.

"I called the guys. They're on their way over. We're going to take a look around. Will you be all right up here by yourself for a while?"

"Of course. Now that you're here, I know that guy won't come back."

Eagle wanted to tell her that he loved her, but this wasn't the time or place. He wouldn't be able to keep quiet for long, however. Everything in him begged to let her know how much she meant to him. That he wasn't going to let her go. Not ever.

But . . . first he had a mystery to solve.

～

Brett scowled as he recalled the way the man Taylor was dating had prowled the parking lot, looking for him. The dumb bitch had ruined his fun by calling the guy. He had no idea how she'd gotten an inkling that he wasn't who he said he was. She shouldn't have been alarmed at all. He knew she couldn't recognize him. He had to have given something away.

But even if he wasn't able to fuck with her head today, he'd loved the way her voice had trembled as she'd talked on the phone. He'd gotten to her—and it had been just as exhilarating as he'd known it would be.

Brett couldn't help but think of how scared she was going to be when he got her into his basement and tied her down. Completely at his mercy. There wouldn't be anyone for her to call to come save her.

It was almost time to put his plan in motion. He'd been following her for months, and the more he got to know his Taylor, the more excited he got. But he had one more face-to-face meeting planned for her . . .

Brett had overheard her talking on the phone when he'd followed her around a grocery store just days ago. It was clear by the obnoxiously flirty banter she'd been talking to her boyfriend . . . and she'd called him Eagle.

It was perfect for his last surprise. Using the man's nickname would make her trust him—then completely freak her out once she'd seen his "delivery."

As for snatching her, he still had to wait until just the right moment. When there weren't any eyewitnesses around to describe him to the police. When it was just the two of them.

When he could overpower her and bring her home.

"Donald?" he heard his mother call out from above his basement lair, and he sighed in frustration.

"I soiled myself again. I need help!" she said in a voice that wavered with fright.

"Fuck," Brett swore. He didn't mind when his girls peed in terror. That was amusing and exciting. But cleaning up his mother's excrement wasn't any fun.

Deciding she could sit in her own shit for a bit longer, Brett went back to planning his last encounter with Taylor. She knew something was up now, which made things trickier, but learning the name of that asshole she was dating would make it easier to gain her trust. She'd find out that she should've been more careful, but not until it was too late.

Yes, while it was fun to mess with her head, it was almost time. Time for the *real* fun to begin.

Chapter Fourteen

Eagle looked over at Taylor and couldn't help but smile. They were hanging out in the basement of Silverstone Towing, and she had a wrinkle on her forehead as she concentrated on the manuscript she was reading. He'd never thought he'd be enamored of how a woman looked while she was reading.

He and the guys hadn't found anything in the parking lot at her complex, nor around it. He'd talked to the manager of the place and verified that maintenance *was* scheduled, but the apartments on Taylor's floor weren't scheduled to have their filters replaced until tomorrow. Eagle didn't want to think about what might've happened if she hadn't had the presence of mind to call him while the man had been in her apartment.

Taylor had been very hard on herself as well, pissed that she'd let the man into her apartment in the first place. He'd tried to reassure her that she'd done nothing wrong . . . but that didn't mean they both weren't taking more precautions with her safety.

She'd been spending the night at his apartment since the maintenance-man incident, as they were calling it. Eagle had been mildly concerned he'd feel stifled, that having her in his space twenty-four seven would be awkward. But in actuality, he loved it. Genuinely liked having her there. They never seemed to run out of things to talk about, and she was equally happy sitting next to him without saying a word.

It was refreshing, and it solidified his decision to do whatever it took to make her want to be with him forever.

During the day, they'd been coming to Silverstone Towing to hang out. She worked while he took a few shifts. He and the team discussed where their next mission would take them . . . it was looking like Africa, to deal with the leader of Boko Haram, who'd recently attacked another girls' school and taken more hostages. They'd learned that in the latest incident, there had been an American kidnapped along with the girls. No one had heard from her or the others who had been taken. It was a clusterfuck, and the leader needed to be stopped.

Along with keeping an eye on international current affairs, the team was also doing what they could to figure out who the man was who'd been in Taylor's apartment. They weren't having much luck. The dementia care center didn't have any information on the man, and in the surveillance videos they'd gotten their hands on from the center and her complex, the guy kept his head down, and they had no opportunity at all to identify him.

It was around lunchtime when Taylor's phone rang. Eagle listened in on her side of the conversation.

"Hello? Yes, this is she. Oh . . . hi. Yeah. Of course I remember, I loved that story. Really? Wow, that's awesome. She would? Um . . . yes, I'm interested—when is it?"

Taylor's eyes met Eagle's when she said, "I'm going to have to check my calendar and get back to you. Of course. I understand, and I'm flattered she even thought of me. A proofreader isn't usually on the guest list for most award ceremonies. I know . . . but still. I'll get back to you as soon as I can. Probably sometime today. Thank you for calling. Okay, bye."

"What is it?" Eagle asked as soon as she clicked off the phone.

"That was the agent for one of my authors. I proofread a book last year that ended up on the bestseller list for a few weeks in a row. The author lives in Bloomington and works at Indiana University. The school is hosting a special awards ceremony for her, and she wanted to invite everyone who had anything to do with her book. Her agent, editors, and me, her proofreader."

"That's great, Tay," Eagle said, happy she was getting some recognition for her hard work. "When is it?"

She bit her lip. "Next weekend. I know it's really short notice, and the agent apologized, but she figured since I'm so close, I could just drive down. But with everything going on, I'm not sure—"

"Accept the invitation," Eagle interrupted.

"But—"

He walked over to her. "You should go. You work really hard, and it'll be nice to get out of Indy for a while. Leave all the stress behind."

"Are you sure?"

"I'm sure."

She looked up at him uncertainly. "Um . . . I can bring a guest. I'm not sure it's really your cup of tea, but I'd love to have you with me. I can ask Skylar if you don't want to go, though, it's just—"

"Of course I want to go," Eagle told her, shocked that she'd think for even one second he didn't want to be by her side.

"Oh, okay."

"Taylor," Eagle said quietly, "I don't know what you think is happening between us, but this isn't casual for me. I was already going to invite myself to go along with you but didn't want to be presumptuous. I'm proud as hell of you, and I want to support your career any way I can. And you being invited to an awards ceremony for one of your clients is definitely something I want to be involved in."

"*I'm* not getting the award," she said wryly.

"Doesn't matter," Eagle said. "You're invited because you had a hand in someone else's success. That's awesome."

She stared up at him for a long moment, then said, "Sometimes I lie awake at night and wonder why in the world you're with me. It makes no sense. I'm the girl who never had a family, never had a true friend, and now you've given me both. Your friends are like your family, and they've invited me into their world without a second thought. It's crazy."

"It's because you were made for me," Eagle said seriously. "We balance each other out. I can recognize everyone, and you can't recognize anyone. Together, we're the perfect couple."

He saw her swallow hard and bite her lip. He hated to see her cry, even if she was happy, so Eagle quickly asked, "Can you get a list of people who might be there? I can study it, find pictures of the big players, and give you a heads-up about who everyone is when we're at the shindig."

She blinked at him. "You'd do that?"

"Flower, I'd do anything for you," Eagle said without hesitation.

"I can ask the agent who will be there and show you their headshots when we get home."

Home. He liked the sound of that. "Great."

Taylor threw herself into his arms, and Eagle chuckled and went back on one foot as he hugged her tightly. "Are you happy?" he asked.

"Yes. So much so, I'm afraid everything's gonna go to hell if I admit it."

"Nothing's going to hell," Eagle said firmly.

Taylor pulled back. "But what about that maintenance guy? We don't know anything about him or what his motivation is."

"We're going to find him," Eagle said confidently.

"How?"

"If he is truly obsessed with you, I have a feeling he'll reach out again. Want to make contact. You're more aware of the people around you now, and you're more careful. If anything unusual happens, you're going to take note."

"I don't understand *why*, though," Taylor said. "I'm nobody. I'm just me!"

"You're not nobody," Eagle said. "You're Taylor Cardin, and you're amazing."

She smiled. "Thanks."

"You're welcome. Are you at a good stopping point? Want to go up and grab some lunch?"

Taylor fiddled with the name tag on his chest that he'd put on when he'd walked into Silverstone Towing. None of the employees had batted an eye at having to wear them, and in fact, most had been very interested in learning more about prosopagnosia.

"Yes, and yes. I'll call the agent back later. I don't want to look too eager and call her back two minutes after I hung up."

Eagle chuckled. "Come on, then, let's go feed you."

"Feed *me*? You know you're the one champing at the bit to see what Shawn made for lunch today."

"True. You got me."

As he walked up the stairs, Taylor's hand tucked into his, Eagle made a mental vow once again to do whatever it took to make her feel safe, even if that meant Taylor eventually wanted to go back to her own apartment. He loved having her in his space, but he wouldn't rush her into moving in. He'd rather she be there because they'd both decided it was what they wanted, not because she was scared and felt as if she had no choice.

∼

Taylor couldn't keep her eyes open. After a large delicious lunch, and after calling the agent back to tell her she'd be in Bloomington the following weekend with Eagle as her guest, and after reading the same paragraph in the manuscript three times and not seeing a word of it, she realized she needed a break.

She could go upstairs into one of the rooms with a bed and take a nap, but she really wanted some time to herself. Taylor was an introvert. She liked her alone time. Had learned over the years that she was comfortable with her solitary life. And for the last week, she'd had very little private time.

She loved being with Eagle. The man was the epitome of a gracious host. But she wanted to sit in silence and just be by herself for a moment.

But she didn't want to go back to her apartment. She didn't really feel safe there anymore, which sucked.

"Eagle?"

"Yeah?" he asked, looking up from the computer he'd been on since after lunch. Taylor knew he and his friends were doing their best to figure out who the mystery man in her apartment was, and dealing with whatever research they were doing for Silverstone. Eagle had been intently clicking away and staring at his computer screen as she'd worked.

"I think I want to go back to your apartment."

Without hesitation, Eagle closed his laptop and started to stand.

"No . . . I mean . . . I'd appreciate if you gave me a ride, but I need some alone time."

He stared at her intently.

"It's not that I don't like being with you. Of course I do. I just . . . I'm used to being by myself a lot. And while the last week has been wonderful, I could use a few hours on my own. I won't go anywhere, promise. I might take a short nap, then I'll make a pot of coffee and work some more."

Eagle came over to where she was sitting at the small table and leaned over and kissed the top of her head. "You don't have to explain, Taylor. I get it."

"You do?"

"Of course. I've lived by myself for a long time. I love having you with me, but I know I can be pretty intense, and it's not a problem if you need a break."

"It's not you," she tried to explain. "It's everyone. I enjoy being at Silverstone. I feel safe here. But sometimes . . . I just need some quiet alone time. I can't explain it."

"You're doing fine. Will you feel safe at my apartment by yourself?"

"Yes," she said immediately. "This is stupid, too, but . . . it smells like you. And your scent calms me. Makes me feel as if you're right there with me. In fact, I might steal one of your shirts and nap in that."

Eagle grinned. "Feel free to steal my clothes whenever you want. I'd love seeing you in my shirt, wandering around my apartment."

Taylor rolled her eyes. "You're such a guy."

"Yup. Guilty," Eagle told her. Then he pulled her up so she was standing next to him. "Anything you need, Tay, I'll bend over backward to give to you. If it's alone time, you've got it. My apartment complex is safe."

"Thanks. And I might not be a supersoldier, but the same goes for you. I never want to crowd you or make you feel stifled. I know I've kinda just moved in over the last week, but I can go back to my apartment if you need me to. I don't want to overstep."

"You aren't overstepping anything," Eagle told her. "I've loved having you in my apartment. Holding you every night is not a hardship. So don't worry about that."

"Okay."

"Okay. Pack up your stuff, and we'll get you home. You want me to pick something up for dinner?"

"Well . . . yeah, if that's okay. I could cook, but I'm not sure what we have. And cooking might break into my nap time." She grinned.

"Perfect. I'll think of something, then. Taylor?"

"Yeah?"

He stared at her for so long, she began to get nervous. Then he said, "Nothing. I'm just so happy we got our heads out of our asses and admitted that we wanted more than a friendship."

"Me too," Taylor said.

~

Three hours later, Taylor felt much better. Eagle had walked her up to his apartment, kissed the hell out of her, then left her alone. She'd changed into one of his T-shirts, taken a forty-five-minute nap, worked a bit more on her current manuscript, and she was currently lying on the couch, watching a cooking show on television.

She was hungry, but Eagle should be leaving Silverstone soon, and he'd be bringing dinner home.

Taylor had no idea when she'd started thinking about Eagle's apartment as home, but she wasn't troubled by it. Pretty much wherever Eagle was seemed like home to her. As a child, she'd moved from foster home to foster home so often, she'd never felt as if she belonged anywhere. And her apartment was fine to sleep and work in, but it had never really felt like a true home.

Here, everywhere she looked, there was something to remind her of Eagle. Not to mention his scent, which permeated every nook and cranny.

A sudden knock on the door had Taylor stiffening.

Shit, not again!

She looked at her phone, hoping she'd missed a text from Eagle, but he hadn't sent her any messages. It was about time for him to be home, but why would he knock on the door? He had a key.

Tiptoeing to the door, not wanting anyone to know she was there, she looked through the peephole. A man wearing a red-and-blue shirt stood there, holding a large flat box that was immediately recognizable. Pizza.

"Who is it?" she asked.

"Pizza delivery," the man responded.

Taylor closed her eyes and tried to decide if she recognized the man's voice. It was impossible to tell. "I didn't order a pizza."

"Right. The guy who did told me to tell you that Eagle ordered it."

The fear in Taylor's gut dissipated at hearing Eagle's name.

"He already paid for it too," the delivery man added.

"Just leave it out in the hall," Taylor told him without opening the door. She'd learned her lesson with the maintenance man. While it was likely Eagle *had* ordered it since the delivery guy knew his name, she wasn't going to take any chances.

"Sure thing, no problem," the man said.

Taylor watched through the peephole as he bent down, obviously placing the box on the floor, and she waited a few moments after he left before cautiously opening the door.

She grabbed the delicious-smelling pizza and locked the door behind her before heading to the kitchen. She wanted to dive into it right then and there, but that would be rude. Since he'd ordered a pizza, that meant Eagle would be home soon. So she opened the oven, set it on low, and placed the box inside, hoping that might keep it warm until Eagle arrived.

Twenty minutes later, Taylor's phone buzzed with a text.

Eagle: I'm on my way up.

Loving how considerate he was, Taylor stood and waited impatiently for him to arrive. She'd unlocked the door and waited for him with the door open once, but he'd scolded her, saying he'd prefer she just stay locked inside until he got there. All it would take was ten seconds for someone to overpower her, and he didn't want that to happen.

Taylor had agreed immediately. It felt rude to let him fumble with his keys to unlock and open the door, but she did as he'd requested.

Within two minutes, she heard the familiar sound of the locks disengaging as Eagle opened his door. "Hey, Flower," he said.

"Hi!" she returned, walking up to him. Going up on tiptoe, she kissed him long and hard.

When they finally broke apart, Eagle grinned and said, "If a little alone time gets me a greeting like that, I'm gonna have to insist you have alone time every day."

She smiled back at him. Lying in bed earlier, surrounded by his scent, had made Taylor very horny. She hadn't touched herself, but she'd thought about all the amazing things he'd done to her in that very bed. She was primed and ready and couldn't wait to show him later how much she appreciated every little thing he'd done for her recently.

A wonderful smell hit her nostrils, and she looked down. Eagle was carrying two paper bags with the logo of the Chinese restaurant they liked to order from. Her brows lowered in confusion. "You got Chinese?"

"Yeah, I told you I was going to bring dinner home."

"But you ordered pizza."

"What?" Eagle asked.

"Pizza," Taylor repeated. "I put it in the oven to stay warm. The delivery guy said you ordered it."

"Me specifically?" Eagle asked, all business now. He walked into the kitchen, and Taylor followed.

"Yes. He said your name. He said"—she closed her eyes to remember exactly what the man had said—"Eagle ordered it."

"Fuck!" Eagle swore. "I didn't, Taylor. I would've let you know if I'd done that. Besides, I would've picked it up and brought it home myself so a stranger wouldn't show up at the door and scare you."

"God . . . I'm such an idiot," Taylor whispered.

Eagle pulled her into his embrace, but she didn't relax or put her arms around him.

"It's okay. You're okay."

She shook her head. "At least I didn't open the door this time. I told him to just leave it outside."

"That was smart," Eagle told her.

Taylor looked up at him. "How'd he know your name?"

"I don't know."

That didn't comfort her in the least. They stood together for another minute or two before Eagle pulled back. He turned from her and opened the oven door. The sight of the pizza, which had smelled so good earlier, made her stomach turn.

Eagle put on an oven mitt and pulled out the box. He placed it on the counter and looked at the information on the receipt at the edge of the box . . . and frowned.

"What?" Taylor asked. "What does it say?"

"It's addressed to Thanatos," Eagle said grimly.

The hair on Taylor's arms stood up. "Are you sure?"

"Yeah."

"That was the name of the guy who rear-ended me," Taylor said unnecessarily. It was obvious Eagle recognized the name.

"It's got your address on it, too, not mine," he informed her. Then he flipped open the box—and swore again.

Taylor walked up to his side and stared down at the pizza. It looked cheesy and gooey, covered in pepperoni, sausage, and chopped olives . . . but the olives were arranged in such a way that they spelled out a word.

Soon.

Taylor shuddered violently.

"I'm calling the cops," Eagle declared and reached for his phone.

Taylor grabbed his arm. "To tell them what? That I let someone into my apartment and he changed my air filter, then left? That a man ran into my car, promised to take care of the damage, and didn't? To tell them we got a pizza we didn't order? They aren't going to take this seriously, especially when I can't describe the guy. Yeah, I can tell them what he was wearing—overalls, a pizza-place uniform—but that's it. We have no evidence of anything!"

By the time she finished speaking, she was almost hysterical.

"I'm going to keep you safe," he told her.

Taylor shook her head. "You can't! He's just fucking with me now. He could've hurt me in my apartment the other day, easily, because I stupidly opened the door to him! Now he's letting me know he can get to me at any time. Even here! But for some reason, he's waiting for something. Toying with me!"

"Listen to me," Eagle pleaded, but she couldn't. Everything seemed to be crashing down on her.

"He knows your name! What's next? He'll go after *you*? We don't even know who this guy is or why he's messing with me!"

"I hope he does," Eagle said.

"No! I don't want anyone coming after you! Or me! It doesn't make *sense*. What'd I do to deserve this? I just want it all to stop!"

"It will."

"When, Eagle? *When* is it gonna stop?"

"I don't know, but—"

"No one knows! It might *never* stop! I could be eighty-seven, and this guy could still be messing with my head!"

"He won't. He'll make a mistake and—"

Taylor was too far gone to listen to his efforts to placate her. "I need to leave. To move. Go someplace where no one knows who I am or where I'm from, maybe then I can—"

It was Eagle who didn't let her finish a sentence this time. He pulled her into him, one hand behind her head and the other arm banded around her waist.

Taylor struggled to get out of his grip, but he wasn't letting go.

"I love you!" Eagle blurted almost angrily.

Taylor froze.

"I *love* you," he repeated a little softer. "I'm not going to let anyone get their hands on you. I've never felt for someone the way I feel about you, Taylor, and I'm not going to let *anyone* fuck up what we have."

Taylor lifted her head, Eagle's hand shifting so his fingers were in her hair. "You love me?" she repeated meekly.

"Yes," he said, simply and without prevarication.

Taylor was literally at a loss for words. No one in her entire life had ever told her that they loved her. Not that she could remember.

"Tay? Say something," Eagle pleaded.

And for the first time, she saw the uneasiness in his gaze. He may not have meant to blurt out his feelings, but she didn't want him to regret them. Not for one second.

"I love you too," she told him, voice breaking. "You've made my life better in so many ways, I can't even list them all." Then she admitted her deep shame. "No one has *ever* loved me before."

"Their loss," Eagle said immediately. "You're the most loveable person I've ever met," he told her.

They stared at each other for a moment before Taylor asked, "What are we going to do about this guy, Eagle?"

"*We* aren't going to do anything. I am. Silverstone and I. We're going to find this asshole, and you're going to keep on living your life as best you can in the meantime. It does mean you probably won't get much alone time in the near future, until we nail his ass."

"I have no problem with that," Taylor agreed without hesitation.

"You're going to have to get used to me being around you every second of every day," Eagle warned.

"Okay," she said. Then asked, "Is that supposed to be a hardship? Because it's really not."

She couldn't believe she was teasing him seconds after a mini break-down. In the past, when she'd been bullied, her foster families hadn't cared. No one had done a damn thing about it. And now here she was, with a former Delta Force soldier completely pissed off and determined to find whoever was stalking her to make him stop. She'd honestly never felt safer in her life.

"Eagle?" she asked.

"Yeah?"

"Remember when you told me last night that you'd teach me how to give a blow job?"

Eagle's eyes widened, and Taylor could see his pupils dilate. "Yes . . ."

"I thought about that all afternoon. I'm ready. I want to please you like you do me. Help me forget about all of this, especially that asshole . . . just for a little while. Please?"

He moved quickly, turning and shutting the lid of the pizza box. He grabbed the Chinese food and put it in the fridge. Then he took hold of her hand and practically dragged her down the hall toward the bedroom.

"We'll eat afterward, and I'll call Bull and the others later to let them know about the fucking pizza."

Taylor couldn't help but smile as she stared at the back of Eagle's head. She should probably still be losing her shit over whoever it was who seemed to delight in scaring the hell out of her, but at this moment, all she could think about was getting her hands—and mouth—on Eagle's cock. He hadn't let her play much up until now, claiming that he'd lose it too fast if she did. But for tonight, all bets were off. She was his, and he was hers. "Sounds good. I love you, Eagle."

"I love you too, Flower."

≈

Brett couldn't stop fantasizing about how freaked out his Taylor must've been when she'd opened the pizza box to find the message he'd left for her. He had no idea if she'd read the name he'd put on the label, but it didn't matter. He was ready to claim what was his.

His to break.

His to torture.

His to kill.

Using her boyfriend's name had been genius. He'd heard the relief in her voice when he'd used it. Sneaking around and spying on her had gained him the perfect information to notch up the torment. Showing up at the boyfriend's place had been a risk, but it was one well worth taking.

He'd have to be ready at all times now. Follow her around and wait for just the right moment to grab her. Brett had no doubt he'd be successful. He hadn't been caught so far because he was smart and careful.

Taylor Cardin would soon be at his mercy. All he needed was a small window of opportunity, and she'd be his. No one would get in his way. Not even that fucking boyfriend of hers with the ridiculous name.

And if the man had to die for Brett to get what he'd waited months to claim . . . so be it.

Chapter Fifteen

"This guy's a ghost," Bull said in frustration. "It's pissing me off."

"He's been lucky," Gramps agreed.

"Lucky?" Smoke spat. "He's managed to avoid every surveillance camera we've found so far. We literally have nothing other than approximately how tall he is and the fact he's got brown hair. Somehow he's managed to avoid the cameras at her place *and* Eagle's. He's obviously very good at staying under the radar, almost as if he's had plenty of practice."

Eagle sat at the table in the safe room listening to his friends discuss Taylor's stalker. They were no closer to catching him now than they'd been five days ago, when the guy had dropped off the fucking pizza at Eagle's apartment. The man knew where they both lived. It was a good bet he knew about Silverstone Towing too. And somehow he'd found out Eagle's name—which all added up to the fact that he'd repeatedly gotten way too close to Taylor for Eagle's comfort.

But the best thing Taylor had going for her was that Eagle wasn't going to let this asshole get anywhere near his woman from here on out.

He and Taylor had practically moved into Silverstone Towing. There was no way anyone was getting through all the security they had there. And while it might not make Taylor comfortable, she was never alone.

Eagle hadn't taken any towing jobs since the pizza incident, and he spent as much time as possible trying to track down the mysterious man. With no luck.

The man really was a ghost, and it was frustrating as hell.

Surprisingly, Taylor had been taking everything in stride. She hadn't complained about basically being locked down at Silverstone. Bull, Smoke, and Gramps were also impressed by her stoic attitude. When Eagle had asked her last night if she was all right with everything, she'd laughed. Actually laughed. Then said, "Eagle, if I have to be on lock-down anywhere, this is where I'd want to be. There's a safe room, I have a personal chef, all the pinball I can play, and you're never farther than a few steps away. What do I have to complain about?"

When she put it like that, Eagle had to agree. But still. He knew this wasn't easy. Knowing someone was out there stalking her, and not knowing why, sucked.

But in an hour or so, they were heading to Bloomington. Eagle had talked it over with her, and they'd decided to go down today, spend the night, hang around Bloomington for the day, go to the awards ceremony tomorrow evening, spend another night, then come back to Indy on Sunday. That would give them both a weekend away to enjoy themselves and have a bit more privacy than they'd had recently, and it would give his team a chance to hopefully figure out who the fuck was messing with her. It was a win-win situation.

But Eagle couldn't shake the feeling of dread that had taken root in his belly.

"When are you guys leaving?" Gramps asked, jerking Eagle back to the present.

"In about an hour or so. We need to stop by both our apartments to grab some things. I need my tux, and Taylor needs to get her dress and a few other things."

"How you gettin' there?" Smoke asked.

"I think we'll go down 37 to Martinsville. I thought about taking the scenic route from there, but it might not be a good idea to get off the main road, just in case."

Bull and Smoke nodded, but Gramps said, "Although it might be harder to follow you if you don't take the main route into Bloomington."

"I've thought about that," Eagle said. "I'm going to play it by ear. If I feel at all uneasy, I'll probably stick to the more populated route."

"If you need us, yell," Bull said.

"You know I will," Eagle reassured them. "I'm hoping this will be a stress-free weekend for Taylor. Even though she's been handling everything well, I know she's nervous leaving Silverstone."

"Sucks," Smoke commiserated.

"How's your arm?" Gramps asked. "Back to full range of motion?"

"Yeah, it's good," Eagle told them. "It was stiff for a while, but now the wound just itches, and it doesn't even hurt when I do push-ups."

"Good."

"Hey, Eagle," Bull said.

"Yeah?"

"Happy for you," his friend said. "It's obvious things between you and Taylor have progressed past the friendship phase. You look happy."

"I am," Eagle said, not embarrassed in the least to admit it. "Things just kind of happened when I got back. I was hurt and thinking about what I might've missed out on if that bullet had been a few inches to the right, and when she saw I'd been wounded, she kinda flipped out too."

"We all like her," Smoke added. "She makes you laugh, which is awesome."

"The test will be to find Gramps someone who makes *him* laugh," Bull said with a chuckle.

"Fuck off," Gramps said with a little shake of his head. "I laugh."

"Not really, and then usually at our expense," Smoke threw in.

"You too?" Gramps growled at Smoke. "I thought you'd be on my side, being single and all."

"Look . . . I know when Eagle first told us about Taylor, I wasn't all that enthused about relationships. But she's grown on me. I've had a chance to get to know her better, and I really like her. And Skylar. Both women have been good for Bull and Eagle." Smoke shrugged. "If I could find someone as great as they are, I might not mind settling down. You know, someone who doesn't give a shit about how much money is in my bank account and likes me for *me*. But I'm not counting on it."

"It'll be hard to find anyone around here who doesn't know you inherited a shitload of money from your uncle," Eagle said.

"I know," Smoke said on a sigh. "But hell, if Bull and Eagle can find women, then there's got to be hope for an asshole like me. I just need to go on more towing calls to find a nice damsel in distress." He grinned.

Bull, Eagle, and Gramps all rolled their eyes at the same time. "You don't want a damsel in distress," Bull told him. "You want a woman who can hold her own when the shit hits the fan. Who doesn't fall apart in a stressful situation. Someone who can fight by your side as easily as she can fight when you aren't there."

"Does a woman like that exist?" Smoke asked.

"Yes," Bull and Eagle said at the same time, then smiled at each other.

"Of course you two think that," Smoke grumbled. "You've already found your women."

"Gramps? You're being awfully quiet over there," Bull said with a smirk.

"I'm not going to speculate on love. I have no idea if there's anyone out there for me. If there is, I'm gonna take her exactly how she is. Short, tall, fat, thin, snarky, sweet . . . timid, or a woman who's not afraid to speak her mind. As long as she can put up with me, I'm good with anything."

"You're not *that* hard to put up with," Eagle said.

"I'm forty-five and have never been married. What does that tell you?"

"I think you're selective . . . as you should be," Bull said. "Don't settle. Trust me, when you find your match, it's worth all the lonely years that came before her."

Quiet settled over the team for a moment.

"On that note, my brain hurts from trying to figure out who this asshole is who's stalking Taylor," Eagle said. "I'm going to leave you guys to it and get out of here. If you need me, or if you find out any information, please let me know. I might be taking the weekend off, but . . . not really. On the off chance this guy follows us to Bloomington, I need to be on the lookout."

"You think he will?" Gramps asked.

"That's the problem. We don't know *what* this guy'll do. He must've followed her to my place at some point. He hasn't acted maliciously, per se, but he's still menacing. Until we find him, and know what his motive is, we have no idea what he's got planned. He might decide to follow us, or he might decide he doesn't want to leave the Indianapolis area to do his stalking. But I'm not taking any chances."

"You'll call if anything happens?" Smoke asked.

"Of course," Eagle told him. "If I need you guys, I'm gonna call immediately."

"Keep your phone on at all times," Gramps said unnecessarily. "We can track it if anything goes wrong. If the need arises, I can call our connections with the local PD and give them a heads-up on the situation."

"If you do that, they're going to want to know why we haven't come to them before now," Eagle cautioned.

"I know. And I'll explain it. But if you're really as concerned about this asshole as you seem to be, there's a reason to be worried, even if Taylor can't describe him or if he hasn't done anything illegal yet."

"I can't explain why this feels fucked up," Eagle began, but Gramps held up a hand, stopping him.

"And you don't have to," he said. "We've been teammates long enough for us to know that if the situation feels hinky, then it's hinky. I'll make sure the cops know this is a serious thing."

"I appreciate it," Eagle said, thankful for the millionth time that he had such an amazing core group of friends.

"Try to have some fun," Gramps said. "I know you're both on edge, but Taylor should be proud of what she's accomplished."

"I will, and she is. Thanks," Eagle said as he stood up. "Have a good weekend."

His friends all said their goodbyes, and Eagle headed out of the safe room. He smiled when the first person he saw was Taylor. She was standing by the pinball machine, trying to give Christine advice as she played.

"There, see if you can hit that—it's worth double points."

"Won't it lock my ball?" Christine asked.

"Yeah, but that's a good thing. Because if you get two more balls, here and here, then it'll drop them all at the same time, and everything you hit is worth double. It's hectic, but the points you get are insane."

"What do I do if—oh crap," Christine said as the ball obviously went between the flippers.

"Aw. It's okay, just keep practicing," Taylor told her.

"Just don't get good enough to beat my Taylor, and you'll be fine," Eagle teased.

Taylor's head whipped around, and she smiled. "Eagle! Are you done?"

"Yup," he said. "You ready to head out?"

"If you're sure you can leave early."

"Take him," Christine begged, her eyes once more glued to the pinball playing field. "He'll just stand here and annoy me if he stays."

"You love it when I annoy you," Eagle told his employee.

"Oh yeah, you just keep telling yourself that," she sassed back.

Eagle chuckled, then asked seriously, "Everything okay with you, Christine? You're early for your shift."

"I'm good, thanks," she said absently. "The kids are at their grandparents' house, and Bob is on an overnight trip. So I decided instead of cooking for myself, I'd get out of the lonely house and come eat some of Shawn's awesome food. And play some pinball."

"Great. Well, have at it, then. As long as everything's okay."

Christine looked up then, and Eagle heard the ball fall between the flippers once more, but she didn't seem concerned. "Thanks for caring," she said sincerely.

"You're welcome," Eagle told her, then he held out a hand to Taylor. "Come on, glamour girl, let's go get your stuff, and we'll be on our way to the ball."

Taylor laughed. "I'm not sure I'll ever be a glamour girl, but thanks for the vote of confidence," she said.

Eagle pulled her close and nuzzled the skin by her ear. Her curls immediately seemed to want to fuse with his fingers as he brushed the strands over her shoulder. "You're *my* glamour girl," he told her softly, loving the way she shivered at the feel of his warm breath in her ear. "I can't wait to make love to you tonight, where we can both be as loud as we want."

"How do you figure? I mean, we'll be in a hotel," she said shyly as he steered them toward the stairs and away from Christine's hearing.

"Right, and I don't give a shit if strangers hear you moaning. But I know you'd be embarrassed if the Silverstone employees heard us."

"True," Taylor said with a small smile.

"No objections?" he asked as they headed up the stairs.

"To you making mad love to me and making me orgasm so hard I can't keep quiet? Um . . . no. No objections. And . . . just saying, the other day when I went down on you, when we stopped at your apartment so you could grab a change of clothes I *know* you didn't really need . . . you weren't exactly quiet yourself."

Eagle couldn't help but burst out laughing. He was busted. Even though he'd known they shouldn't linger in his apartment, he'd figured since it was the middle of the day, and he was with Taylor, it would be all right. He'd needed to get her alone. And when she'd gone down onto her knees as soon as the door was shut and locked behind them, he'd realized she'd needed to be alone with him just as much.

They'd made love at Silverstone, and it'd been sweet and easy. The sex they'd had in his apartment had been frantic, passionate, and almost out of control. Eagle enjoyed both kinds of sex, but most of all he loved seeing Taylor lose all her inhibitions.

"Guilty," Eagle said calmly as he held open the door for Taylor at the top of the stairs.

She smiled at him, and Eagle did his best to memorize the moment. He'd been doing that a lot lately. Storing up memories of his Taylor to bring out when he couldn't be with her.

"Do you think Shawn would mind if we took a snack with us?" Taylor asked.

Eagle huffed out a breath. "Do I need to worry about you dumping me so you can marry our resident chef instead?"

Instead of getting irritated, she smiled wider and snuggled into him, her arms going around his waist. "Jealous?" she asked.

"I'm never going to be able to make you a delicious home-cooked meal," Eagle admitted.

"I don't need you to cook for me," Taylor said seriously. "I need you exactly how you are. You have no idea how happy you've made me simply by being yourself. You're the only person who's looked past my condition to see *me*. It would be hypocritical to get upset that you can't cook. I love you, Eagle. I've enjoyed getting to know Shawn better, and I might love the food he cooks, but I don't love *him*."

"It's a good thing," Eagle told her with a small smile. "Because I'd hate to have to beat him up."

Taylor rolled her eyes. "Whatever. You won't touch him, because you like his food just as much as I do."

"True. I love you, Flower. So much."

She beamed at him. "Thank you for going with me to Bloomington. I probably would've declined if you couldn't or didn't want to go. And not because of whoever seems to be following me. I don't like parties like this. I'm always uncomfortable."

"That's in the past," Eagle said. "I told you before, and I'll tell you again, I've got your back. Now and forever. You showed me the list you got from the agent of people who will be attending. I looked them all up online, so if they approach you, I'll just whisper who they are."

Her eyes shone with love. "That's literally the nicest thing anyone's ever offered to do for me."

"You're with a man who remembers every single person he's ever met," Eagle said easily. "I think we're a pretty good pair."

Taylor rolled her eyes. "I'm probably getting the better end of the bargain here."

Eagle looked around and, seeing they were alone, moved his hands down to her ass and squeezed. His fingers were within an inch of her pussy, and he had to force himself to not touch her intimately right there and then.

She went up on her tiptoes. "Eagle!" she exclaimed.

"You gave yourself to me," he told her. "I don't take that lightly, and you're both the best friend *and* the best fuck I've ever had. I love you, so much it scares me sometimes. I definitely got the better end of the bargain."

"We'll have to agree to disagree, then," Taylor said, and brushed her fingertips across his nape. He'd never thought he was sensitive there until she touched him. "And I can't believe I'm saying this, but I'm kind of excited about the party. I've never had someone have my back like you do. I've always been the awkward girl standing on the side, looking at her watch, wondering if she's stayed long enough to be polite and if she can leave already."

"Not tomorrow, you won't."

"Nope. And . . . one of the people who'll be there is an author I'd die to proofread for," Taylor admitted. "I think if I can make a good impression, she might consider hiring me."

"She will," Eagle said confidently. "How could she not?"

"Thanks, Eagle. Your support means the world to me."

"Back atcha," he said. "Now, as much as I'd like you to put your legs around my waist so I can carry you into a room and make love to you until you're limp as a noodle and I feel the same, we need to get going."

Taylor took a deep breath, then nodded. She stepped back, and Eagle dropped his hands reluctantly. It was insane how he wanted to touch her all the time. He wondered if the feeling would ever fade, then decided he hoped it wouldn't. He wanted to be eighty-five and still so madly in love with his woman that he needed to hold her hand, or be otherwise touching her, all the time.

"What are you thinking?" she asked, her head tilting in question.

"Just how much I like being with you," Eagle told her. Then he grabbed her hand and pulled her toward the kitchen. "Let's see what Archer left in the fridge. I won't tell our employee you pilfered anything if you hurry."

He grinned as she pulled her hand out of his grip and rushed ahead to see what goodies there were for her to take with them to snack on.

This would be their first road trip, and Eagle was eager to see what kind of traveler Taylor was. Would she sleep? Want to talk? Listen to the radio? Need to stop every thirty minutes to pee? He couldn't wait to find out. Every little thing he discovered about her made him love her more. Bloomington wasn't that far a drive from Indy, only around an hour, but he'd drive across the country with her if that's what she wanted to do.

Knowing he was smiling like a crazy man, and not caring, Eagle put his hand on the small of Taylor's back as they walked out of Silverstone Towing minutes later. He couldn't wait to get to the hotel and show his woman how much he loved her.

Chapter Sixteen

Taylor couldn't remember being this happy. Ever.

Which was pretty amazing, considering tomorrow night she'd be standing among the people she most wanted to impress in the book industry. Agents, authors, editors, other proofreaders. In the past, she'd have been in a full-blown panic by now.

Instead, Eagle had given her the confidence to actually look forward to what was ahead. She'd seen firsthand how he'd studied the pictures of the people who were going to be in attendance tomorrow night. She had no doubt he'd be able to stealthily let her know who was approaching or who she was talking to without making it seem weird. She'd seen him do it time and time again in the last couple of months.

She still had to pinch herself to believe she'd somehow found a man who seemed to respect and cherish her the way Eagle did. At first glance, she was aware that they looked a little odd together. He was tall, muscular, and gorgeous . . . or so Skylar had informed her. And she knew longing and admiring looks when she saw them, and that was what she saw on a lot of women's faces when they looked at her man. In contrast, Taylor thought she was the definition of average looking. Her best feature was her curly hair, but she wasn't sure that made up for her average height, average hair color, and average weight.

But Eagle loved her body. And said her height was perfect for him. And he loved *her*. As for Taylor, she didn't care how attractive others found Eagle; he was hers, and she wasn't giving him up.

If he decided one day that he didn't love her anymore, it might utterly destroy her. But for now, he *did* love her, and she loved him, and life was good.

She looked over at Eagle as he drove like he did everything else—with confidence. He had one hand on the steering wheel, and the other was currently holding hers on the console between them. Every now and then, his thumb would brush against the back of her hand, sending goose bumps down her arms. She couldn't help but look forward to getting to the hotel and seeing what dirty things Eagle had planned for the two of them.

There hadn't been much traffic on 37, and as they approached the interstate that would take them into Bloomington, Eagle asked, "You want to take the scenic route?"

Taylor bit her lip. "Is that dangerous?"

"I don't think so. I've been monitoring the vehicles behind us and haven't seen anything suspicious," he said.

"In that case, I'd love to," Taylor said eagerly. "This part of Indiana is so beautiful. Anytime I can take the back road instead of the interstate, I'm all for it."

"Great. We'll get off at Martinsville. There's a road called Low Gap that I've driven before. It goes right through the Morgan-Monroe State Forest. It's beautiful. We'll be a little later arriving at the hotel, but I think it's worth it."

Taylor sighed in contentment. "If I forget to tell you later, I had a great time this weekend."

He grinned. "Ditto."

They drove for a bit, then Taylor asked, "Can I ask you some stuff about Silverstone?"

Eagle immediately nodded. "Yes, but there might be some things I can't tell you."

"I know, I'm just curious about how you decide where to go and what missions to take on."

"Sometimes it's a simple matter of listening to the news. Other times we consult with our FBI contact. We look at the most-wanted lists, both national and international. We also have contacts around the country who might call and ask us to consider taking something on."

"Like a referral?" Taylor asked.

"Sort of. Because of our time in the military, we have some Special Forces contacts. For instance, there's one guy who lives in Pennsylvania—he's an expert at digital sleuthing," Eagle told her.

"What does that mean?"

"His computer is his weapon. There's literally nothing he can't do with his keyboard. He can find people no matter where they are and track down the smallest bits of information. He's a miracle worker, and my team and I were grateful for his help when we were on active duty. He's asked us for a few favors since we formed Silverstone, and we haven't hesitated to grant them."

"He sounds impressive," Taylor said.

"He is. He's helped us gather intel before missions a time or two, and been spot on with his info every time. There's another guy out in Colorado who specializes in finding missing women and children. His own wife was kidnapped when they were on vacation in Las Vegas over a decade ago. He was frustrated with the lack of information generated by the authorities, so he formed his own team to rescue people who've been kidnapped into the sex trade."

"Wow."

"Yeah, the best part is that he did eventually find his wife—*alive*. It took ten years, but they're now living happily ever after in Colorado."

Taylor's eyes filled with tears. She had no idea why she was so emotional over a couple she'd never met, but she was. "That's . . . I don't know what to say." They'd turned onto the scenic road now, and it was as pretty as Eagle had promised. The densely packed trees on either side of them lent an additional aura of intimacy to their conversation, as did the frequent gentle curves in the road.

Eagle squeezed her hand. "Silverstone had never said yes so fast when he called and asked us to go down to Peru to take care of the leader of the sex trafficking ring that had taken his wife."

"Really?" Taylor whispered. "You killed him?"

Eagle nodded once.

At that, she started crying harder.

"Tay?" Eagle asked with concern. "I'm sorry! I never would've said anything if I knew you'd get so emotional."

"I'm just so proud of you," she choked out. "You probably saved so many people."

Eagle shrugged. "Unfortunately, someone will step in to replace him. They always do."

"I know, but that man and his wife have to be so relieved, knowing her tormentor won't ever come after her again."

"They are," Eagle said with confidence.

"I love you," Taylor told him. "I know I'm probably supposed to be appalled and think that what you do is morally wrong . . . but I can't. I was never abused sexually when I was growing up—which was a miracle, considering how many foster homes I lived in—but I knew other kids who had been. I'll *never* understand how adults can think that's okay. Never. But knowing there are people like you and your team, and like the man who lives out in Colorado, who are fighting for the less fortunate . . . it makes me feel good."

"I'm glad."

"I talked to Skylar about Silverstone when you were on your last mission, and she told me a bit about her kidnapping. But what intrigued me most was the rating scale."

"The one-to-ten thing?" Eagle asked.

"Yeah."

"Bull told us about that."

"It makes more sense now that you told me about the sex trafficking guy. Anyone who would keep a woman hostage for a decade is most definitely a ten," Taylor said with feeling, wiping the last of her tears off her face.

"All of us have different definitions of that scale," Eagle said.

"You do?"

"Yeah. Of course terrorists like Khatun and Mullah are tens. Their entire goal was to kill as many Westerners as possible. And that piece-of-shit sex trafficker was up there too. But while Bull might consider Ricketts, the pedophile who kidnapped Skylar, a three . . . I don't."

"What would you rank him?"

Eagle sighed. "Are you sure you want to talk about this?"

Taylor nodded.

"Okay. I would've classified him as an eight and a half—and I wouldn't have had any problem taking him out. He wasn't a serial killer, but he was a serial child molester. And in almost every case, men like him don't just grow out of that. The more they do it, the more they like it. If he'd have gotten away with Sandra, he wouldn't have let her go. He would've abused her until she got too old for him, then he would've found someone else. And the cycle would have continued.

"I'm babbling a little, but basically, taking the future away from just one child could have a ripple effect on everyone he or she might've touched in their future. That's why I wouldn't have hesitated to put a bullet in his head."

Taylor listened in fascination. She hadn't really thought about it that way before.

"Did I scare you?" Eagle asked. "You're being quiet."

"No. I just hadn't thought about it in that light."

"And I'll tell you something else," Eagle added.

When he didn't immediately speak, Taylor squeezed his hand. "Yeah?"

"Anyone who *dares* fuck with you is an automatic ten to me."

Taylor's eyes got big, and she stared at him. Eagle's attention was on the road in front of him, but she saw a muscle in his jaw clench. She wasn't sure what to say, but she didn't have to say anything, because he went on.

"I don't mean someone who merely says crap to you, because it's not like I'm gonna kill anyone for that. But I'll defend you, and I *will* make sure they know if they ever disrespect you again, they'll regret it. I'm talking about physical violence against you. If someone thinks they can rob you, or break into our home, or in any way cause physical hurt to you . . . I'll end them."

Taylor shivered. "Eagle?"

He glanced over at her then. "Yeah?"

"I really wish we'd taken the interstate."

"Shit. Why? Are you carsick? Do I need to pull over?"

She shook her head. "No. I'm fine."

"Then, why?"

"Because I want to fuck you so hard, and show you exactly how much everything you just said means to me. No one has ever stuck up for me before. I was always the weird kid everyone made fun of. I've been kicked, spit on, and punched, and not one person ever gave a shit. I've never liked violence, but knowing you'd resort to it on my behalf doesn't scare or disgust me . . . it makes me feel valued. Granted, I don't want you going around shooting people or beating them up if they accidentally run into me, but I can't help feeling even safer just knowing you'd *want* to."

"I'm not exactly proud of the fact that I'm that kind of man," Eagle admitted. "But the thought of you being hurt makes me crazy. I'm sorry

I've been so over-the-top protective this past week. But the more I think about this guy coming into your apartment, and what he could've done to you, the more nervous I get."

"I don't understand who he is," Taylor admitted softly.

"I don't *give* a shit who he is," Eagle retorted. "He doesn't get to scare you. If he's thinking about putting his hands on you, he's not going to get the chance. We're going to find out who he is, and I'll have a little talk with him."

"I don't want you to get into trouble," Taylor said worriedly.

"I won't," Eagle responded. "I'm good at what I do, Flower," he added softly.

That made Taylor feel a little better. She just had to trust that Eagle knew what he was doing. He'd been a Delta Force soldier; it wasn't like he was a hotheaded punk who flew off the handle at the slightest provocation.

She opened her mouth to tell him she trusted him—but never got the chance.

A car hit them from behind. *Hard.* The curves they'd been going around had prevented either of them from seeing the vehicle until it was actually upon them.

Eagle's Wrangler immediately spun. Taylor's seat belt locked in place, but her head whipped to the side and barely missed hitting the window next to her.

She screamed as the car was hit again. This time the driver's side was T-boned, and their Jeep went careening off the road into a shallow ditch, rolling once before landing on its roof.

Hanging upside down, Taylor was dazed. She looked over at Eagle and saw that he was limp, blood dripping from his head. She couldn't see the wound, but judging by the blood pooling below him, she knew it had to be bad.

"Eagle?" she yelled frantically.

"Miss?" a voice called from next to her, and Taylor screamed in fright. She turned her head and saw a man kneeling next to her broken window.

"Sorry for scaring you, but we need to get you out of there. The engine's smoking."

Taylor could smell the smoke, but her head was still spinning.

The man produced a knife, and she flinched back.

"Easy, now. I'm going to cut your seat belt. Brace yourself so you don't fall on your head."

His voice was low and soothing, but it didn't make her feel any better. Before she could tell him to just leave her where she was and to help Eagle, he'd already sliced through her belt.

She fell with a grunt onto the ceiling of the Wrangler. Her hands landed on broken glass from the side windows, and she cried out.

Before she could orient herself, the man had a hold of her upper arm. "Come on, this way. I've got you. Good, crawl this way."

Overwhelmed, Taylor let the man help her out of the upside-down car.

"I'm an off-duty paramedic," the man said. "I was driving behind the other car when I saw that guy hit you. What an asshole. Let's get you to my car, where you can sit down. I've already called the police."

Taylor stumbled as she walked toward the man's car. She looked back at Eagle's Wrangler and gasped. The driver's side was completely smashed in.

"Eagle!" she exclaimed.

"I'll check on him in a second," her rescuer said. "I want to get you settled first. Come on."

Taylor stumbled again and realized the man had a very tight grip on her biceps. He was practically marching her toward his vehicle.

The second she saw it, Taylor's insides instantly froze. She tried to stop walking, but the man wouldn't let her.

"No, I'm okay. Let me go," she said. Her voice wavered, wasn't nearly as strong as she would've liked.

"I don't think so, Taylor," the man said, strengthening his grip.

Adrenaline had already been coursing through her veins, but her heart started beating even faster at hearing the man say her name.

She recognized the car he was hauling her toward. A dark-brown Cadillac.

The same one that had hit her bumper a while back; she'd bet everything she owned on it.

She looked at the man and racked her brain, trying to find *anything* familiar about him. Was this the same guy who'd been so apologetic after he'd run into her? Who'd asked for her insurance information?

Inhaling deeply to try to slow her racing heart, Taylor only managed to increase her panic. She recognized his smell.

Disinfectant, urine, and bleach.

This *was* the same man who'd creeped her out at the dementia center. He was the maintenance man who'd changed her air filter. And she'd bet anything he was the guy who'd brought her pizza with the word *soon* spelled out in olives.

Looking around frantically, Taylor realized they were in the middle of nowhere. There were no cars in either direction, and she couldn't see even one house. She was in big trouble.

She began to struggle in the man's grip, but he held her effortlessly. "Oh, you aren't getting away from me that easily," he said. "I've waited and planned far too long for you to get away from me now."

Taylor had to do something. If she didn't, she knew no one would ever see her again.

Looking back at the car in the hope that she'd see Eagle climbing out and coming to her rescue, Taylor wanted to cry when all she saw was a bit of smoke lazily rising from the engine.

"Eagle!" she screamed, continuing to struggle.

But the man holding her just laughed. "He's dead," he said bluntly. "He can't help you now. No one can. Now, come *on*," he growled as he jerked her arm viciously.

It hurt, but Taylor ignored the pain. The thought of Eagle being dead made her want to collapse on the ground and sob.

She suddenly realized the front of the Cadillac was smashed. Not so badly that the vehicle couldn't be driven, but his lights were broken, and the grill was completely messed up.

He'd been the one to hit them.

If he drove off with her, there was a chance a police officer would stop them because of the condition of his car . . . but she couldn't risk her life on it. If she allowed the man to put her in his car, she was all but dead.

Instead of opening the passenger door, the man walked around the back and reached to open the trunk.

The thought of being stuffed in there made Taylor's resolve double. He had his keys in his hand, arm outstretched, and Taylor acted without thinking, bringing the edge of her hand down hard on his forearm.

He cried out, probably more in surprise than actual pain, and dropped the key ring.

"Bitch!" the man exclaimed, and backhanded Taylor so hard, she flew backward and landed on the ground.

Ignoring the pain in her face and from the wreck, she leaped up and sprinted for the trees lining the side of the road. The man had made a mistake in letting go—and she was going to take advantage of his screwup.

Running as fast as she could, Taylor plowed into the dense trees.

"Get back here!" the man yelled, but she didn't even slow down.

Dodging tree trunks and leaping over scrub bushes, Taylor resisted the urge to look behind her. She could hear the man in pursuit. He was swearing and yelling about how much Taylor would regret running from him.

Frantically glancing around as she dashed through the woods, she tried to figure out where she should go. Where she could hide. It wasn't likely that she could outrun the man, but maybe she could outsmart him. Maybe he'd get tired of chasing her and go back to his car and leave, and she could double back and check on Eagle.

He couldn't be dead. He just *couldn't*!

The thought of the man she loved being dead wouldn't compute.

The aches and pains from the accident were slowly making themselves known. Her ribs throbbed, and her right foot really hurt. Flicking her gaze down, Taylor noticed for the first time that she was wearing only one shoe. She had no idea when she'd lost the other one, but at least she had on her sock.

Surprisingly, she didn't feel like crying. Not in the least. She was terrified for Eagle, but not hysterical. Her body was on autopilot, as if she subconsciously knew she had to keep herself together if she was going to survive. Under no circumstances could she let this man put her into his trunk.

Taylor had no idea how long she'd been running when she suddenly realized she couldn't hear the man chasing her anymore, and he was no longer yelling.

Stopping in her tracks and attempting to control her harsh breaths, Taylor tried to listen. Was he still following? Had he given up and gone back to his car? Eventually someone would have to drive by and see the wreck, right?

She was about to circle around to head back the way she'd come when she heard a stick snap to her right.

Taylor turned her head and saw the man standing just thirty feet away. They locked eyes—and Taylor could see the insanity in his glare.

He lunged toward her without a word, and Taylor spun and ran.

The chase was back on. It was obvious now that the man wasn't going to stop until he'd caught her. But she wasn't going to let that happen.

She had to find a place to hide. That would be her only chance.

Taylor ran and ran, weaving in and out of the trees, zigzagging and turning, plunging through thickets of bushes that ruthlessly raked at her exposed skin. The harder the path she took, the harder it would be for the man to follow. She was smaller than him—she could get into spaces he couldn't.

Gradually, the distance between them lengthened, until the sounds of pursuit faded once more.

She had no idea how long she'd been running this time, but when she saw a hollowed-out log in the distance, a plan came to mind.

Glancing behind her, Taylor saw no sign of her pursuer. She had no idea when he'd catch up. He was out there somewhere, though. She had no doubt. When she reached the log, what she thought was the best hiding place she was going to find, she fell to her hands and knees and sucked in a breath before squeezing into it.

Taylor did her best to cover her tracks, trying to make her hiding spot look as natural as possible and disguising anything that might give her away. Then, with her ribs throbbing and her heart beating out of her chest, she concentrated on breathing quietly in and out through her mouth.

She was running out of time. Surely the man would be there any second.

Praying there weren't any snakes or poisonous creatures lurking in her hiding spot, Taylor got onto her stomach and wiggled and contorted her body until she was as concealed as she could get. Hoping it was enough, that she'd covered herself sufficiently, Taylor once again did her best to slow her breathing. Something tickled her leg, but she ignored it. Freaking out about an ant or spider right now could literally get her killed.

Within thirty seconds of getting into her hiding spot, she heard the man nearby. Sticks broke under his feet, and leaves rustled as he stalked her.

Closing her eyes so he wouldn't feel her gaze on him, Taylor prayed.

Chapter Seventeen

Eagle wasn't sure why his head hurt so badly. Groaning, he opened his eyes, and it took a second for what he was seeing to register. He was hanging upside down in his Wrangler, and his head felt as if it was going to split in two.

Eagle couldn't remember what had happened or where he was, but he couldn't hang upside down forever while he tried to recall what was going on.

Fumbling for the seat belt release, he grunted when he pressed it and fell in a heap onto the ceiling of his beloved Jeep. Pushing on the door, he discovered it was too mangled to open. He probably could've fit through the broken window, but decided not to risk cutting his torso to shreds on the glass. He began to crawl over to the passenger-side door, when something caught his eye.

A purse.

Not just any purse—Taylor's purse.

He froze, and everything came back to him in a flash.

He and Taylor had been driving down to Bloomington to attend the awards ceremony for one of her authors.

Taylor.

Fuck.

Where was she? Was she hurt? Had she gotten out of the car?

Eagle noticed the passenger-side door was open. He glanced down and saw the seat belt she'd been wearing had been sliced in half. For a second, he was relieved that she'd gotten out. Someone had to have stopped to help.

But the second he emerged from his wrecked vehicle and looked around, he knew she was in trouble.

The brown Cadillac on the shoulder was obviously the car that had hit them, based on the damage he could see on the front end. But more than that, he clearly remembered Taylor mentioning that the exact same make and model car had run into her Rio.

She'd commented that it had looked older than she was.

This was no coincidence. And the Cadillac behind him now was definitely an older model. Cars were made sturdier back then, which explained how the driver had been able to force him off the road. He'd done a PIT maneuver. A pursuit intervention technique.

Eagle had trained with police officers when he'd joined Delta Force to learn how to most effectively get another car to stop in a pursuit. Whoever was driving the Cadillac had obviously been familiar with the movement as well, or had gotten lucky when he'd hit them. Then the bastard had T-boned him for good measure, sending his Jeep into the ditch and onto its roof.

But Taylor and whoever was driving the car were nowhere to be seen.

Was her stalker working with someone else? Had they ditched the Caddy and gotten into another car, taking Taylor away?

Eagle blinked, his vision fuzzy because of blood dripping into his eye from a cut on his forehead. Damn head wounds always bled profusely. He used his arm to wipe his face, not caring about his injuries at the moment. All he cared about was Taylor.

Able to see again, but knowing the wound continued to bleed, he jogged to the Cadillac and walked around it, looking for clues. When he got to the back, he spotted a key ring on the ground.

Upon further inspection, Eagle noticed footprints in the dirt on the shoulder, leading into the dense forest next to the road. The same forest he and Taylor had admired as they'd driven south.

He'd been such an *idiot* taking the scenic route! He'd known better, but he'd gotten careless. Had thought since he hadn't seen anyone following them, it would be safe.

He'd kick his own ass later. Right now, he didn't have time for anything but finding Taylor.

Pulling out his phone, Eagle dialed Smoke's number.

"Hey, you in Bloomington already?" Smoke asked as he answered.

"I need you to trace a license plate," Eagle said.

"Shit, what's wrong?"

"I don't know if it's active—it looks old, and the registration sticker expired six years ago."

To Smoke's credit, he didn't ask any more questions. "Give it to me."

"LLC 432."

"Got it. What else do you need?"

"A chopper. I was PIT-ed and T-boned on the way to Bloomington. I'm between Martinsville and Bloomington, somewhere in the Morgan-Monroe State Forest. Looks like Taylor ran, and someone followed. I'm going after her, but the chopper can use FLIR to find her. Trace my phone to give the pilot coordinates," Eagle told his teammate.

"Will do. We're on the way," Smoke said.

Eagle cut the connection, knowing his friend would be as good as his word. If they could get the chopper with the forward-looking infrared camera in the air, there was a chance Taylor could be found within the hour.

But Eagle's gut rolled. She might not have an hour. If the man chasing her was the stalker—and he'd bet everything that he was—her life was in serious danger.

Slipping his phone back into his pocket, knowing his team would get to him as soon as they could, Eagle set off into the forest.

He had to stop and wipe blood out of his eyes every several minutes, but nothing was going to keep him from finding his woman. Not the way his head was spinning. Not the blood oozing from the cut on his forehead.

Eagle had been trained to track targets, and he was more than thankful at the moment for everything he'd learned. He could tell when Taylor had been running and when she'd stopped for a moment. The man following her hadn't lost her, either. Eagle had hoped he might've gotten turned around in the forest.

Even if the man *was* lost, Eagle wouldn't go after him. No, his mission was Taylor. He needed to make sure she was safe and unharmed. She'd been in the Jeep with him. She could have broken bones, or the man could've hurt her before she'd run.

The forest was unnaturally silent. Even the birds weren't chirping, and he couldn't hear any sign of a pursuit. His own steps were nearly silent, as he avoided stepping on anything that might announce his presence to Taylor's stalker.

He steadily followed Taylor's trail deeper into the forest. He was impressed at her clear attempts to shake the man. She stayed off the easy, more obvious trails, choosing instead to cut through brambles and thick copses of trees. And Eagle was doing a good job of keeping himself calm and focused—until he saw blood smeared against the trunk of a tree.

He had a feeling it was Taylor's. The tree was directly behind a particularly nasty group of blackberry bushes. He remembered the short-sleeve T-shirt she'd been wearing to travel to Bloomington and could only imagine how scraped up her arms would've gotten by cutting through the thorny bushes.

Gritting his teeth, Eagle wiped at his face once more, annoyed by the blood that wouldn't stop seeping from his wound. He paused for a second, closing his eyes and straining to hear something. Anything.

Amazingly, he thought he heard a shout not too far ahead.

He had no idea how much of a head start Taylor and her stalker had on him, and was thrilled at hearing even the slightest evidence he might be getting close.

He opened his eyes and began jogging in the direction of the noise, not bothering to pay as close attention to the tracks at his feet anymore. The shouting could only have been made by one of two people, and instinct told him that Taylor and her stalker would be together.

The faster he jogged, the easier it was to hear the voice somewhere in front of him. If the woods had been quiet before, they weren't now.

It was clearly a man's voice Eagle was hearing, and the words made his blood run cold.

"You can't hide from me, Taylor!" the man was shouting. "I'll find you no matter where you try to hide. You know why? Because you're perfect! You'll never be able to recognize me. When I have you chained up in the basement, I'll show you what helpless *really* feels like!"

Eagle ran faster, staying light on his feet. He had to be close, but he couldn't quite pinpoint where the man was, his voice seeming to echo around him. It didn't help that he was still dizzy from hitting his head.

"I can't wait to wrap my hands around your neck and watch you stop breathing. But don't worry. I'll resuscitate you so we can do it all over again. And the best part is, you'll have no idea if it's the same man strangling you or a different one each time! That's why you're so damn perfect!"

Eagle regretted not grabbing his firearm before he'd left his car. He always carried it, but he'd been disoriented and not thinking straight when he'd climbed from the wreckage.

But he didn't need a gun to kill this asshole.

He could do it just as easily with his bare hands.

He had no idea how much time had passed since he'd set off after Taylor, but it obviously hadn't been enough for a helicopter to get to them yet. He was on his own, and that was all right too.

Slowing down and silencing his footsteps further when the man's voice got louder, Eagle peered through a dense wall of trees when he was within yards of the stalker to get an idea of the terrain and to make a plan.

A man who looked to be in his early forties was in a small clearing. He was a bit shorter than Eagle. His hair was brown, and he was a little on the heavy side. From his current angle, the man looked completely ordinary. There was nothing about him that stood out. Even if Taylor didn't have prosopagnosia, she might not have been able to describe him to the cops in a way that would make a sketch very valuable.

There was a large tree trunk lying on its side close by, with vines and weeds growing up thick around it. The man had a knife in one hand and was rooting around one end of the trunk with the other, talking to Taylor, as if he knew she was hiding within the hollowed-out tree.

"You might as well come out, Taylor. There's only going to be one outcome to this. You're coming back with me to my house . . . and we're going to play."

Without a word, and remaining completely silent, Eagle slipped up behind the man.

A mere few feet away, he stepped on a small branch—and it snapped.

Cursing his fuckup and wishing Smoke were here—he would've been able to approach the man without making a sound—Eagle braced as the man spun.

The smirk on his face faded, replaced with disbelief and rage, and Eagle recognized evil when he saw it. He'd seen more than his fair share of pure malevolence, and this man was right there at the top of the list with the worst of humanity.

Eagle had no idea what his name was, or what he'd done in the past, but there wasn't a doubt in his mind that Taylor wasn't his first victim. He'd done this before. Stalked and kidnapped women to torture them.

Moving faster than his target could react, Eagle punched him in the face as hard as he could.

The man staggered but didn't fall. He growled and lunged at Eagle, knife swinging.

Eagle sidestepped as the man got close and hit him again. This time he went to his knees, dropping the knife and instinctively reaching for his broken nose.

Before the man could get up, Eagle was on him. He got behind the man and put him in a headlock, wrapping an arm tightly around his neck. They were both on their knees, and the man frantically thrashed and bucked in his hold, throwing wild punches behind him, trying to dislodge Eagle, with no luck.

Neither spoke a word, both concentrating too hard on winning this fight. It was to the death, and they both knew it.

Eagle tightened his hold, not feeling an ounce of remorse when the man went from trying to hurt him to clawing at the arm around his throat to get it to loosen. Eagle remembered what the man had said while trying to find Taylor—that he wanted to choke her out over and over again. How he'd gloated that she wouldn't even know if it was the same man strangling her or if she was being tortured by several different men.

The thought of his Taylor in that situation, being in *any* situation where someone would psychologically and physically hurt her to satisfy their own sick desires, made Eagle tighten his arm even harder.

But it would take too long to kill him this way. As much as he wanted the man to undergo the same suffering he'd obviously planned for Taylor, Eagle needed to get this done. He needed to find his woman and make sure she was all right.

The man was making gurgling sounds deep in his throat as he tried to get air into his lungs. Moving quickly, Eagle released him. As he'd hoped, the man was too relieved to finally be able to breathe to fight him. The sound of the guy gasping for breath echoed, but Eagle barely noticed. He was concentrating too hard on what he had to do.

Without hesitation, without saying even a single word, Eagle grabbed the man's head and wrenched it to the side as hard as he could.

The snap was loud in the quiet forest, but Eagle felt no remorse whatsoever. The man had threatened Taylor. Had bragged about the horrible things he'd planned for her. The world was a better place without him in it—and more than that, Taylor was safer without him breathing.

Dropping the man facedown in the dirt, Eagle stood. Now that he'd mitigated the threat, his entire concentration was on finding Taylor. Wiping his eyes once more, he called out her name.

"Taylor?"

There was no answer.

Kneeling on the ground next to the dead man, Eagle parted the vines and looked into the hollowed-out log.

It was empty. She wasn't there.

Confused, Eagle stood. Why had the man been looking at the tree trunk if Taylor wasn't hiding there?

Dread blossomed in his chest, and he looked around frantically. Desperate to see some sign of Taylor, his eyes scanned every inch of the small clearing.

The sound of a helicopter high above suddenly echoed throughout the forest, but Eagle couldn't feel relieved that the cavalry had arrived. Was Taylor lying somewhere hurt, unable to move or respond?

For the first time in his life, Eagle panicked. Was he too late?

No, he wouldn't accept that.

"Taylor!" he yelled as loud as he could. "Where are you?"

There was no answer to his desperate call, only the sound of the helicopter's blades rotating overhead.

～

Taylor barely dared to breathe. Her heart was beating so hard it was difficult to hear anything over the sound it made in her head. So much so, she'd heard her stalker talking but hadn't been able to make out most of his words.

She'd chosen her hiding spot carefully, praying the nearby tree trunk and vines would make her kidnapper think that was where she was hiding.

It was just a decoy.

When he didn't find her there, Taylor hoped he'd assume she was still running, would then take off in the direction he thought she'd gone. Leaving her free to double back to Eagle's car, where she could hopefully find her phone, or Eagle's, and call for help.

She refused to believe that the man she loved was dead. Her stalker had to have been lying to make her panic. At least, she hoped that was what he'd done.

To the side of the tiny clearing had been another huge patch of blackberry bushes. Without hesitation, Taylor had gotten down on her hands and knees and backed into them, using dirt, sticks, and leaves to bury herself further. She had no idea if she'd completely covered her clothes and hair, but she tried to control her breathing and not move even an inch.

Flinching when she heard her name being yelled loudly in the forest, Taylor did her best not to whimper in fright. If the stalker found her, he was going to kill her.

The next sound she heard was the ringing of a phone.

It was such an odd thing to hear in the middle of the forest. Taylor had no idea who her stalker was talking to—the thumping of her heart prevented her from understanding the soft conversation.

Just when she thought she'd gotten lucky, that the man had left the clearing to search for her elsewhere, the leaves above her rustled.

This was it. The man had found her—and she was going to die.

"Flower?" a man cried.

But it didn't sound like Eagle. This man sounded unsure, frightened.

Torn between wanting to reveal herself to the man who'd used Eagle's code word and wanting to sink into the earth, Taylor remained frozen.

Her stalker could've discovered the code word. He knew Eagle's nickname, and he'd found them on the road today. He could be trying to trick her, to make her give up her position.

"Oh my God, Flower!" the man said again.

This time, Taylor could feel the dirt being brushed away.

Knowing if she was going to make a move to run, she had to do it now, Taylor lifted her head.

The second she did, she met a pair of blue eyes looking back at her in shock.

There was nothing recognizable about the man kneeling in the dirt beside her. He had blood dripping from a nasty gash in his forehead, which he'd somehow smeared all over his face and hair. But something in his gaze made her frantic heart stutter . . .

"Flower, are you hurt?"

Without the leaves and other camouflage covering her ears, or the thudding in her chest drowning him out, she could finally hear the man clearly.

The second he said her name again, Taylor knew it was Eagle.

Flying out of the bushes and flinging dirt and sticks everywhere, Taylor threw herself at Eagle. He caught her, falling back on his butt yet somehow managing to hold on. The blackberry thorns had caught in her hair and scraped up her already-bleeding arms as she'd launched herself out of her hiding spot, but Taylor didn't care.

Eagle was alive—and he'd found her.

She knew without a doubt that this was the man she loved. Her pursuer could've somehow learned Eagle's code word, but Taylor's gut told her that he hadn't.

And she recognized Eagle by his scent. By the way they fit together. By the feel of his arms around her.

"Eagle!" she exclaimed.

"Fuck," Eagle swore in an agonized tone.

They held each other a long moment before Taylor tried to pull back in a panic. "We have to get out of here. He's going to find us!"

"He's dead," Eagle said, not letting go.

"What?"

"Dead. I killed him," Eagle rasped, using his head to motion behind him.

Looking over his shoulder, Taylor could see a man's body lying in the dirt, near the tree trunk where she'd first considered hiding.

The sound of a helicopter registered, and she looked up, not able to see it through the thick leaves on the trees. Yet she panicked once more, trying to pull out of Eagle's arms.

"We need to go! We'll tell them the guy ran off and we don't know what happened to him. Then maybe we can come back later and bury him or something!"

"Taylor, it's okay."

"No, it's *not*! You can't go to jail. I'd never survive that!" She was hysterical, but she couldn't help it.

"I'm not going to jail," he said calmly.

"Yes, you are! You *killed* him, and I can't identify him as the man who's been stalking me. I mean, I knew he was because of the way he smelled, but no one will believe me. Lawyers will tear any self-defense argument apart!"

"His scent was still that strong?" Eagle asked.

"How can you be so calm?!" Taylor practically screamed. "Yes! He said he was a paramedic and wanted me to sit in his car while he went to check on you, but I recognized his piece-of-shit car from when he hit me before. That, and the way he smelled. He was trying to put me in his trunk, but I hit his arm and made him drop his keys. Then he hit me, and I ran."

"He hit you?" Eagle growled, bringing a hand up to gently push the hair away from her face so he could examine her.

"Eagle, please!" Taylor begged, struggling in his arms.

"As much as I love that you want to protect me, it's not necessary," Eagle told her, his voice calm once more, even as he tightened his hold and took in her swollen cheekbone. "My team will be here in minutes, and everything will be fine."

"Your team?" Taylor asked in confusion. "We're almost an hour from Silverstone Towing."

"They were in the helicopter. After the FLIR found our heat sources, they rappelled out and are hotfooting it to our location."

Taylor's head spun. "*What?*"

"No one's going to jail," he reassured her.

Wanting to believe him, Taylor shook her head, still dazed. "You're bleeding," she said.

"I know," he replied. "I also have a concussion. What about you? Did he hurt you any other way than hitting you?"

"No. But my ribs are killing me, I lost a shoe and my foot hurts, and I got scraped up pretty good by all the thorns in this forest."

Eagle just closed his eyes and pulled her even closer.

Taylor understood. She didn't want to let him go either. Everything had happened so fast, and they'd both come close to dying.

Two minutes later, that was how Bull, Smoke, and Gramps found them. Sitting on the ground, Taylor in Eagle's lap, holding on to each other as if they'd never let go.

Chapter Eighteen

Taylor sat in an interrogation room at the police station near Silverstone Towing. It was two days after her stalker had purposely run into Eagle's Wrangler and had tried to kidnap her. They'd missed the awards ceremony in Bloomington, but considering all that had happened, it didn't seem all that important anymore. She and Eagle were still feeling a bit rough, but she wasn't going to put off this meeting even one day longer. She needed answers, and she knew Eagle felt the same way.

Bull, Smoke, and Gramps had also asked to sit in on the meeting. Familiar with the men, the police allowed it, and Taylor had no problem with that either. She owed the men everything. They'd gotten to her and Eagle quicker than she could've imagined. They'd been like the brothers she'd never had. She wouldn't deny them information about what she'd gotten them in the middle of.

Taylor looked over at Eagle. He'd refused to wear a bandage over the large cut on his forehead today, saying it itched and he'd rather let the stitches get some air. She couldn't decide if he looked better with the bandage on or off. At the moment, the wound was red and slightly infected, and the black stitches looked like antennas from bugs trying to crawl out of his forehead, so she was leaning toward him looking better with it on.

Eagle caught her watching him, and he reached for her hand. He scooted his chair closer, then rested their clasped hands on his thigh. "What'd you find out?" he asked the detectives.

Instead of answering Eagle, both the man and woman who'd been tasked with updating them on the investigation looked at Taylor. They had similar looks of sympathy on their faces.

Taylor tensed.

"First of all, in case you were worried, there will be no charges against Mr. Trowbridge," Detective Allen said. She was dressed in a pair of jeans and a black polo shirt featuring the police department logo.

It took a second for Taylor to remember Mr. Trowbridge was Eagle. She nodded.

"The man who caused your car wreck was Brett Williams. He was forty-three, and we have evidence to suggest he was a prolific serial killer."

Taylor gaped at the detective in shock. "What?"

"We're positive he's responsible for almost a dozen young women's deaths over the last three years," the other detective said. He'd already introduced himself as James Wolfe.

"How do you know?" Eagle asked.

It was just as well, because Taylor was literally speechless. She couldn't think of even one thing to ask; she was too horrified.

"He had pictures of his victims," Detective Wolfe said. "Polaroids. They look like they were taken after he'd killed them. All of the women had been reported missing, but there were never any clues as to where they might have gone."

"He lived with his mother, who's suffering from Alzheimer's. When we got to her house, she was locked inside a bedroom. She'd soiled herself and was suffering from dehydration. She was completely confused and kept asking where her husband, Donald, was, as well as her little boy, Brett," Detective Allen explained.

Taylor felt horrible for the woman. The way Brett smelled made more sense now.

"How did Brett become fixated on Taylor?" Eagle asked. "Where did they meet?"

Detective Wolfe opened a folder in front of him, studying a report. "In a search of the basement, where it looks like he spent most of his time, a diary of sorts was found. It clearly implicates him in the deaths of the women we saw in the photographs. He wrote extensively about how he felt as he tortured them. He also went into detail about how he'd strangled them until they were unconscious or dead. Then did rescue breathing, if necessary, to bring them back to life. Apparently, that's what got him off. As far as we can tell from his diary, he kept each woman for anywhere from a few days up to two weeks."

Taylor swallowed hard, and she jerked in surprise when she felt Eagle's fingers on her cheek. She'd been crying and hadn't realized it.

"I know you do this all the time," Eagle told the detectives in a harsh tone, "but can you please lighten up on the details? My girlfriend narrowly escaped being one of his victims."

Both detectives looked contrite.

"Sorry," Detective Wolfe said.

"To answer your question," Detective Allen continued, "based on the journal, it looks like he first met Ms. Cardin after an incident at a grocery store. He was a witness and was interviewed by the police officers at the scene. Of course, nothing about him stood out as being off, so he wasn't detained or even looked at twice."

Taylor leaned forward in her seat. "Was that when the two guys got in a fight over a parking spot?" she asked.

The detective looked down at the notes in front of her and nodded. "Yes."

"I remember there were a bunch of people who were interviewed," Taylor said. "I don't recall anyone being creepy or anything, though."

"Well, Mr. Williams wrote in his journal that he'd found his next 'plaything' that day. He went on and on about how perfect you were, that since you wouldn't be able to recognize him, he could mess with your mind. He was planning to pretend to be several different people once he got you in his basement."

Taylor felt sick. She wanted to claim Brett's plan wouldn't have worked, that she'd have known she was being tortured by the same person. But honestly, Taylor wasn't sure *how* she would've reacted or *what* she would've thought. If he'd changed clothes, maybe worn a hat, she wouldn't have known she was being tortured by just one man, over and over.

She closed her eyes in humiliation.

As if Eagle knew what she was thinking, he squeezed her hand and told the detectives, "Taylor knew he was the man who'd been stalking her. She refused to get in his car as a result."

"How?" Detective Wolfe asked.

Taylor opened her eyes and looked at the man across the table. She saw only curiosity in his gaze.

"The way he smelled," she admitted. "I noticed it after he sat next to me at the dementia care center. And it makes sense now, because he was caring for his mother at home. Bleach, disinfectant, and urine," she clarified. "That, and I also recognized his car from the time he rear-ended me. I guess he figured since I couldn't remember faces, I wouldn't recall his car, either, but that old Cadillac didn't exactly blend in."

"I'm impressed," the detective said. He glanced briefly at his partner, then back at Taylor. "And you said that you believe he pretended to be a maintenance man to get into your apartment, and that he delivered a pizza, too, right?"

Taylor nodded.

"You're very lucky," Detective Allen said. "He wrote about both incidents in his journal. He'd planned to grab you when you let him into your apartment, but your boyfriend was on the way."

"What else did he do?" Taylor asked, not really wanting to, but unable to *not* know.

Detective Allen looked down at her notes. "Looks like he mostly followed you for a couple of months after he met you. A lot of fantasizing about what he was going to do when he finally got you back to his house. Let's see . . . he talked to you at the post office, at the library . . . you know about the fender bender. He paid for your food when you went through a drive-through one day. He was actually inside, and he told the cashier he wanted to pay for your meal, but to say it was the car in front of you. It looks like he also saw you and a friend having lunch at a diner, and he paid for that meal too.

"There are quite a few references to your boyfriend, how irritated he was that you'd started seeing more of him and spending nights away from your apartment. He bitched that it took him so long to find out who he was. Seems clear that dating Mr. Trowbridge made it harder for him. He didn't want anyone to see him interacting with you and possibly remembering him."

Taylor couldn't believe that literally *all* the times she'd thought strangers were simply being nice, it had been Brett. That he'd been . . . what *had* he been doing? Not really messing with her mind, since she hadn't known he was the one behind the gestures. She supposed he'd simply been enjoying the thrill of the chase and reveling in the fact that she had no idea he was watching her.

"As I said," the detective went on, "you were very lucky. But you did everything right when he did finally decide to make his move. You didn't allow yourself to be put in his car. Sometimes it's best to be docile and let a kidnapper feel as if they're in control, to wait for the perfect time to run, but in this case, fighting back was absolutely the right thing to do. You gave your boyfriend time to recover from the accident and come after you."

"I never even saw him following us," Eagle said. "One second we were the only ones on the road, and the next he'd run into us. I didn't see him come up on us because of the curves in the road."

Taylor knew he still felt horrible about that. He'd been the one to suggest taking the scenic route, which had made things so much easier for Brett. He would've made his move at some point over the weekend anyway—there was no doubt about that—but taking the road through the forest, one that wasn't well traveled, had given him the chance to wreck their car and attempt to snatch Taylor.

"We suspect that he'd honed his surveillance skills enough that he was very good at stalking," Detective Wolfe said matter-of-factly.

It was Taylor's turn to squeeze Eagle's hand. He'd been beating himself up for getting knocked out and not being able to prevent Brett from taking her out of the car. But the officers at the scene had said if it hadn't been for Eagle's driving skills, they both could've been killed in the accident.

"Anyway, I know you already know this," Detective Allen said, "but there will be no charges for Williams's death. It was obviously self-defense, and"—her voice lowered—"you saved the city and state a lot of money, because now we don't have to put him on trial. The families of his other victims will finally get closure. Williams put extensive notes in his diary about where he buried each woman—we think so he could go back and relive everything he'd done to them. It'll be a long time before the families can process what happened, but thanks to both of you, they can finally put their loved ones to rest."

Taylor wasn't so sure learning your wife, sister, or daughter had been killed by a serial killer would make anyone feel better, but she supposed it was preferable to not knowing anything at all about where they'd disappeared to or what had happened to them.

Detective Wolfe went on, "Williams apparently went out in the middle of the night and buried his victims in various wooded areas around the city. And he buried them deep; it would've been years before they were ever found, *if* they were ever found."

"What will happen to his mother?" Gramps asked from his position against the wall.

Taylor jumped. She'd completely forgotten the other three men were standing behind her.

"We haven't been able to find any kin," Detective Wolfe said. "For now, she's in the hospital, but she's going to have to be moved soon. There's a place on the west side that takes in indigent people who have little money and no one to care for them."

Taylor could tell just by his tone that the home probably wasn't very good. Even though she hated Brett Williams with every cell in her body, his mother hadn't known what he'd been doing, and she was ultimately one of his victims as well.

"I'll pay for her to be in a specialty care center," Smoke said.

Taylor turned to gape at him.

He didn't take his eyes from the detectives. "I've got the money. I'll get in touch for the details about where she is and take care of it. The woman didn't deserve what happened to her."

Taylor was crying again, but she couldn't help it. How she'd somehow found the most generous, compassionate friends, she had no idea, but she vowed never to take them for granted.

"Generous of you," the detective said. "I'll be in touch with the name of her doctor."

Smoke nodded. "'Preciate it."

"Do you all have any more questions?" Detective Allen asked.

Taylor's mind whirled as the Silverstone men asked several more questions. All she could think about was how close she'd come to disappearing exactly like the eleven women before her. She'd been extremely lucky. A serial killer had fucked with her for *months*, and she'd had no clue.

Not only that, but she'd put Eagle in danger. And Skylar. And everyone at Silverstone Towing. What if Brett had seen Skylar and decided he wanted her too? Or little Sandra? Or Christine or Leigh? He could've sabotaged his own car and called for a tow. Would the others have been as lucky?

Taylor's head throbbed, and the longer she sat in the small room, the more claustrophobic she felt.

But as usual, Eagle was in tune with her and noticed. "I think that's enough for today," he announced, and Taylor lifted her head to look at him.

"If we have any more questions, we'll be in touch," he went on, scooting back his chair and standing. Since he hadn't let go of her hand, Taylor had no choice but to stand as well. As soon as she was on her feet, Eagle released her hand and wrapped an arm around her waist, pulling her into his side. She might've protested his heavy-handedness, but she was more than happy to get out of the police department.

Eagle shook both detectives' hands, then Taylor did the same before Eagle steered her out of the room and down the hall. Feeling as if she was in a daze, she allowed herself to be led outside, taking a deep breath of fresh air the second they were in the parking lot.

Eagle turned her to him then, keeping one arm around her waist and using his other hand to lift her chin so she had to look at him. "You okay?"

Taylor nodded, but said, "Not really."

She hated the look of concern on his face.

"How do your ribs feel?"

"They're okay," she told him.

"And your foot?"

Sometime during her flight from Williams, she'd stepped on a piece of glass, which had imbedded itself in the arch of her foot. It was infected, but the doctor said because she was otherwise healthy, and with the antibiotics she was taking, it should clear up quickly.

"Sore, but not bad."

Her arms itched from where she'd been scratched by all the thorns in the forest, but she wasn't going to complain. She'd been very fortunate; having a few scrapes was nothing more than an inconvenience at the moment.

"Come 'ere," Eagle said, then wrapped both arms around her.

Taylor immediately snuggled into him, grabbing him as if she'd never let go. She rested her head on his shoulder and inhaled his clean scent.

"Christ," he muttered. "I can't believe how close I came to losing you. For the record," he said without letting go, "I never would've stopped looking for you. And I would've found you, and rescued you too."

She wasn't sure she believed that, but she loved the thought that he wouldn't have given up trying.

How long they stood pressed together in the parking lot, she didn't know, but eventually Bull wandered up to them and asked if they were ready to get out of there. Eagle nodded and opened the back door of Bull's Altima. The other man had driven them to the police station, as Eagle hadn't gotten his Jeep replaced yet.

No one said much on the way back to Silverstone Towing until Bull parked. He turned to look at her and Eagle in the back seat.

"So you know, this wasn't my idea. In fact, I tried to talk Skylar out of it, but she insisted."

"Out of what?" Eagle asked wearily.

Taylor wasn't in the mood to really do anything other than go and lie down, but she had to admit she was curious as to what Skylar had done.

"Everyone's inside," Bull said.

"Everyone?" Eagle asked.

"Yup. All of Silverstone's employees. Archer made a shit ton of food, and there's a huge party going on."

"Take us to my apartment," Eagle clipped.

Taylor put her hand on his arm. "It's okay."

"It's *not* okay. You're stressed way the fuck out, and so am I. Neither of us are in the mood to pretend to be happy about this. I don't want to hurt any of their feelings by being short and grumpy, and I know you don't either."

She didn't. And it felt good to have Eagle so firmly on her side. She'd never had a champion, and it would never feel anything less than amazing.

"I think it'll be good for us," she said softly. "I don't want to dwell on what we learned today. I don't want to think about how close I came to dying at the hands of that crazy bastard. I've never had a surprise party before, never had friends who cared enough to do something like this for me. And . . . Shawn made food . . . I'm not sure you have anything edible in your apartment, and I sure don't feel like cooking. Besides, I'm starving."

Eagle studied her. "You aren't just saying that, are you?"

"No."

"Okay. But the second you've reached your limit, let me know, and I'll get you out of there."

Taylor nodded. "I will."

"Skylar didn't mean anything bad by this," Bull explained. "She knows firsthand how it feels to escape death. She just wanted to help."

"I know," Taylor reassured him. "I'm lucky to have a friend like her."

"Come on, let's put everyone out of their misery. I'm sure they've been watching the security camera, wondering what the hell we're talking about out here," Eagle said, reaching for the door handle.

Taylor scooted after Eagle and followed him out of the car. She could've gotten out on her side, but she wasn't ready to let go of his hand yet. She felt somewhat weird that she needed to keep in physical contact with him, but he didn't seem to mind.

The three of them walked into Silverstone Towing, put on their name tags—which were the last three attached to the metal board next to the door—and headed into the great room.

Bull hadn't lied; every single employee of Silverstone Towing was there—those who weren't out working, that was. Everyone yelled out a greeting when they entered, and Taylor couldn't help but tear up. How she'd gone from living a lonely existence to this, she didn't know . . . but she *did* know she'd do whatever it took to keep it.

Skylar came rushing up to them and gave Taylor a long heartfelt hug. When she pulled back, she asked, "Are you okay?"

"I am now," Taylor said with a smile, and it was true. A minute ago, no matter what she'd told Eagle and Bull in the car, she hadn't really been sure she wanted to be around anyone other than Eagle. But now that she was here, and after seeing how genuinely relieved and happy everyone was that she was all right, Taylor didn't want to be anywhere else.

As she and Eagle walked around the room saying hello to everyone, Taylor was once again reminded how good it was to be alive. Everyone was wearing their name tags, so she didn't have to ask their names. She might not have recognized their faces, but she knew a lot about each of them. Robert hated pinball, but was a master at foosball. Jose was a complete softy. Christine bitched about how messy everyone was, when she herself was, in fact, a closet slob. She'd learned about everyone's children, and each person's favorite shift at Silverstone.

Taylor might not've been an employee, but she'd spent enough time there to know everyone well . . . and they'd gotten to know her in return.

This was just what she needed. To be surrounded by friends.

Shawn came up to her then, and Taylor almost cried again, feeling overly emotional about everything at the moment. He didn't say anything, simply wrapped his huge arms around her. They hugged for a long moment before he pulled back and looked deep into her eyes. Then he nodded. "You're okay," he declared.

"I am," Taylor agreed.

Then Shawn leaned down and whispered into her ear, "When you're hungry, I made a caramel-peanut-butter pie just for you. I hid it in the crisper drawer of the second fridge. It's got aluminum foil over the top, and I wrote 'Touch this, and I'll never make another dessert again' on it. No one has dared to even peek under the foil to see what it is. It's all yours."

Taylor smiled, stretching up on her tiptoes and kissing his cheek. "Thanks."

"You're welcome." Then he turned and went back into the kitchen, shooing Robert and Shane out of his domain.

"What was that about?" Eagle asked. He hadn't gotten more than an arm's length away from her as she'd made the rounds at the party.

Taylor put her arm around his waist. "Nothing. You've got some pretty amazing friends."

"*We* have amazing friends," he corrected.

Taylor beamed. "Yes, we do."

~

It was one o'clock in the morning before the last person left Silverstone and Eagle could get Taylor alone. He loved how well she got along with everyone, but he badly needed her to himself. After learning what that bastard Williams had done over the last couple of months, he couldn't think of anything other than holding her.

They'd commandeered an empty room at Silverstone so no one had to go out of their way to take them back to his apartment. He would've asked someone to drive them home if he'd had the slightest indication that Taylor wanted to leave, but she'd seemed content to climb into one of the full-size beds at the garage.

The second he got under the covers, she snuggled into his side, holding on to him as if she never wanted to let him go. They were skin to skin, nothing between them, and her warmth seeping into his side went a long way toward making him feel better.

He was also relieved he wouldn't be charged for killing Williams, but even if he were sitting in a jail cell right now, he wouldn't have done anything differently. He'd told Taylor he'd kill anyone who hurt her, and he hadn't been lying. The thought of her being in the clutches of that madman was enough to make him paranoid about letting her out of his sight ever again.

"I'm okay," Taylor said softly, obviously picking up on his unease.

Eagle did his best to relax his muscles. She was all right. She was safe in his arms.

"I love you," he said.

"I love you too."

She looked up at him, and he saw her gaze go to the gash on his forehead.

"It'll heal," he said quickly. "Compared to all the other wounds I've gotten over the years, this one is nothing."

"When I first saw you, you were literally covered in blood," Taylor said softly.

"Head wounds bleed a lot," he said. "I had to constantly wipe the blood from my eyes so I could see."

Taylor nodded. Then she brought a hand up to his face and touched his stitches with a barely there caress. "It's going to scar."

"Probably," Eagle said with a shrug. "Does that bother you?"

Taylor gave him a weird look that he couldn't interpret. Then she came up on an elbow and hovered over him. "I hate that you were hurt because of me, but—"

"I wasn't hurt because of you," Eagle interrupted, not liking that she thought such a thing for even a second. "I was hurt because Brett Williams was a sick fuck who decided to take something that wasn't his."

Taylor gave him a small smile. "You didn't let me finish," she scolded.

"That's because you were talking crazy," he retorted.

"You're bossy," she informed him.

"Yup," Eagle agreed.

She smiled, and he loved how relaxed she was around him.

"Anyway, what I was saying was that while I hate you were hurt in the first place, I'm also kind of glad."

Eagle didn't know where she was going with this line of thinking, but he didn't take offense. He knew she'd have a good point—he just had to wait for her to make it.

Her free hand came up and once again traced the wound on his forehead. "You're going to have a scar. On your face . . . where you can't hide it." Her gaze came to his, and he could see tears forming in her eyes. He opened his mouth to comfort her, to reassure her once again that he didn't give a shit what he looked like, as long as she loved him. But she spoke first.

"I'll be able to recognize you."

The six words made Eagle's throat close up with emotion.

"I'll be able to tell at first glance who you are. That you're *my* man. I won't have to wait for you to call me Flower, or to give me some other clue. I can be like any other normal woman and know immediately that you're mine."

"Fuck," Eagle whispered, not sure what else to say.

"I know that's weird, and if you want to see a plastic surgeon to fix it, that's okay."

"No fucking way," Eagle told her. "I'm going to wear this scar with pride."

Taylor smiled again and rested her head back down on his shoulder. "Remember when we had that talk about kids, and I said I didn't want any?"

"That's not what you said," Eagle told her. "You said that you didn't think you'd make a good mother."

"I can't believe you remember exactly what I said," she huffed.

Eagle smiled. "I remember everyone I've ever met or seen a picture of. Why wouldn't I remember what you say?"

"True. Point made. But it's annoying. If you're always going to be reminding me of my exact words, that might not bode well for our relationship in the future."

"Got it," Eagle said, grinning. He could tell she wasn't really pissed at him. She was kinda cute when she was ruffled. "Go on."

"Right . . . I've thought about it a lot," Taylor said.

"And what did you decide?" Eagle's heart was beating faster, and he wasn't sure why. Once again, he didn't know where Taylor was going with this conversation, but he had a feeling whatever she said next was going to be life changing.

She lifted her head again. "I want them. With you, at least. You've helped me realize that part of my problem growing up was *me*. I should've been more open and honest with my friends and foster families. Should have communicated more. I took their confusion about my condition as them not liking me. I think if I'd just talked to them, tried to explain more clearly how my brain worked, maybe things would've been different."

Eagle rolled, trapping Taylor under him. "Say it again," he ordered, the emotion easy to hear in his voice.

She blushed, but shrugged. "I could see myself having children . . . as long as you were the father."

"Yes!" he said, a little more forcefully than he'd meant to.

She grinned.

"Will you marry me?" he blurted.

Taylor blinked in surprise. "I didn't tell you that to get you to propose," she protested. "I just wanted you to know that I'd thought about it, and that you were right. Even if my kids have prosopagnosia, I'll never give them up. I'll teach them what it means and give them tricks to get through life."

"*Our* kids," Eagle corrected. "Even if *our* kids have prosopagnosia."

Taylor licked her lips and stared up at him.

"I can't imagine my life without you in it, and hearing those detectives talk about what Williams had in store for you made it crystal clear. I want to spend every day for the rest of my life with you. Taylor Cardin, will you marry me? Have babies with me? Beat me in pinball and keep me on my toes for the rest of our lives?"

"Yes." Taylor nodded. "Yes! Of course I will!"

Eagle lowered his head and kissed her as fiercely as he had their first time. He couldn't get enough of her. Wanted to show her how much he loved her. "I don't have a condom," he whispered, wanting desperately to plunge inside her and plant his seed in her womb. But she hadn't said she was ready for children right that second, only that she wanted them at some point.

"I don't care," she panted, shifting her legs, opening herself to him.

"You aren't on birth control," Eagle reminded her.

"I know."

Wanting to be clear, Eagle leaned down and kissed her, then lifted his head a fraction of an inch. His lips almost touched hers as he spoke. "If I fuck you now, I'm going to do it bare. I have no idea where you are in your cycle, but I could get you pregnant."

Taylor reached up and palmed the side of his face. "I *know*," she repeated.

"Fuck," Eagle growled, his excitement ramped up a thousandfold. He rose up on one hand and looked down between them. Her legs were spread wide around his hips, and his cock was as hard as he could ever remember it being.

He took hold of himself and brushed the tip of his weeping cock around her opening.

Taylor groaned. "Please, I need you."

He couldn't deny his Flower anything. Slowly, making sure she was truly ready for him, Eagle pushed inside her welcoming body.

When he was balls deep, she hooked her ankles around his ass and lifted her hips.

"Hold on," he croaked.

He waited until Taylor nodded, then he proceeded to show her how much she meant to him. How much he loved her. How grateful he was that she was in his life.

And every time he bottomed out inside her, Eagle thought about how he could possibly get her pregnant. Right here, right now.

He hadn't thought much about children, but suddenly he couldn't think of anything else. He wanted a little girl with the same out-of-control curls as her mother's. A little boy with her beautiful brown eyes.

Excitement almost overwhelmed him, and Eagle knew he was going to come faster than he wanted. The thought of his sperm filling her up made him even harder. The feel of her hot, wet walls tightening around his bare cock was something he'd never felt before, and it was fucking heaven.

"I'm going to come," he warned, hating that he hadn't made sure she was right there with him.

"Do it," she encouraged, then she squeezed her inner muscles around him, hard.

That was all it took. Eagle let out a bellow he was sure everyone in the garage could hear, and then came. Emptying what seemed like gallons of come inside his woman.

As soon as he recovered, Eagle sat up so he was resting on his heels, not breaking their connection, pulling Taylor's hips up and onto his thighs.

"Eagle!" she exclaimed in surprise.

"You didn't come," he informed her, although he was certain she was well aware.

"It's okay," she soothed.

"Nope. Not okay," Eagle told her. "Just lie back and relax."

His cock was still inside her body, even though he'd gone half-hard. She felt even hotter and wetter than before, and he knew it was because she was full of his come. He prayed that one of his sperm was able to make the journey to her womb, because he couldn't wait to see her round with his child.

Holding on to her hip with one hand, he pressed his thumb against her clit with the other. She moaned as he began to play with her.

"That's it," he encouraged. "Let go, let me make you feel good."

Taylor's eyes were closed, and her mouth was open as she panted. She was so damn beautiful, Eagle had no idea how he'd gotten so lucky.

It didn't take him long to push her over the edge. As her orgasm approached, she tried to shut her legs, but couldn't. Eagle didn't lighten his touch either. "Come for me, Flower," he urged.

Within seconds, she'd tightened all her muscles and was thrown over the edge. Eagle felt some of their combined juices leaking out of her and smearing against his thighs. It only increased his enjoyment of the moment.

Sweat beaded on her temples as she thrashed in his grip, and Eagle finally relented, taking his thumb off her clit and holding her hips to him, making sure not to let his cock slip out of her core.

"Holy crap," she mumbled, and Eagle smiled. Being careful not to lose her, he maneuvered them so they were lying flat on the bed once again.

"You're still inside me," she mumbled.

"Yup," Eagle agreed. "I've never been able to do this before. I've always had to pull out and take care of the condom. I love being inside you."

"I love you being inside me," she admitted.

"You'll marry me soon, right?" Eagle asked.

"What about your parents, and your brother?" Taylor asked, opening her eyes and looking up at him.

"They'll be happy for me, but honestly, they aren't really a part of my life. My family is here."

"So maybe we can do it here? At Silverstone Towing?" Taylor asked uncertainly.

"Yes," Eagle said immediately. "I can't think of a better place to officially make you mine."

"No one's ever wanted me before," Taylor said softly.

"I not only want you, I *need* you," Eagle said. "And I know I didn't ask properly with a ring and all that, but I'm gonna get you one soon."

"It's okay. Just don't go overboard."

Eagle grinned.

"Seriously. I can't type with a big-ass ring on my finger. Besides, something big would attract attention, and you wouldn't want me to get robbed, would you?"

"Shit," Eagle said, "I hadn't thought about that."

Taylor giggled, and he felt his cock finally slip out of her body.

They both sighed at the loss.

Eagle moved them into a more comfortable position, with Taylor on her side in front of him. He wrapped his arm around her, pulling her back against him. His cock nestled against the small of her back, and he couldn't remember ever feeling more content.

"I promise, Flower, I'll love you and our children so much, you'll get annoyed with my hovering and overprotectiveness."

"I'll never get annoyed with that, especially when I've never had it."

"Thank you for being strong. For not letting that asshole get you into his car."

"Thank you for coming after me."

"Always. I'll always come for you," Eagle vowed.

As he held his fiancée and listened to her breaths even out and get heavy, her body completely relaxed as she fell asleep, Eagle let out a long, slow breath. It was almost scary how much he loved the woman in his arms. No one would ever take her from him. She was his, just as he was hers.

He finally understood how Bull could put everything on the line for Skylar. He'd do *anything* for Taylor. Absolutely anything.

His mind wandered to Smoke and Gramps. He wanted them to find their own women to love. He was grateful they liked Taylor and that they'd protect her with their lives, but he wanted his friends to be as happy as he was right at this moment. Somewhere out there were women who could make their lives as wonderful as his . . . they just had to find them.

Epilogue

A mere month later, after Eagle and Taylor had gotten married and they'd announced that Taylor was pregnant, the team made the decision to go overseas and take care of a situation they'd been anxiously following for a while now. Everyone knew it was hard for Eagle to leave his newly pregnant wife, but this mission was important, and they needed all the manpower they could get.

Though Smoke was happy for Eagle and Taylor, he was itching to get to Africa. He'd been watching the situation with the extremist group Boko Haram closely.

In 2014, they'd kidnapped two hundred and seventy-six girls from a school, taking them into the Konduga area of the Sambisa Forest. They'd forced the non-Muslim girls to convert to Islam. Many of the captives had been forced into marriages with members of Boko Haram. Others had been taken into Chad and Cameroon. Some of the girls who'd briefly managed to escape had been returned to their captors and whipped.

The entire situation turned Smoke's stomach. He hated everything about the repression of those young girls. They'd had their entire lives ahead of them, and while they'd been trying to better themselves, to learn all they could, they'd been stolen and repressed by adults who should've been celebrating their successes.

As of today, over a hundred of the girls in the original attack were still unaccounted for, something that haunted Smoke. He hated to think of those young women living lives that were forced upon them. They may not be able to save those girls . . . but there was still a chance they could keep the same thing from happening to a new group of innocents.

They'd gotten reports a few weeks ago that Boko Haram had raided another school. This time in Askira, a town just south of Chibok, where the original group had been kidnapped. Seventy-two girls were taken this time, stolen away into the Nigerian forest. A lot fewer than in the previous attack, but as far as Smoke was concerned, that was seventy-two girls too many.

Boko Haram wasn't nearly as strong as it had been back when the Chibok girls had been taken, but they obviously had a large enough following to once again steal innocent kids away from their homes and parents.

And this time, there was also an American woman among the missing. No one had heard from her or the students who'd been taken. At first, it had been hoped that she'd fled into the forest to hide when the school she'd been visiting was attacked. But after a day or two, it had become obvious she'd disappeared along with the girls.

Smoke was ready to go. To find Abubakar Shekau, the leader of Boko Haram, and get rid of him once and for all. It wasn't just that he'd gone too far and abducted an American—it was also that he'd dared to steal away innocent schoolgirls for a second time. It was abhorrent, and everyone at Silverstone agreed he needed to be stopped. The man had been reported dead several times, yet he always seemed to pop up in propaganda videos, doing his best to incite his followers. It was assumed that he used body doubles to try to protect himself, but Smoke and his fellow Silverstone teammates knew they could find and kill him.

And hopefully along the way, they'd find the missing girls as well. And Molly Smith, if she was still alive.

This mission wouldn't be as quick as many of their most recent ones had been. They could be gone for months; trying to find a single man in the African jungle wasn't exactly easy, even if they had intel on the whereabouts of Boko Haram. So Smoke understood why Bull and Eagle had been putting the mission off. They didn't want to leave their women, and Smoke couldn't blame them.

But he couldn't help but picture Molly Smith's face. She was petite, around five foot two, and if she weighed more than a hundred pounds, he'd be surprised. She'd earned both her undergraduate and master's degrees from Northwestern. She was smart, and hopefully resourceful. Her grandparents had raised her after her parents had been killed in a freak train accident on their way home from their jobs in the city one day.

In a recent photo, Molly had shoulder-length black hair, and brown eyes that seemed to hold a lot more pain than the average person's. Smoke couldn't stand the thought of her being held against her will.

The woman had gotten to him. Smoke didn't understand why, but he couldn't shake it. He'd even had a nightmare about her just last night.

She'd been in a cage magically suspended in the air somewhere in the African jungle, and every time she'd tried to jump out, lions and tigers would appear below, preventing her from escaping. Then someone had materialized out of thin air in the cage behind Molly, shoving her toward the opening in the bars.

The scream that had come from her mouth as she'd fallen toward the ravenous animals had jerked him awake, and he hadn't been able to go back to sleep.

This morning, he waited in the safe room in the basement of Silverstone Towing for his teammates to arrive, and they'd begin working out the details of their trip. He'd gotten there early since he couldn't sleep.

One by one, Bull, Eagle, and Gramps finally arrived, and it was all Smoke could do not to get right to the Boko Haram situation. After some small talk, they finally got down to business.

"What do we think about Nigeria?" Gramps asked. "It'll be a long, hard mission, with no guarantee we'll find Shekau."

"Any word on the girls?" Eagle asked.

"Nothing concrete," Gramps said.

"And Molly Smith?" Smoke asked.

Gramps shook his head.

"I'm in," Smoke said eagerly.

"Me too," Gramps agreed.

They looked at Bull and Eagle.

"I'm not thrilled at the open time frame," Bull admitted.

"Me either. What if we give ourselves a time limit?" Eagle asked.

Smoke hated to agree to that. His worst nightmare would be to call it quits and later find out they'd been only one day away from finding the kidnapped girls or Shekau.

"What were you thinking?" Gramps asked.

"Two months?" Bull suggested.

Smoke breathed out a sigh of relief. That was more than fair. "Agreed," he said quickly.

"Same," Gramps said.

Eagle took a deep breath, but finally nodded. "I hate to leave Taylor that long, but she's in good hands here."

Silverstone had changed a bit with both Bull and Eagle finding women. And now that Eagle was married with a child on the way, everyone knew things would change even more. It wasn't that they wanted to stop going after the worst of humanity, but there was more on the line if they failed. Smoke understood that, as did Gramps. They didn't hold anything against their friends and would protect them even more fiercely now.

"I'll get with Willis at the FBI and see what information he can give us and what contacts he can hook us up with in Nigeria. I'm thinking we go wheels up in a week. That acceptable to everyone?"

The men around the table all nodded. Smoke would've preferred to leave immediately, but he felt better knowing they'd be on their way soon.

A week was an eternity when you were a kidnapping victim, but when you had to say goodbye to the woman you loved, it wasn't nearly long enough. He could be patient . . . he just hoped the missing children, and Molly Smith, could hang on long enough to be found.

~

Molly was terrified out of her mind. She had no idea where she was, other than at the bottom of a hole somewhere in the African wilderness. She'd been in the wrong place at the wrong time. Which was the story of her life.

She'd been nicknamed Folly Molly when she was little, because bad luck seemed to follow her everywhere.

Someone would drop a lunch tray right after she walked by.

The bus she was riding in would get a flat tire.

She'd once told a boy she liked him, and the next day he came down with chicken pox.

The list of things that had happened when she was little went on and on. But that wasn't the end of her bad luck. As she'd gotten older, it had only gotten worse.

Surprise quizzes, her bike getting stolen—then, in junior high, her parents had been killed. They'd stayed late at work in downtown Chicago, because they'd both taken the next day off to treat Molly to a musical she'd been dying to see. They'd taken the later train to get to their home in the suburbs, and it had derailed.

The only two deaths had been her parents.

Molly had moved in with her paternal grandparents, and she was grateful every day that they'd taken her in.

Her mother's parents had wanted nothing to do with her, telling her to her face that she was nothing but bad luck.

Molly knew she'd never have survived high school, or gotten her college degrees, if it wasn't for her nana and papa. She'd recently moved back in with them after a man she'd dated for a while had gotten violent when she'd tried to break things off. He'd continued to harass and stalk her, so Molly had taken a job with a group of scientists traveling to Africa.

Nana had tried to talk her out of it, but Molly had thought if she got out of the country, and out of Preston's reach, maybe he'd move on.

Things had been going well in Africa. Molly'd thought that maybe, just maybe, the curse of her bad luck had finally ended.

Until the day she'd gone to the school in Askira to be a guest speaker. To talk about the importance of science and the research she was doing in Africa. She'd been relieved that English was the official language of Nigeria, even if many people spoke Hausa, a Chadic language, because she'd be able to share her knowledge of what she was doing without having to worry about a translator.

She'd been sitting in the back of a classroom, awaiting her turn to speak, when men had stormed in with guns and machetes, separating the girls and boys. They'd forced all the girls to walk to trucks parked a few miles away from the small town.

Everyone had been crying and hysterical. Molly had tried to get her kidnappers to let her go, telling them that she was an American scientist, but they'd pushed her right along with the girls. They'd driven for hours before being forced to march through the jungle.

Once they'd reached the camp the men had set up, they'd been crammed into small huts, sleeping practically on top of each other. The young girls hadn't taken to Molly. They'd shunned her, speaking in their native language so she couldn't understand them. At this point, she had no idea what was happening to the girls.

Molly also had no idea how much time had passed, but she guessed it had been at least a few weeks. She'd tried to escape twice, and after the second time, she'd been forced to climb down a rickety ladder into a pit in the ground. At only five feet, two inches tall, she couldn't reach the top of the hole without assistance. It was only about seven feet deep, but that may as well have been a mile. There was no way she could climb up and out of it without the ladder, and most of the time she was ignored by her captors.

Every other day or so, someone would throw down a piece of stale bread, but that was the extent of their interest in her. Luckily, she'd been able to dig down a bit farther in her prison and find water. It wasn't much, just enough to keep her alive. She supposed her kidnappers were probably wondering why she hadn't died yet.

Molly kind of wondered that too. The world might be better off without her. She'd heard more than once that if she didn't have bad luck, she wouldn't have any luck at all.

Folly Molly.

It was a childish name, but as she languished in a hole in the middle of the African jungle, Molly couldn't help but think that it still fit her well.

Sitting on her butt in the dirt, making sure not to disturb her precious water hole, Molly put her head on her knees. She was beyond dirty, and starving, and had no idea what was in store for her.

She assumed her captors would eventually make her climb out of the hole, and they'd attempt to get a ransom for her or sell her to someone. As far as she could tell, the group was desperate for money. They were a ragtag bunch of men who didn't seem to have any real plan in mind for the girls they'd kidnapped. Someone had to be calling the shots, but she didn't know who that was.

The second she got the chance, Molly would do what she could to escape again. She might end up lost in the jungle, but that was better than being at the mercy of terrorists. Or stuck in a hole, dying from lack of food and water.

Looking up, she could just see a few stars in the night sky. She wondered if there was someone else, somewhere in the world, looking up at the same stars. It made her feel not so alone.

Molly didn't want to die. Her grandparents would always wonder what had happened to her. Preston would probably laugh and say she deserved it. Fuck him. She was going to get out of here, no matter what. But she couldn't deny that she could use some help.

A shooting star suddenly flashed across the sky, and Molly closed her eyes and made a wish. Her nana had always told her wishing on a shooting star was good luck.

"I wish someone, *anyone*, would find me and get me out of here," she whispered.

A part of her knew she was being ridiculous. She was a nobody. A scientist with a family who couldn't afford to hire any big-name private investigator. She'd have to rely on herself. Once she was out of this hole, she'd run into the jungle and hide. Then she'd walk for weeks if that was what it took.

But another part of her prayed for a miracle.

She put her head back on her knees and cried. She was too dehydrated for her body to produce tears. Molly knew her time was coming to an end, but she still refused to give up.

She'd set her wish loose into the world, and now she just had to wait for it to reach the right person.

About the Author

Susan Stoker is a *New York Times, USA Today*, and *Wall Street Journal* bestselling author whose series include Badge of Honor: Texas Heroes, SEAL of Protection, and Delta Force Heroes. Married to a retired army noncommissioned officer, Stoker has lived all over the country—from Missouri and California to Colorado and Texas—and currently resides under the big skies of Tennessee. A true believer in happily ever after, Stoker enjoys writing novels in which romance turns to love. To learn more about the author and her work, visit her website, www.stokeraces.com, or find her on Facebook at www.facebook.com/authorsusanstoker.

Connect with Susan Online

Susan's Facebook Profile and Page

www.facebook.com/authorsstoker

www.facebook.com/authorsusanstoker

Follow Susan on Twitter

www.twitter.com/Susan_Stoker

Find Susan's Books on Goodreads

www.goodreads.com/SusanStoker

Email

Susan@StokerAces.com

Website

www.StokerAces.com